The Last Sentinel

"The numerous action scenes are depicted with precision and authority, including technical details of armaments and vehicles. Gervais's action-packed odyssey of a righteous American Everyman continues in fine fashion."

—*Kirkus Reviews*

The Blackbriar Genesis

"Gervais blows the doors off the hinges with this series-starting thriller that introduces a pair of characters that readers will love. Hands down, *The Blackbriar Genesis* is the best thing to come out of Ludlum's universe since *The Bourne Ultimatum*."

—The Real Book Spy

"[In] this worthy addition to the Ludlum enterprise . . . Gervais delivers the exciting action, colorful heroes and villains, and seamless plots that readers have come to expect from this dependable franchise. Ludlum would be proud."

—*Publishers Weekly*

"Gervais, a talented thriller writer, launches a new Ludlum series . . . and his style fits right in. An action-packed thriller worthy of the Ludlum legacy."

—*Kirkus Reviews*

The Last Protector

"Gervais's brisk series kickoff, which jumps around the world, is built on the tension underlying the tenuous alliances among the sort of power-hungry villains who will stop at nothing. Well-modulated action scenes alternate with showdowns that reposition the pawns."

—*Kirkus Reviews*

"[A] solid thriller from Gervais."

—*Publishers Weekly*

"Gervais has already cemented himself as one of the supreme writers in the genre, and this newest novel only adds to it. This is a book that thriller fans won't want to miss."

—Stuart Ashenbrenner, Best Thriller Books

"A thrill ride from the first page to the last! Simon Gervais is coming in hot with *The Last Protector*. Looking for action, intrigue, and suspense? This is your novel! Move it to the top of your list!"

—Jack Carr, #1 *New York Times* bestselling author of *The Devil's Hand*

"*The Last Protector*, by Simon Gervais, is a perfectly built, spellbinding thriller with true heart and depth woven into the blood-soaked and bone-crunching action. Relentlessly paced, authentic, and utterly engrossing, *The Last Protector* knocked me off my feet."

—Mark Greaney, #1 *New York Times* bestselling author of *The Gray Man*

"Simon Gervais writes with an insider's knowledge, putting us in the shoes of someone working close-protection assignments. Tightly plotted and lightning fast, *The Last Protector* is a must read."

—Marc Cameron, *New York Times* bestselling author of *Stone Cross* and *Tom Clancy's Code of Honor*

Time to Hunt

"An action-packed thrill ride with plot twists around nearly every curve."

—*Kirkus Reviews*

"Gervais consistently entertains."

—*Publishers Weekly*

"Gervais weaves both villainous story lines together with action, intrigue, and suspense."

—*Mystery & Suspense Magazine*

Hunt Them Down

"In *Hunt Them Down*, Gervais has crafted an intelligent and thoughtful thriller that mixes family dynamics with explosive action . . . The possibilities are endless in this new series, and this will easily find an enthusiastic audience craving Hunt's next adventures."

—Associated Press

"[An] action-packed series launch from Gervais."

—*Publishers Weekly*

"Nonstop action meets relentless suspense . . . The blood flows knee deep in this one as Gervais uses his background as a drug investigator for the Royal Canadian Mounted Police to bring a gritty authenticity to his latest thriller."

—The Real Book Spy

"Gervais dishes out lavish suspense to keep a reader glued."

—Authorlink

"Superbly crafted and deceptively complex . . . This is thriller writing at its level best by a new voice not afraid to push the envelope beyond traditional storytelling norms."

—*Providence Journal*

"Another simply riveting read from author Simon Gervais, *Hunt Them Down* showcases his mastery of narrative-driven storytelling and his flair for embedding his novels with more twists and turns than a Coney Island roller coaster."

—Midwest Book Review

"From the first page, *Hunt Them Down* is a stick of dynamite that Simon Gervais hands you, masterfully lights, and then dares you to put down before it explodes. Don't. It's worth a few fingers to read to the end."

—Matthew Fitzsimmons, bestselling author of *The Short Drop*

"Your hunt for the next great adventure novel is over. If Jack Reacher started writing thrillers, he'd be Simon Gervais."

—Lee Goldberg, #1 *New York Times* bestselling author of *True Fiction*

"A huge thriller with intense action and emotion. *Hunt Them Down* had me squirming in my seat until the last masterfully crafted page!"

—Andrew Peterson, bestselling author of the Nathan McBride series

THE LAST GUARDIAN

ALSO BY SIMON GERVAIS

The Blackbriar Genesis

CLAYTON WHITE SERIES

The Last Sentinel
The Last Protector

PIERCE HUNT SERIES

Hunt Them Down
Trained to Hunt
Time to Hunt

MIKE WALTON SERIES

The Thin Black Line
A Long Gray Line
A Red Dotted Line
A Thick Crimson Line

THE LAST GUARDIAN

SIMON GERVAIS

THOMAS & MERCER

Published by Thomas & Mercer, Seattle

www.apub.com

Amazon, the Amazon logo, and Thomas & Mercer are trademarks of Amazon.com, Inc., or its affiliates.

ISBN-13: 9781662510762 (paperback)
ISBN-13: 9781662510779 (digital)

Cover design by Kirk DouPonce; DogEared Design
Cover image: © Roman Babakin, © photo-lime / Shutterstock

Printed in the United States of America

THE LAST
GUARDIAN

PART ONE

PART ONE

CHAPTER ONE

Near the US–Mexico Border
Southern California

Clayton White loosened his tie and undid the button of his shirt's sweat-stained collar. The sun was high, bright, and sizzling, and the temperature inside the black Suburban was quickly becoming unbearable. Sweat prickled at his spine beneath his soft body armor. The unbridled intensity of the sun reminded White of his time in the scorching heat of the Iraqi desert.

"You're killing me, brother," White said, rolling his sleeves. "There were four other SUVs in the parking lot. Why did you have to pick the one with the faulty air-conditioning?"

Chris Albanese, who was slouched in the front passenger seat, wiped the perspiration off his forehead with the back of his hand. "C'mon, Clay. How was I supposed to know the air-conditioning was going to quit on us?"

"I have a feeling you did this on purpose. Would it have anything to do with how easy it was to humiliate you on the firing range yesterday?"

"I have no idea what you're talking about," Albanese replied, brushing White's comment off with a wave of his hand.

"Is that so?"

"Are there any witnesses to back up that outrageous claim?" Albanese asked. "I'll wait."

White had known Albanese for years. They had first met when White had been sent to Albanese's unit within the Protective Intelligence Division following White's graduation from the Secret Service Academy. Though Albanese had been White's boss at the time, the two men had quickly formed a solid friendship.

The previous day, Albanese—now a team leader within the Presidential Protective Detail—and White had spent the afternoon at a firing range owned by one of White's friends, a former colleague from his days as an air force combat rescue officer. Albanese wasn't a bad shot by any means, but White had kicked his ass. The price of defeat had been an expensive dinner at one of San Diego's most renowned steak houses. The total bill for the meal had been more than seven times the per diem Albanese was getting, and White knew his friend was still fuming about it.

Albanese opened the glove box, from which he pulled a micro-USB portable mini fan. He plugged it into the charging port of his cell phone, and the fan's three small soft plastic blades began to spin. Albanese placed the fan next to his face and smiled.

White was searching for a smart-ass comment when the portable radio crackled to life.

"Specter Actual, this is Grizzly-One, over."

"Go ahead for Specter Actual," a woman's voice replied.

Specter Actual was the task force commanding officer's call sign. The commander was a tough-as-nails woman who had moved up the DEA ranks due to her ability to send high-profile drug dealers behind bars for long periods of time.

"Specter Actual, Grizzly-One. The Sierras have confirmed there are no tactical changes at the objective. Permission to continue toward the objective. Over."

"Permission granted, Grizzly-One."

"Good copy, Specter Actual. Grizzly elements are proceeding as planned and should be on target in four mikes. Over."

4

"Good luck, Grizzly-One. Specter Actual out."

This was it. In four minutes, a DEA-led task force of DEA special agents and officers from the US Customs and Border Special Response Team was going to hit a safe house belonging to the Jalisco New Generation Cartel—formerly known as Los Mata Zetas—in which investigators believed cartel members and their associates had stockpiled over 2,500 pounds of fentanyl. It was an unimaginably large quantity, and White doubted its accuracy. Confidential informants often lied or exaggerated about such things. Still, even the seizure of a fifth of the claimed volume would be a significant bust and deliver a massive blow to the JNGC.

Not to mention how many lives it would save.

It was time to bring Hammond up to speed.

CHAPTER TWO

The White House
Washington, DC

President Alexander Hammond was standing behind his desk, hands on his hips, looking out the window. At six-four, Hammond was a physically imposing man, and he had towered over his heads of state counterparts in the group photo at the latest G20 summit. Like most days, Hammond was wearing a perfectly fitted dark blue suit that accentuated the width of his broad shoulders. His white shirt contrasted with his dark hair, and his blue tie matched the color of his eyes. Hammond looked down at his watch.

Ten minutes.

That's how much time he had before he would walk out onto the South Lawn and board Marine One for a quick trip to Andrews Air Force Base. From there, he would board Air Force One—which Hammond guessed was being pulled from its hangar at this very moment—and travel to London to meet with the British prime minister. Hammond hoped his visit would help restore the special relationship Washington and London had enjoyed since the end of World War II—a relationship that had weakened due to the twin realities of the United Kingdom's decision to leave the European Union and Hammond's predecessor's harsh critique of the British prime minister caught on a hot mic during a state dinner in Washington.

But as crucial as his trip to the United Kingdom was, Hammond's mind wasn't focused on foreign policy. Quite the contrary. All he could think about were the seventeen teenagers who had lost their lives to a fentanyl overdose in Southern California the day before.

This has to stop!

A major spike in fentanyl seizures by the DEA and border officials in and around San Diego and Imperial County during the last six months had made the area the epicenter of fentanyl trafficking in the United States. The five thousand pounds of fentanyl they'd seized represented close to 60 percent of all the fentanyl seized in the country during that time.

Hammond couldn't begin to imagine the quantity of the deadly substance that passed unnoticed through the southern border every day. What he did know, though, was that fentanyl killed indiscriminately. Fentanyl-related deaths had reached an unprecedented level, and the crisis was far from over. Fentanyl wasn't the kind of narcotic you could experiment with. A dose the size of a few grains of sand could kill you.

Two weeks ago, following the overdose of eleven high school students in San Diego, Hammond had come out publicly about his determination to do more to stop transnational criminal organizations from importing fentanyl into the United States. The DEA had received the message loud and clear and had gone to work. After he was briefed by the DEA administrator about an ongoing investigation in Southern California, Hammond had sent Clayton White to San Diego to be his eyes and ears on the ground. Hammond had personally called the DEA administrator to let her know White was on his way. Hammond hoped that White's presence would emphatically demonstrate to the local, state, and federal law enforcement agencies that the war on fentanyl was a priority for him.

"Mr. President?"

Hammond turned around. His secretary, a short, stern-faced woman who Hammond was sure would vote for anyone but him at the next election, took two steps into the Oval Office.

"What is it, Madison?"

"Clayton White is on the line."

"Patch him through, please," Hammond said.

Hammond picked up the phone.

"Clayton? I had hoped to hear from you sooner."

"Lots of moving pieces, sir," White said. "But the task force is about to hit the safe house."

"Good. Were you able to establish who owns it?"

"The DEA did. They're confident it belongs to the Jalisco New Generation Cartel."

The JNGC. Hammond's eyes narrowed. As the former commanding officer of the Joint Special Operations Command, Hammond was well versed on the topic of Mexican drug cartels. The JNGC was one of the most powerful cartels in Mexico, and their tentacles often reached deep into the United States. The cartel was well known for its use of extreme—and often very graphic—violence to crush out any semblance of resistance from local populations. The JNGC's enemies were often found hanging from bridges on federal highways in Mexico, and rumors of new sicarios being forced to cannibalize their first victim had begun to surface on social media. The JNGC, the primary drug trafficking organization in most of Mexico's thirty-two states, now controlled the movement of approximately one-third of all drugs entering the United States.

And the bastards are playing by an entirely different set of rules, Hammond thought.

Unlike the old-school drug cartels that for decades had shied away from targeting top government officials to avoid a clash with the state—though local politicians had always been fair game—the JNGC, by sending dozens of commandos armed with military-grade weapons to assassinate Mexico City's police chief at his home, had shown the world it couldn't care less about the *old rules*. During a recent phone conversation Hammond had had with his Mexican counterpart, the Mexican president had admitted he was at a loss as to how to curb the JNGC's growing influence. Hammond's guess was that short of a full-scale military intervention, the Mexican president's only option was to wait for the JNGC to obliterate all its opponents so that a relative peace could return under its control. Hammond, who was pissed at the Mexican government for their lack of a coherent policy and at the persistent corruption within its ranks, grudgingly understood the Mexican president's position. Years of laissez-faire had left the man in a no-win situation.

Hammond wasn't going to make the same mistake and let himself be pushed into a corner by the cartels. It was time for him to send a strong signal to the JNGC and the other Mexican cartels. As president, Hammond would do everything in his power to eradicate their presence on US soil.

"Tell Special Agent Albanese to get ready, Clayton. I want to show the cartels who's the boss."

The British prime minister could wait a few more hours. Hammond was going to California.

CHAPTER THREE

Near the US–Mexico Border
Southern California

White felt his friend's eyes on him.

"What did he say?" Albanese asked.

"He's coming. He wants to do a press conference on site."

"Shit."

"Isn't that why you and your team are here?"

"Yeah, but I was hoping the president would be in London by the time the task force raided the safe house. It's gonna be a bitch to secure the site."

White agreed with Albanese, but he also understood why the president wanted to come to California. It wasn't just politics. By doing a press conference at the location of a fruitful raid against a JNGC safe house in California, Hammond would show all the Mexican cartels, not just the JNGC, that he wasn't afraid of them.

White didn't know all the details of the investigation that had led to the raid—the task force was understandably playing this one close to the vest—but the newly sworn-in administrator of the DEA, a former air force general who had President Hammond's full support, had herself greenlighted the upcoming raid after reviewing the ops plan. Apparently, a trusted confidential informant had stipulated that the fentanyl would be on location only for another seventy-two hours before being distributed all over the West Coast through the cartel's channels. White thought it was a risk to move in before proper surveillance and patterns of lives had been established around the safe house, but he understood the need for speed, so he didn't voice his concern.

Not that anyone had asked for his opinion anyway.

The DEA special agent in charge of the operation had justified his decision to expedite the raid by reminding everyone at the briefing that the amount of firepower that would land on the objective would annihilate the will to fight of whoever was inside the safe house.

In White's opinion, this was wishful thinking, despite the well-thought-out plan he'd been allowed to look at. In addition to the trio of two-sniper teams that had been inserted under the cover of darkness the night before and the two Sikorsky UH-60M Black Hawk helicopters filled with operators in tactical gear presently converging on the safe house, the ops plan called for another twenty task force members to be on location to secure the perimeter and assist with the arrests. These extra assaulters would reach the safe house by using the two paved roads leading to the cluster of mobile homes located in the vicinity of the safe house.

The team leader, although he'd never met or worked with White before, knew White by reputation and had penciled him into the operation, albeit in a support role.

White had become somewhat of a celebrity in law enforcement circles after he'd saved the life of Veronica Hammond, a renowned archaeologist specializing in aerial archaeology who happened to be the US president's daughter, in San Francisco the year before. He'd again made the national news when his knife fight in the streets of New York with Reza Ashtari, a rogue Iranian intelligence asset, had been recorded by a bystander, then televised nationwide. Though White didn't personally keep track of such things, someone at the White House had told him that the video of his confrontation with Ashtari had been viewed over twelve million times. The fact he was now engaged to Veronica—who was herself quite popular on social media—did nothing to diminish the copious amount of attention White was getting from traditional and social media alike.

Though White would have given a month's salary to participate in the air assault and be aboard one of the two choppers making their way to the safe house, he understood this was no longer his job. As the special assistant to the president for the Office of Special Projects—an important-sounding title that simply meant that White took care of anything Hammond felt he couldn't run through career bureaucrats, regular channels, or political appointees—White was here to witness the raid from afar and give his report to Hammond. He was no longer an air force combat rescue officer or a Secret Service agent. That was all behind him now, a fact that brought enormous joy to his pregnant fiancée. Veronica had been through a lot during the last two years, both professionally and in her personal life. She deserved some peace and quiet. The last thing she needed while carrying their child was to worry about him. If that meant White couldn't join in on a raid against a cartel safe house, that was fine by him.

White stretched his legs and looked outside the dust-covered Suburban. As per the team leader's wish, he had parked the SUV on the shoulder of a narrow dirt road half a mile from the objective. The JNGC safe house was a two-story, once-white wooden house with a porch and overhanging tin roof. A medium-size junkyard was also part of the property. It didn't look like much, but wasn't that the point? Although the two paved roads leading to the small town were the main access points to the objective, the dirt road still needed to be monitored. From his current location, a small hill obstructed White's view, but he knew the safe house was located at the eastern end of the town next to a faded brown-painted gas station. Cheaply built houses and mobile homes in various states of decay lined both sides of the main road that ran across the town, and a mini convenience store attached to a restaurant that had seen better days was at the junction where the two paved roads met. A chain-link fence topped with barbed wire surrounded the safe house and the junkyard beside it. The snipers had reported the presence of four guard dogs, all of them sleek, powerful Dobermans. The first operators on the ground would take care of them with tranquilizer guns. Once the choppers were on their final approach, White would move the Suburban forward a couple hundred feet in order to watch the raid in real time.

"Let's switch to the assault team's channel," White said, adjusting the frequency of the portable radio.

Seconds later, the distinctive *thump thump* of the rotor blades of two low-flying helicopters filled the air as a pair of Black Hawks raced past the parked SUV at an altitude of less than fifty feet, leaving behind them a mini dust storm. White shut his eyes as he tried to close the windows, but he was too late: the interior of the Suburban was already chock full of sand and dust as small rocks pinged off the SUV's metal frame.

By the time White managed to start the engine and move the Suburban past the small hill, the dust had settled, and the two choppers had landed, their contingent of operators already moving toward the safe house. White was too far away to discern who was doing the shooting, but the unmistakable sound of automatic gunfire reached the SUV.

The portable radio kept White in the loop about how the raid was progressing. The voices of the task force operators—calm and unruffled even when they were under fire—confirmed that White's first impression of them had been correct. They were highly trained professionals who knew exactly what they were doing.

White grabbed the binoculars from the center console and pressed them against his eyes. Most of the operators were now inside the house, while two of them had remained outside to link up with the additional assaulters, who were just arriving at the objective aboard dark SUVs. White witnessed the lead SUV ram the gate of the chain-link fence, sending it flying into the air. A couple of flash-bang grenades exploded, followed by controlled bursts of automatic gunfire.

Through his binoculars, White saw two men jump out of the house from a first-floor window, unaware that agents were posted outside for this exact reason. Half a dozen agents rushed the two men and wrestled them to the ground. Movement at one of the second-floor windows caught White's attention, just as Albanese shouted, "Shit! Shooter on the second floor!"

White adjusted his binocs, then felt his heart lurch into his throat. A man wearing a chest rig and armed with an assault rifle was leaning out the window, about to fire at the unsuspecting agents below him.

CHAPTER FOUR

Near the US–Mexico Border
Southern California

For White, it was as if time had stopped like a photograph. He watched it all play out in his mind in slow motion. The agents, still grappling with the two suspects, hadn't seen the shooter about to unleash death upon them. White's right hand hadn't even reached the portable radio when the single unmuffled crack of a high-caliber rifle rang out. The shot had come from one of the hills, some distance off. At the window, the armed man pitched back, his head split open by a sniper's bullet.

White heard Albanese breathe a sigh of relief. White did the same.

Shit. That was too close. Way too close.

A couple of minutes later, White heard the assault team leader confirm that the first and second floors were clear.

What about the basement? White thought.

Then, as if someone had read his mind, the radio came alive.

"Grizzly-One from Four, I've got something here. Basement level, second room to your right. You have to see this."

"Copy that, Four. On my way."

White resisted the urge to request a more complete sitrep, but it wasn't his operation, and he didn't want to distract the team with useless chatter.

"Do you think they'd mind if we got a bit closer now that the fire-fight is over?" Albanese asked.

White didn't think they would. He was about to take his foot off the brake pedal when the team leader's voice came back over the radio.

"Specter Actual, this is Grizzly-One, message over."

The commander's reply was instantaneous. "Go ahead for Specter Actual."

"Jackpot. I say again, jackpot. There's at least two thousand pounds of substance here, equally divided between powder and pills. Six tangos are KIA, plus three more critically injured. Four are under arrest. No friendly casualty. I say again, no friendly casualty. I request immediate medical assistance for the injured tangos."

"Grizzly-One, Specter Actual copies all. Medical teams are on their way."

"Specter Actual, Grizzly-One. Please note that there are two tunnels leading out of the safe house. One is heading south, the other east. There are indications that numerous tangos have run away through these tunnels with backpacks loaded with fentanyl."

"Specter Actual copies. I'll advise air support. Please state your intentions, Grizzly-One."

"We're going after them, but progress will be slow, ma'am. They've probably laid booby traps in their wake. Grizzly-One out."

Albanese looked at White and asked, "Do you think these tunnels lead to Mexico? Could they be long enough to reach across the border?"

White thought about it for a moment. He wasn't a specialist in drug trafficking or Mexican cartels, but he knew that the longest illicit cross-border tunnel ever discovered along the southwest border had stretched nearly a mile and had included a rail track, electricity, and a ventilation system. White confirmed the Suburban's exact location on the GPS. They were more than three miles away from the border. There was no way the cartels had succeeded in building a three-mile-long tunnel.

"We're too far out, Chris," White said.

"Yeah. That's what I thought," Albanese replied, unbuckling his seat belt. "Then we better keep our eyes open."

White nodded and turned off the engine. He held the portable radio close to his mouth and pressed the transmit button.

"Specter Actual, this is Tahoe-One. Over."

"Hmm . . . go ahead for Specter Actual," came in the commander, clearly surprised to hear from White.

"Tahoe-One and Two will be on foot approximately five hundred meters south of the objective," White said. "We'll keep an eye out for bad guys exiting tunnels, and we'll be wearing Secret Service jackets. We'll advise if anyone pops up in our area."

"Specter Actual copies. I appreciate the help."

White climbed out of the Suburban and scanned the area around him. His head swiveled as he took in the surrounding terrain. It was brown and desolate, with a few scrappy bushes here and there. Off to his right was a hilly area dotted with medium-size boulders. White walked to the back of the SUV and joined Albanese, who had opened the rear hatch of the Suburban. Inside the truck's cargo area were two black plastic Pelican cases. White unsnapped the fasteners of the larger case and opened the lid, revealing two SR-16 CQB rifles, each mounted with a Spitfire 3x scope. There were also eight thirty-round magazines, four flash-bang grenades, two tan-colored plate carriers, and two dark blue Secret Service wind jackets. White considered skipping the plate carrier since he was already wearing soft body armor under his shirt but decided to don it anyway. Albanese did the same. White pulled one of the SR-16s free from its foam insert and slammed a full magazine into the rifle's grip before racking a 5.56 mm round into the chamber. White dropped additional magazines into the front pouches of his plate carrier. Despite the heat, he grabbed a wind jacket. He preferred to be hot than be misidentified as a bad guy by one of the task force operators.

White opened the smaller Pelican case and took out a miniature drone. White unfolded its arms, then powered it up. He was about to sync the drone to his phone when Albanese tapped him on the shoulder. White turned in his friend's direction. Albanese had his rifle up, aiming at something White couldn't quite see.

"What are you seeing?" White asked, getting down on one knee and using the sights mounted on the SR-16 to search for a target.

"Not sure yet, partner," Albanese said, slowly moving to cover behind the SUV. "But I caught movement about one hundred and fifty meters away in this direction."

"Understood." White grabbed the drone and moved it to the driver's side of the SUV, a few feet away from where Albanese had taken cover.

"Let's get this baby up in the air, shall we?" White said.

White synced the drone to his phone and selected from a drop-down menu the type of mission he wanted the drone to accomplish. He pressed the green "Go" button, and the drone took flight, rapidly gaining altitude. White wished the drone had been one of the newer and quieter models, but he'd have to make do with this one and the typical buzzing sound that accompanied it. Still, having their own eye in the sky allowed them to monitor the area without breaking cover.

"Anything?" Albanese asked, his eye glued to the scope of his rifle.

White switched to the infrared camera, hoping to catch a heat signature, which he did.

"Yep. I got something," he said, enlarging the screen with his fingers. "Right about where you said you saw movement."

"Good," Albanese said. "How many tangos?"

"Sorry, brother, but I think you spotted a coyote," White said as he flew the drone farther east at a slow speed. Mindful of their proximity to the Mexican border, he quipped, "The four-legged variety, not two."

"Shit. I was sure I—" Albanese started but was interrupted by a hail of gunfire.

White heard a sound similar to a baseball hitting a wet catcher's glove at high speed, which was instantly followed by a loud grunt from Albanese's lips. White watched helplessly as his friend was driven forward against the SUV, his knees buckling underneath him as he sagged to the ground.

CHAPTER FIVE

Near the US–Mexico Border
Southern California

White grabbed Albanese by the collar and started to drag the Secret Service agent to the other side of the Suburban as incoming rounds kicked up dirt around them. Others hit the SUV with loud clangs. White hadn't made two steps when Albanese began to shout at him to let him go.

"I'm good! I'm good!" Albanese said. "The round caught the ceramic plate."

But White didn't let go until he and Albanese had reached the other side of the Suburban.

"Stop staring at me like that, for God's sake," Albanese said. "I lost my breath for a second. That's all."

White was about to take a firing position over the hood when more rounds thumped against the SUV, forcing him back to cover.

"Did you see who's shooting at us?" Albanese asked as he got to one knee next to White.

"No, but I will," he said.

White peeked over the hood.

The last thing he expected to see was three men rushing toward the SUV almost at full sprint. But that's exactly what he saw. One of the running men must have seen White's head pop up from behind the hood because he stopped and brought his rifle to his shoulder.

Before the man could fire, White pressed the trigger of his SR-16 three times. The man dropped his weapon and fell forward into the sand. The other two men fell flat on the ground but didn't fire back.

"I don't see weapons on the other two," White said, aiming his SR-16 at the two remaining traffickers.

"I don't either," Albanese replied.

"Keep them in your sights, Chris. I'll contact Specter Actual."

Resting his rifle on the hood and keeping it aimed toward the threat, White used his left hand to unclip the portable radio from his belt. Before White pressed the transmit button, he looked around him. Being caught in the open with his pants down had left a sour taste in his mouth. Focusing on the drone footage, he and Albanese hadn't paid enough attention to what was going on around them. They'd made a serious mistake, and it could have cost them their lives. White had no intention of repeating the error.

"Specter Actual, this is Tahoe-One," he called once he was satisfied nobody else was about to surprise them from behind.

"Go for Tahoe-One."

White gave the task force commanding officer a quick sitrep and the grid coordinates of the two traffickers.

"Roger, Tahoe-One. I'll send a team your way. Specter Actual out."

"Damn! They're getting up, Clay," Albanese said. "They're walking toward us with their hands up."

Careful to leave his finger on the trigger guard, White placed the dot of his Spitfire scope on the closest man. He was Caucasian, in his early twenties, with a strong build, and dressed in a dirty pair of jeans and a green muscle shirt. He had short black hair and carried a backpack on his shoulder. The backpack might have contained drugs, but it could also be a bomb. White wasn't about to let the man get too close.

He angled his rifle toward the second man, who was now less than fifty meters away.

He looks Asian, White thought, somewhat surprised.

The man wore white pants, which were now stained and dirty, and a black long-sleeved shirt. His head was shaved. He was tall but slightly built, and, in contrast to his friend, he wasn't carrying a backpack.

"We need help! Please don't shoot us!" the Asian man yelled, waving his hands above his head.

White studied the man's face.

Tensed. Ready to pounce. And unafraid. His facial expression didn't match the words coming out of his mouth. Not the behavior White had hoped for.

"These guys aren't victims," White said.

"Yeah," Albanese agreed. "I figured that much."

The portable radio crackled. "Tahoe-One from Sierra-Four."

"Go for Tahoe-One."

"Tahoe-One, this is Sierra-Four. Following your last transmission, I've repositioned. I'm now in an elevated position one hundred meters behind you. I have good visual on both approaching male tangos."

"Good copy, Sierra-Four. Thanks for having our back."

White felt good knowing he had a sniper in overwatch.

"Tahoe-One, Sierra-Four. The man you shot is still alive. Down, but still moving."

"Copy. If he makes a move toward his weapon, take him out," White said.

"Will do. Sierra-Four out."

While White had been busy with the comms, Albanese had started issuing orders to the two men. They were twenty-five meters away and nearing rapidly. White noted that the Asian man had closed the gap with his companion. There were less than two meters separating the two. Seeing that Albanese was still using the engine block as cover, White moved to the rear of the Suburban, preferring that he and Albanese covered the suspects from two different angles.

"You with the green shirt, slowly use your left hand to unshoulder your backpack," Albanese ordered.

White's eyes were on the Asian man. He was taking long, deep breaths as if calming himself before making some kind of move. White was about to remind him not to try anything stupid when the crack of a high-velocity round breaking the sound barrier distracted him for half a second.

To his credit, the Asian man didn't hesitate and took three long side steps to his left, positioning himself behind his companion, effectively blocking White's line of fire.

In the background, White heard the sniper's voice through the portable radio confirming his kill. The trafficker White had shot and injured was no longer a threat. The .308 caliber round the sniper had sent through the man's throat had seen to that. Though he was grateful for the sniper's contribution, White didn't have time to acknowledge the transmission. He had a more pressing issue to deal with. The Asian had pulled a pistol from a waistband holster hidden under his shirt and was now pointing it at the other trafficker's head while keeping the rest of his body shielded behind him.

White still didn't have a shot. The only way White could get an angle on the shooter was to move out of cover. The Asian man began to move forward, guiding the other man with his nongun hand.

"Stop right there!" White yelled. "You have nowhere to go!"

"We'll see about that," the Asian man said. "Move back and away from the vehicle, or I'll kill him."

From the corner of his eyes, White saw Albanese preparing a flash-bang grenade. White needed to keep the shooter's attention focused on him.

"The truck's keys are in my pocket, dumbass," White said. "How are you going to start the engine without them?"

A flicker of confusion crossed the shooter's face; then Albanese's flash-bang grenade landed three feet to his right. White had just had time to duck back fully behind the SUV when the grenade exploded in a white-hot blinding flash. A wave of flying dirt and small rocks showered the Suburban. The rocks hadn't yet fallen back onto the dirt road when White pivoted out of cover, his SR-16 aimed at the shooter. The stun grenade had done its job. In the wake of its sound shock, the shooter had lost his balance and was in a state of confusion, his left hand covering his eyes.

But he was still holding his gun.

"Drop your weapon! Now!" White yelled.

But the shooter didn't. He jerked the pistol up. White and Albanese fired within half a heartbeat of each other, both striking the shooter center mass. The man was dead before he hit the ground. White shifted his aim toward the man with the green muscle shirt. He had fallen on his ass, his face a bloody mess, though the cuts looked superficial. White suspected the flying rocks had caused the lacerations.

"Face down on the ground! Face down on the ground!" White barked, knowing that the man's ears were probably still ringing from the explosion. As his were.

The man obeyed, and White covered him with his SR-16 while Albanese handcuffed him.

White headed to the dead shooter. Once he had secured the pistol, he searched the body. White found a cell phone. From the dead man's back pocket, White pulled out a black leather wallet that contained a driver's license and two credit cards. And a Sam's Club Plus membership card.

White read the man's name off his driver's license. *John Lee.*

White used his phone to take pictures of all the cards.

"What's your name?" Albanese asked the handcuffed man. "And don't tell me you don't speak English."

"Shane. Shane Brooks."

"All right, Shane. What's in the backpack?" White asked, helping the man to his feet.

"Fentanyl pills."

"Glad you didn't try that 'it's not mine' bullshit," White said.

Albanese picked up the backpack and unzipped it. He took out what looked like a pack of Skittles. He tore it open and poured part of its contents into his hand.

When White realized that what had come out of the candy package weren't Skittles but fentanyl pills designed to look like candy, his blood pressure skyrocketed. Picturing his yet unborn child putting one of these in his mouth almost drove him over the edge.

"You sonofabitch!" he muttered between clenched teeth.

With an almost uncontrollable rage, White drove his fingers deep between the brachioradialis muscle and the flexor carpi radialis on the front of Shane's left forearm. Shane squealed in pain and fell to his knees.

"What's that for?" Shane cried out, pain filling his eyes with tears.

White wanted to gouge the man's eyes out, but Albanese placed a hand on his shoulder.

"DEA's coming, Clay," Albanese said. "Don't worry, they'll take care of him all right."

A gray Dodge Durango slowly drove up to their position. The Durango eased to a stop, and three operators dressed in dark green tactical gear climbed out, one woman and two men. The woman was small, not more than five foot two, with red hair pulled back into a sleek ponytail. She walked to White with purpose, her intense green eyes fixed on him.

"You guys okay?" she asked.

"We're good," White said, then offered his hand. "Clayton White."

"Yeah, I know who you are," she replied, shaking his hand without offering her name.

Albanese showed the DEA agent the fentanyl pills disguised as candy. "Were there more of those at the safe house?" he asked her.

"I'm afraid so," she said, then looked at the dead trafficker sprawled in the middle of the dirt road. "Interesting."

"Why? Because he's Asian?" asked White.

Instead of replying to White's question, the woman gestured for her two male colleagues to bring Shane Brooks to the Durango. White didn't challenge her. It wasn't his case, and he didn't want the extra paperwork that came along with booking a prisoner. Still, he knew he would have plenty of form filling to do. Firing one's weapon during a law enforcement operation was an entirely different ball game from running a black op overseas. White was willing to bet he'd soon get an email requesting his notes.

The DEA agent was getting ready to leave, but White had a few questions for her. "If you know who I am, then you know who I represent—the president. I asked you a question, and I'd like to hear your answer."

The DEA agent—at least that's the agency White believed the woman was working for—gave White an exasperated look. "Really?"

White nodded but kept a smile on his face. There was no point in pissing the woman off. "Yeah. I'd like to hear your thoughts."

She inhaled loudly, then said, "To be honest, I'm glad you caught one alive. The other team wasn't as lucky. The tunnel heading east ended one hundred meters in, and instead of surrendering, the bad guys decided to dish it out with one of our teams. It didn't end well. For the bad guys, I mean."

"They went in knowing the tunnel wasn't completed?" White asked, not understanding why the traffickers would willingly head into a dead end.

"My guess is they didn't know. Our intervention might have forced them into action sooner than they had anticipated and before they were fully briefed," she said. "But we'll never get a definitive answer. None of the traffickers who entered that specific tunnel survived the firefight."

"What about the two I saw jumping through a window?"

"Right. We're not gonna get anything from those two clowns. They clammed up and requested to speak with a lawyer. Plus, their faces are covered with tattoos marking them as cartel members. They won't talk to us, but the white trash you picked up might. We'll see."

"And what about this one? What did you find interesting about him?" White asked, looking at the dead trafficker.

The DEA agent crouched next to the corpse. "You see this tattoo right there?" She indicated a red-ink dragon tattoo on the inside of the man's wrist. "This guy is a fully fledged member of the Red Dragon Triad."

White had to admit this was indeed noteworthy. As far as he knew, at no point during the investigation had there been a mention about a link to a triad. "I've heard about the Red Dragon Triad before, but I didn't know it had much of a presence in the United States."

"That's the thing," the DEA agent said, dusting off the front of her cargo pants with her hands. "They don't. At least, that's what we thought until a few months ago, when reports started to come in suggesting that the Mexican cartels were now importing the chemicals necessary to make fentanyl pills from China. If we're to believe that, then I don't think it's much of a stretch to imagine that the triads now want a piece of the actual distribution pie. This is where the real money is being made."

"I get this," White said. "But why would the cartel willingly give up a share of the market they've fought and bled for? That's not like them."

"That, Mr. White, is the billion-dollar question."

PART TWO

Two Months Later

CHAPTER SIX

Macau Special Administrative Region
China

Geng Peiwu grimaced and slowly replaced the phone receiver in its cradle, his heartbeat faster than it had been in months. He reached into the inside pocket of his black Zegna suit jacket and pulled out a matchbox and a new bright red pack of Chunghwa cigarettes—his third of the day. He swiveled his office chair away from his desk and toward the floor-to-ceiling window that faced the ever-expanding Macau skyline.

Peiwu had noticed many changes since Lisbon had officially handed Macau back to China in 1999. With Peiwu's father's help, the Chinese government had developed Macau into a leisure destination that no longer played second fiddle to Hong Kong, its prolific neighbor on the opposite shore of the Pearl River. Vegas-style hotels and megacasinos—rather than office and condo towers—had replaced many of the Portuguese-style village squares that had once populated the charming, laid-back former colony. Although numerous structures that clustered around the historic center of Macau had been added to the UNESCO World Heritage List two decades ago to recognize the enclave's role as the first instance of European architecture on Chinese soil, the Macau of Peiwu's youth was long gone, its once-vibrant cultural heritage falling deeper every day into the shadows of its blinding neon lights and opulent shopping malls.

Peiwu couldn't care less.

Macau's modern trajectory, the consumerist dystopia it had become, had made his father rich beyond his wildest dreams. Following his father's passing, and with the quiet blessing of Beijing, Peiwu had taken over the Macau branch of the infamous Red Dragon Triad his old man had commanded with an iron fist. Under Peiwu's leadership, the criminal organization had expanded tenfold and now controlled over 50 percent of all drug trafficking activities in and out of the South China Sea. The casinos, which two decades ago had provided his father's triad with the bulk of its income, were now the heart of Peiwu's money-laundering operations. By his own calculations, he'd need to build three more hotels and at least that many more casinos within the next ten years in order to keep up with all the cash generated by the drug trafficking arm of his triad. But acquiring the land necessary for such growth had proved more difficult than he had anticipated.

His latest batch of requests for development permits, usually approved within hours of being submitted to the proper administrative forums for review, were being snubbed by the local administrators. When the secretary of economy and finance and the director general of Macau customs—both highly paid *consultants* of his—stopped responding to his emails and didn't pick up their phones when he called, Peiwu had worried about a possible regime change in Macau. That would have been bad for his business.

Had the local government lost the confidence of the State Council in Beijing?

While Macau still enjoyed a high degree of autonomy due to the "one country, two systems" policy, China had begun to tighten its grip. A regulatory overhaul and the implementation of a special tax aimed at the gambling industry had been the first two salvos. The third had been to incorporate Macau into a cooperation zone with Guangzhou, the capital of Guangdong Province. The mainland was flexing its muscles, a clear sign that Beijing wanted to regain full control over Macau's society and businesses. Still, despite the hurdles he'd encountered obtaining his new development permits, Peiwu's business had been somewhat spared from the crackdown he'd seen happening to many of his rivals on the gambling side of his business.

And now this?

Two minutes ago, as Peiwu had been getting ready to head home for the night, his assistant had called to report that an unannounced guest had shown up in the lobby of Peiwu's office tower requesting to be seen immediately.

This had triggered Peiwu's interest. No one made that kind of request. Not to him.

"Who is it?"

"Director Ma Lin."

Peiwu had jumped to his feet, standing ramrod straight, as if a five-foot javelin had been shoved up his ass.

"Sir, should I ask security to escort him out?"

"Absolutely not," he had barked into the phone. "Is he by himself?"

"Yes, sir. He's alone."

Strange. Ma Lin always traveled with a protection detail.

"Send him up immediately."

Ma Lin. This was unexpected. Or was it?

Ma Lin was the director of the 4th Bureau of the Ministry of State Security—or MSS. The MSS 4th Bureau was responsible for all intelligence work in Taiwan, Hong Kong, and Macau. If Geng Peiwu was Macau's prince, then Ma Lin was its uncontested king. The two men rarely spoke, but when they did, Peiwu listened.

Not that he had much choice in the matter.

As Peiwu waited for Ma Lin to make his way to the thirty-eighth floor, he unwrapped the pack of Chunghwa, the crackling of its plastic loud in the dark and solitude of his office. He pulled a cigarette from the pack and brought it to his lips. He struck a match and lit it, immediately inhaling a lungful of smoke. As he exhaled, he wondered about the reason behind Ma Lin's visit. Peiwu wasn't naive. He was aware that the

4th Bureau had intervened on his behalf against the charge Beijing was leading against the gambling industry in Macau. Contrary to those of some of his competitors, Peiwu's gambling operations had been afforded the privilege to continue running without too much interference.

Although he had been caught off guard by Ma Lin's visit, Peiwu had always known that it was only a question of time before the MSS contacted him to collect their due. Peiwu, and his father before him, had managed to thrive where so many others had failed only because the MSS had sanctioned their success from the get-go. In Macau, one's business acumen and ruthlessness could only carry one so far without Beijing's support. Without the backing and protection offered to him by the 4th Bureau, Peiwu wouldn't only have had to dedicate significantly more manpower to ensure the security of his business ventures; he would have probably ended up in jail a long time ago.

Or at the bottom of the Pearl River, he thought as he exhaled another cloud of smoke, wondering which was worse.

Over the last decade, Peiwu had witnessed Ma Lin's efficiency numerous times. Immediately coming to mind was the 4th Bureau's intervention in disqualifying twenty-one prodemocracy candidates during Macau's last legislative election, which had effectively shut down the political parties the rulers in Beijing had felt weren't loyal enough.

Or had become too powerful.

Only last month, Wan Chi-li, one of Peiwu's fiercest rivals, had been arrested in Macau on allegations that he ran a cybergambling platform that was accessible from mainland China, a place where gambling—other than in the state-run lottery—had been deemed illegal since the Communist Party had come to power in 1949. The war the president of China was waging against the gambling industry was real, but Peiwu doubted this was the true reason behind Chi-li's arrest. In Peiwu's opinion, it was the little black book Chi-li had kept that had sealed his fate. Crammed with the names of some of Beijing's top politicians and other government officials who had partaken in illegal activities, the black book hadn't offered Chi-li the protection or the leverage he had expected. Quite the opposite. It had put a target on his back. Wan Chi-li had played a dangerous game, and he had paid the price.

As mighty as he was in the underworld, Peiwu was under no illusions. In China, if the president—or the MSS, for that matter—wanted you gone, there was very little you could do to escape.

Two quick knocks on the door to his office pulled Peiwu's eyes away from the Macau skyline. His assistant leaned in the doorway and said, "Ma Lin's on his way, sir. Is there anything specific you want me to do?"

Peiwu dismissed him with a wave of his hand. "No, go home. I'll see you in the morning."

His assistant, who was in fact a former officer in a mountain infantry regiment of the People's Liberation Army, didn't look pleased about leaving his boss alone with the head of the 4th Bureau but bowed his head and did as he was told.

Peiwu stubbed out his cigarette in a pewter ashtray on his desk, and, moments later, Ma Lin walked into Peiwu's opulent office, carrying a brown leather briefcase in his left hand. Peiwu, who prided himself on his ability to size up those who appeared before him, quickly assessed his visitor. Ma Lin was in his midfifties and of medium height, but solidly built, with a bland face that wouldn't get noticed in a crowd if it wasn't for its asymmetric lips that gave him a kind of weird and permanent smirk. His thinning black hair, combed flat and straight back on his high forehead, had streaks of gray at the temples. Ma Lin's well-known friendship with the Chinese president made him not only a powerful and influential member of the Chinese intelligence community but also someone who commanded deference, or, more accurately, a healthy dose of fear.

At some point in the near future, this man will be the next minister of the Chinese Ministry of State Security, Peiwu thought.

"Director Lin," Peiwu said, walking across the marble floor and approaching the man, his right hand extended. "An unexpected visit, but a true honor to welcome you to my office."

Ma Lin shook his hand, but before he said anything, his gaze shifted to somewhere over Peiwu's left shoulder, an appreciative grin spreading across his face.

"Zhang Daqian's *Mist at Dawn*, isn't it?" Ma Lin asked.

Peiwu turned on his heel to face the painting. "A replica, I'm afraid," he said.

"Yes, of course," Ma Lin replied, his dark, mischievous eyes locked on the painting. "You keep the original, which you bought for more than twenty-five million US dollars last year, in a secure vault in the basement of your most recent resort. My mistake."

Peiwu felt perspiration break out on his upper lip. He forced a toothy smile.

"There isn't much you don't know, Director."

"Very true. Talking about knowledge, are you familiar with the rumor that Zhang Daqian was a master forger?" Ma Lin asked.

"I admit that I am not," Peiwu said, keeping his tone neutral.

"Then I think you'll find this fascinating," Ma Lin said, taking a seat in one of the two armchairs facing Peiwu's desk and motioning his host that he, too, should sit down.

Peiwu, not liking how quickly Ma Lin had made himself at home, obeyed, but his jaw tightened.

Ma Lin continued. "Zhang, who at a young age was selected to help copy centuries-old Buddhist paintings found in Dunhuang's caves, was so skilled that many of his forgeries are indistinguishable from other pieces that are often more than a thousand years old. It is even said that some of our own museums, which specialize in Chinese art no less, have undetected Zhang forgeries."

"Interesting," Peiwu said as he tried to determine the subtext, if there was any.

34

"Isn't it? What's even more impressive is the fact that despite the many technological advancements of recent years, Zhang's fakes are still being shown as originals from different tenth-century Chinese painters."

"That speaks volumes about his talent," Peiwu offered.

"There's that, but it shows how difficult it becomes even for subject matter experts to distinguish what is real and what's not, don't you agree?"

Peiwu nodded.

"And I'd add that it is especially true in the academic world when esteemed colleagues of yours have declared something to be original," Ma Lin said. "Going against their verdict could sink their reputations, even their careers, if you're right."

"Or yours if you're wrong," added Peiwu, which earned him a nod from Ma Lin.

"In my world, similar rules apply," the 4th Bureau director said. "Do you know why?"

Here we go, Peiwu thought. *He's about to tell me why the hell he's here.*

"I'm not sure I do," he said.

"Oh, but you do, Mr. Peiwu. You see, the intelligence-gathering business has some similarities with the kind of business you're running. It is sometimes difficult to differentiate friends from foes once your enemy's spies have penetrated your lines of defense."

Peiwu could relate. In many ways, his triad was like a large business or government organization. Despite his and his top lieutenants' efforts to keep police informants, rival triads' moles, or even Chinese and foreign intelligence officers out of his organization, there was no way to seal all the gaps that might be exploited. Getting fully accepted within Peiwu's triad and getting high enough within the organization to be able to inflict real damage took years, but once one was in that position of trust, and after all the hurdles and stress tests one had to endure to secure it, it would be a challenging task for anyone to unmask a turncoat.

"I don't disagree," Peiwu said after a moment. "But I'm curious as to why you're telling me this."

"I believe you and your organization are in a unique position to help me accomplish certain objectives that were personally given to me by the minister of state security," Ma Lin said.

Peiwu tried to hide his surprise but doubted he did a good job at it. Before he could say anything, Ma Lin asked, "You have a relationship with Henry Newman, is that right?"

Peiwu wasn't in the habit of discussing his business dealings with anyone but his most trusted associates, but he felt he had no choice when it came to the director of the 4th Bureau.

"Yes . . . I do," he said, not willing to share anything more than that until he knew why Ma Lin was interested in Newman.

Henry Newman, an American real estate developer, was the chairman and CEO of Newman Horizon Development, which owned and operated two of the largest casinos in Macau. Despite his relatively young age at the time, Newman had already been an established real estate developer in the United States when he'd built his first casino in Macau in 1998. Peiwu's father had taken a liking to the young American capitalist and had given him enough latitude to let Newman Horizon Development flourish—in exchange for 5 percent of its casino's gross income. Ten years later, another deal had been struck for Newman's second casino, an arrangement that proved lucrative for all parties. And, whenever sudden surpluses had prevented Peiwu from laundering cash through his own casinos in a timely fashion, he had often turned to Newman for help. Over the years, Newman had gained Peiwu's trust, enough so that a year ago Peiwu had used Newman's network and contacts in America to significantly expand his triad's footprint in the United States. In exchange for a reduced rate against the payments he owed Peiwu for the gambling income he generated in Macau, Newman provided members of the Red Dragon Triad with green cards and employment through several of his corporations in the United States.

I wonder if Ma Lin knows about that . . .

"In the very near future, I'll need you to . . . leverage that connection, Mr. Peiwu. Will that be a problem?"

Though Peiwu had no idea what Ma Lin had in mind for Newman, he replied with the only answer he knew would be acceptable. "It won't. At least not on my end. He owes me quite a few favors."

Ma Lin fished a gold-colored cigarette case from the breast pocket of his jacket. He selected a long, slim cigarette out of the case, then clicked it shut. Peiwu watched as Ma Lin patted his other pockets in search of a lighter. After a moment, Peiwu leaned over and lit the man's cigarette.

Ma Lin nodded his thanks, then inhaled deeply before blowing a thick, grayish stream of smoke toward the ceiling.

"You don't seem confident about Henry Newman. Why is that if, as you said, Newman owes you favors?"

"Newman is a shrewd businessman and isn't the kind of man that can be easily manipulated," Peiwu said. "Without knowing what it is you want from him, it's hard for me to say how he'll react to any type of request. He won't cooperate unless there's a clear benefit to him."

"Can't we squeeze him?" Ma Lin asked, taking another deep drag from his cigarette. "Your track record indicates you're quite good at that. And so was Wan Chi-li, until he wasn't, of course."

Peiwu cocked his head to one side. Had Ma Lin just threatened him? Were there 4th Bureau agents about to break into his office and arrest him, too, like they had done to his competitors?

"I'm told Wan Chi-li kept detailed notes on high-ranking party members," Peiwu said. "I don't."

Ma Lin blew another puff of smoke into the air. "Maybe. Maybe not. I'll be the judge of that."

Peiwu's blood pressure rose another notch. "I've never crossed you, or anyone in Beijing, so why are you making these threats?"

"I haven't made any threats, Mr. Peiwu. Now, tell me why you feel Henry Newman can't be blackmailed into helping us?"

Peiwu had learned that not everyone could be coerced, bribed, or bullied into playing ball. Most men could, but a select few couldn't.

"Director Lin, you must understand that Newman's holdings in Macau represent less than twenty-five percent of his total net worth and no more than thirty percent of his legitimate business income. If I were to put too much pressure on him, or find something really compromising about him, there's a chance he'd simply fold and head back to the United States," Peiwu replied, leaving out the fact that Newman could also decide to fight back, which wouldn't be good for anyone's business.

"Don't you have compromising information already on file about him?"

"None I can use that won't hurt me."

Ma Lin didn't say anything for a while, seeming content to smoke his cigarette.

"Newman Horizon Development is a publicly traded company," he finally said. "I don't think its shareholders—or its board of directors, for that matter—would be too happy if Newman was to pull out of Macau."

"You aren't wrong, but Newman has a firm grip on the company, and he has the trust of the board. Under his helm, the company has steadily provided good returns to its investors. I'm not saying he couldn't be pushed out, but what would be the point in that?"

"Hmm . . . hmm. But he likes money, doesn't he?"

Peiwu smiled. "Who doesn't?"

"So maybe in Newman's case the carrot is better than the stick."

"I think that would be a fair assessment," Peiwu said, relieved he wouldn't have to threaten or blackmail Newman.

But the relief didn't last long because Ma Lin was quick to add, "But I still prefer the stick."

With that, Ma Lin rose to his feet and used Peiwu's ashtray to extinguish his cigarette.

"The matter is settled," Ma Lin said. "Clear your schedule for tomorrow and the day after that. You're coming back to Beijing with me. My assistant will call you in an hour with the details."

"Excuse me? I can't simply—" Peiwu started, but was immediately cut off by Ma Lin.

"Yes, you can. And you will," Ma Lin said, his face hardening and his words hitting Peiwu like brutal blows. "You've been living like a king since you took over your father's business. Don't you think it's about time you show us some gratitude?"

Peiwu had to bite his tongue to remain quiet.

"But it is not my intention to fight with you," Ma Lin said in a gentler tone. "And, as a gesture of good faith, I've made a call on your behalf."

From his leather briefcase, Ma Lin pulled a paper file. "Inside you'll find the building permits you've asked for."

"I assume these permits will be revoked if I don't go to Beijing?"

A light chuckle escaped Ma Lin's lips as he shook his head. "No, no, Mr. Peiwu. You've got this all wrong," he said, pointing his index finger at Peiwu's chest. "It is not the permits that will be rescinded if you don't show up at my office tomorrow, it is you who will be swapped with a more willing participant. And, for the record, *that* was a threat."

Peiwu thought about the QSZ-92 semiautomatic pistol in the top right drawer of his desk. It would be so easy to grab it and put a round in the middle of Ma Lin's forehead for his insolence and lack of respect. But to what end? What would that accomplish? He'd be hunted down like a dog and lose everything he and his father had dedicated their lives to. There would be no safe place left in the world for him, his wife, and his four children. He had no option but to go ahead with whatever was on Ma Lin's mind.

For now.

CHAPTER SEVEN

Macau Special Administrative Region
China

Once Peiwu was sure he had reined in his anger in a way that his voice wouldn't betray his frustration, he asked, "Can you at least tell me why I need to be on a three-hour flight to Beijing tomorrow?"

"Because I want you to attend a meeting that's scheduled for tomorrow afternoon at the MSS headquarters. But don't worry, you'll be flying with me. You'll be back in time to kiss your lovely wife good night."

Peiwu wasn't looking forward to stepping into MSS headquarters. It was the kind of place that could make someone disappear into thin air. "And what's this meeting about? Does it have anything to do with Henry Newman?"

"It does. There's someone who'll be in attendance I want you to meet. His name is Yuri Makarov."

"Who is he?" Peiwu asked. He had never heard the name before.

"Yuri keeps a low profile, but he's very much like you. Same line of work. Anyhow, he's the person the Russian president sent our way to negotiate on his behalf."

This left Peiwu perplexed and feeling as if he was missing something. "Why do we need to negotiate with the Russians?" he asked. "I'm not seeing the connection between Russia and Newman."

"Yuri Makarov has something we need. You'll understand tomorrow."

"That doesn't tell me much, Director."

Ma Lin seemed to think it over for a moment, then sat back in his chair and crossed his legs.

"With the fiasco of their special military operation in Ukraine, our friends in Moscow opened a door for us," he said.

"A door to what exactly?"

"As I just said, everything will make more sense tomorrow," Ma Lin replied. "But know this. Our president believes—he told me so personally—that the reunification with Taiwan must be fulfilled as soon as possible. The chaos Russia created has not dissipated. We need to seize the moment. The Americans are still distracted by the ongoing humanitarian crisis in Ukraine. That, combined with the neck-deep political infighting you will help generate, should allow us to launch our attack on Taiwan. By the time they realize our intentions, it will be too late. Taiwan will be ours."

Did he just suggest that I get involved in a sanctioned MSS operation in the United States? Has he gone mad?

Peiwu observed Ma Lin for a moment. The man's excitement was palpable, but Peiwu didn't share his enthusiasm. Quite the opposite. Even before Ma Lin's reference to Peiwu's involvement in some kind of intelligence operation in the United States, Peiwu's mouth had gone dry at the mention of Taiwan. His wife's parents were originally from Taiwan, and his eldest son was currently studying medicine in Taipei. Taiwan's armed forces were no match against the Chinese military, but the Taiwanese wouldn't simply roll over and welcome the Chinese invaders with open arms. They would fight back, and the Americans would be on their side. There would be a war. An ugly one.

"And what's to be my role in this?" Peiwu asked.

41

"You will use your relationship with Henry Newman to do three things. The first one will be to smuggle certain precious items into the United States."

"What items?"

"We'll discuss this at length tomorrow, but I don't mind giving you a bit of background. But before I do so, it's imperative you understand that this information isn't to be shared with anyone else without my consent. Your wife's and children's lives depend on it."

Peiwu fought to keep the white-hot surge of anger welling up inside him out of his facial expression while Ma Lin's cold, dark eyes assessed him. Peiwu met Ma Lin's gaze without flinching, which seemed to please the MSS spy.

Then Peiwu nodded, and Ma Lin began.

"In their haste to leave Afghanistan, the Americans left behind more than seven billion dollars' worth of military equipment," he said. "That includes armored vehicles, aircraft, and thousands of crates of weapons and ammunitions."

"I've read about this," Peiwu said. "The previous American administration tried to downplay this by claiming that the hardware was actually the property of the Afghan government at the time it was abandoned."

"Yes, they did. And for a few news cycles, the American political left and right were at each other's throats about it, blaming the other side for the collapse of the Afghan US-backed government as soon as the last aircraft flew out of the country. It was a thing of beauty."

"The Taliban are ferocious fighters, but they don't have the training necessary to use the more advanced equipment the Americans abandoned in their poorly planned retreat," Peiwu said, not sure where this conversation was headed. "So, who cares who the military equipment belonged to at the time?"

"We do!" Ma Lin snapped. "You see, Mr. Peiwu, political enemies in the United States have the tendency to hold a grudge for a very long time. You were correct about the Taliban being unable to make good use of the equipment they inherited, so Yuri Makarov bought it for pennies on the dollar."

"I see," Peiwu said, though he was still puzzled as to why this concerned him.

Reading right through him, Ma Lin let out an amused chuckle, as if to say: *No, you don't.*

"Buried among the various weapons crates he had purchased, our friend Yuri was surprised to find two dozen FIM-92 Stinger surface-to-air missiles."

Now Peiwu finally understood. "The precious items you mentioned," he said through tight lips.

"Yes. You will send these missiles to the United States via the same routes you've established for your other activities," Ma Lin said. "The ones you're using to supply the Mexican cartels with the necessary precursors for the fentanyl pills, in case you aren't sure which routes I'm talking about. I'm aware that one of them was recently shut down by American federal agents, but I believe there are two others in California that remain operational and six more between the states of Arizona, New Mexico, and Texas, isn't that so?"

Peiwu's heart skipped a beat and he remained silent, shocked—although he knew he shouldn't be—that Ma Lin knew so much. It could mean only one thing.

Someone with intimate knowledge of my organization is leaking information to the MSS.

Ma Lin continued. "It's my job to exploit the vulnerabilities you and your kind uncover," he said, matter-of-factly.

"My kind?" Peiwu growled, his eyes moving once again to the drawer where he kept his pistol.

"Don't fool yourself. Criminals like you have a purpose, but you are allowed to exist because the state permits it. You work for us, remember, not the other way around."

Peiwu ground his teeth. *Insolent bastard.* His growing frustration was in no small part due to knowing that Ma Lin was speaking the truth.

"Don't look so distraught, Mr. Peiwu," Ma Lin said. "As long as your endeavors and those of your triad weaken the Americans, the MSS will not interfere. In fact, we've been keeping track of your activities with great interest and have been discreetly intervening on your behalf with our friends in the United States."

"What do you mean?"

"There's a reason why the Red Dragon Triad hasn't faced significant headwinds in the United States," Ma Lin said. "Let's just say that the MSS sees it as a priority that the network you've built up remains stable."

"Because you don't want any issue with the delivery of the surface-to-air missiles," Peiwu said. "And to whom will the missiles go?"

"You don't have to worry about this, but we will require you to assist with the positioning of our national assets in the United States. To do this, we want you to exploit the same system you tapped into to expand your triad's footprint in America."

"Through Henry Newman?"

"Yes."

"And what do you mean by *assets*?"

"Saboteurs, some criminals, but mostly intelligence operatives. People able to teach the left- and the right-wing radicals in the US how to operate the American-made surface-to-air missiles."

"You're planning to shoot down an aircraft in the United States?"

"No, not one aircraft. Several of them, all at the same time. And the Americans will do it for us."

As crazy as it sounded, Ma Lin's strategy made sense. American radicals from both sides of the aisle taking down airliners with weapons the United States had themselves left behind in Afghanistan? Peiwu had to give it to Ma Lin. The plan was bold and ambitious, but it could work, and, if it did, it could very well ignite a second civil war.

Which would clear the way for Beijing to annex Taiwan, Peiwu thought. But there was one problem.

"Director Lin," Peiwu said with a newfound respect for the 4th Bureau director. "Henry Newman might not walk the straight and narrow, but he's far from being stupid, and he'll see soon enough that the people you're sending into the US aren't Red Dragon members. He'll recognize them for what they are, and I doubt he'll be willing to betray his country. Even for money."

Ma Lin, who was in the process of lighting another cigarette, looked up at Peiwu over the top of his glasses. "Who said anything about him doing it willingly?"

Peiwu exhaled loudly. "I already told you I have nothing I can use against him that won't affect me or my business."

"Then we will have to create something, won't we?"

Peiwu was about to reply, but Ma Lin raised a hand, silencing him before he had even opened his mouth. "About Henry Newman," Ma Lin said, tapping his cigarette over the precariously full ashtray on Peiwu's desk. "Did you know that the FBI director is considering opening an investigation into the Red Dragon's activities in the United States?"

The question took Peiwu by surprise.

"Of course you didn't," Ma Lin said, making no effort to hide his condescending tone. "The look on your face betrays you. Then I assume you also don't know that one of Newman Horizon Development's initial investors happens to be Patrick O'Donnell."

"The FBI director?" Peiwu asked, feeling the muscles in his jaw tightening.

"Yes."

"I . . . no, I didn't," Peiwu confessed, conscious of the negative ramifications this might have. "As you know, it was my father who initiated contact with Newman, but I admit that I did read through the due diligence documents, and I didn't see anything that would—"

"Don't be overly concerned about this," Ma Lin interrupted. "We ourselves only came by this information a little over a year ago, when you decided to use Newman's organization as a conduit to expand into the United States. The tools and the technology we have access to nowadays are vastly superior to the ones we had two decades ago."

"Is Newman the cause of the FBI investigation you mentioned?" Peiwu asked after a moment.

"Doubtful. He has nothing to gain and everything to lose if the FBI was to investigate the Red Dragon Triad. As far as we can tell, Newman has contacted Director O'Donnell only four times in the last twelve months."

Peiwu was skeptical. "How can you possibly know this? And how do you know the FBI is coming after my organization?"

"Have you forgotten who I work for, Mr. Peiwu? The MSS has a variety of resources at its disposal. You'll learn how in due time."

Peiwu's mind was racing. The progress he'd made in the United States in less than a year was astounding, especially with his human and drug trafficking rings. Ma Lin's confession that the MSS had provided support along the way explained why he hadn't encountered as many problems as he had anticipated. There had been a few hiccups here and there, including the death of his lead man in San Diego two months ago in a shoot-out with the DEA, but his network was getting stronger by the day. He'd always believed that the local gangs would fight tooth and nail for their territory, but it hadn't been the case. His alliance with two of the Mexican cartels had certainly helped, but Peiwu assumed the MSS had facilitated that too. There was no doubt in his mind that an FBI investigation would slow the Red Dragon Triad's momentum and potentially allow other organizations to throw their weight around— two things the MSS couldn't allow to happen. There was a lot more on the line than Peiwu had ever thought possible, which made him realize that he was only a small cog in a big, powerful machine.

But an important cog nonetheless, he thought. *That's why Ma Lin is here. Despite his threats and intimidation tactics, he needs me.*

"Let me guess," Peiwu said. "You want to use Newman to pressure the FBI director to back down."

"Yes. With what you've learned this evening, I'm sure you understand why the minister of state security and the prime minister have made it abundantly clear that it is a matter of national security that this investigation never occurs."

Peiwu nodded.

"We've done what we could to delay any kind of investigation into the Red Dragon Triad, but our influence within the FBI is very limited. Certainly not strong enough to stop a directive coming from the director's office."

"But you're hoping I can."

"Through Henry Newman, yes," Ma Lin confirmed, taking a final drag of his cigarette.

"Tell me again, Director Lin, what is it that you want me to do in order to . . . convince Newman he should cooperate?"

What might have been a smile seemed to rise from Ma Lin's bland face and asymmetrical lips. "I'm glad you asked."

CHAPTER EIGHT

Key West
Florida

White stared at his fiancée, his eyes soft with love. Veronica was clearly in a state of pure bliss. Seated in the middle of a large sofa and surrounded by plush pillows and baby catalogs, she had spent the better part of an hour looking at changing stations, baby chairs, cribs, and other *necessary* baby items. White had had to call his credit card company twice in the last month to bump his credit limit. Who would have thought high chairs and strollers were so expensive?

Now that they were splitting their time between the White House's Executive Residence and their oceanfront three-bedroom apartment in Key West, Veronica had insisted that they needed two sets of everything. White had acquiesced. They had the money—or at least the extra room on the credit card. Truth be told, he wasn't worried about their finances. The only thing that made him anxious was the number of hours his fiancée worked per week. Veronica was still working ten-hour days at SkyCU Technology, a Silicon Valley start-up, and was collaborating with NOAA—the National Oceanic and Atmospheric Administration—on a major project for which she would be the ambassador. Veronica being Veronica, she was still going at it at full speed, despite her doctor's recommendation to significantly cut down her hours.

White had tried to bring up the subject a couple of times, but she had pointed out to him that he hadn't slowed down, either, and that most of her work was done online without the need to travel to SkyCU's office in California. Reluctant to pick a fight over this, White had backed down, but he hoped Veronica's obstetrician would take the opportunity at their next appointment—which, thankfully, was scheduled later in the day—to gently remind Vonnie to reduce her workload.

"How're you feeling?" he asked, taking a seat next to her.

As usual, Veronica radiated positivity. She kissed him on the lips; then he snugged her closer, wrapping an arm around her.

"I'm feeling great," she said, resting her head on his shoulder. "I have no morning sickness, no stomach cramps, I really can't complain. How about you?"

"Same," he said. "No morning sickness or stomach cramps either."

She laughed and smacked his thigh.

God knew how much he treasured the carefree sound of her laughter. He always had. White loved the way Veronica's laugh changed her attractive features into luminous ones and how her vivid green eyes reached into his soul when she did. This was also one of the rare moments when he could see the vulnerability his fiancée tried so hard to hide.

"I might have gone slightly overboard with my latest shopping spree," she said a moment later. "You wouldn't believe how many cute, adorable outfits there are for newborns. It's mind boggling!"

White chuckled and wrinkled his nose. "It's my fault," he said. "I shouldn't have gotten you so many magazines. Too many options for you to choose from. I'll cancel the monthly subscription."

"Don't you dare."

He kissed the top of her head and closed his eyes, enjoying the moment. The silence stretched on for a few minutes; then she said, "I'm nervous about this afternoon, Clay."

He squeezed her tighter against him. Veronica wasn't the only one anxious about the upcoming scan. He was scared too. More than he was ready to admit to her. This afternoon's appointment with their obstetrician was for a detailed scan—their fifth since the beginning of her pregnancy. This one would tell them if everything looked normal. The doctor would look at the baby's brain, spine, and vital organs for anything out of the ordinary. The first four appointments hadn't revealed anything unusual, but each visit had been a nerve-racking experience.

White fished his phone out of his jeans pocket and selected the photo app. He opened the top folder and angled the screen so that Veronica could see it too. He slowly scrolled through the four photos, each one showing a different image of their unborn baby. The difference in the fetus's size between the first picture, taken at the eighth week, and the most recent one was astonishing.

"Baby's growing so fast," Veronica whispered.

"Have you changed your mind about asking the doctor the baby's sex?" he asked.

He felt Veronica stiffen a little. She gently pushed herself from him. "Have you?" she asked, raising an eyebrow.

White shook his head. "No. I still prefer if we kept it a surprise, and I think you do, too, but I just wanted to let you know that I'm fine with the idea of knowing if you had changed your mind."

"I feel the same way," Veronica said. Then she sat straighter, lifted her sweater, and took his hand, pressing it against the naked flesh of her stomach.

White felt a flutter; then her belly rippled underneath his palm, and he suddenly found himself overwhelmed by the reality of it all. He looked at his fiancée in amazement. A beautiful smile had lit her face, and her eyes were sparkling. A sense of wonder swelled through him.

The featherlight touch I felt against my hand is an actual human being growing inside the woman I love, he thought. White wondered, and not for the first time, if he'd be up to the task of raising a child. *Do I have what it takes?*

His phone buzzed, pulling him out of his spiral of self-doubt. He looked at the screen. Recognizing the number, he took a deep breath.

"It's your father," he said.

"Then you better answer."

White did.

"You're on speaker, and I'm with Veronica," he said, taking the call, his mind still reeling at the realization that he'd felt his baby move for the first time.

"Hi, Vonnie," the president said.

"Hey, Dad."

"I wish I could talk longer, but I only have a minute."

"That's fine. You wouldn't have dialed Clay's number if this was a social call," Veronica said.

"Right. Sorry. Listen, Clayton, I need you to make a short trip to the US Virgin Islands," Hammond said. "Rest assured, it's the kind of trip where you can bring Veronica with you if her schedule allows for it."

White frowned, surprised by the request, though he had to admit a trip to the Virgin Islands sounded nice, knowing it might force Veronica to take a well-deserved break.

"Okay. Why, and when?"

"It's not urgent, and I know you guys have a doctor's appointment later this afternoon, so later this week is fine."

White was delighted to see Veronica going through her agenda. He noted that her lips were curled up.

She's happy her father remembered the doctor's appointment, he thought.

By the way she was scrolling through her schedule, White was pretty sure she'd find a way to make room for a short trip to the Caribbean.

"As for the why," Hammond continued, "I need you to meet with the FBI director, Patrick O'Donnell. He has a vacation home in Saint John. I'll go into more details later tonight, but I wanted to give you a heads-up."

"Can you at least give me a hint?" White asked.

"Sure. It's about the Red Dragon Triad."

CHAPTER NINE

Macau Special Administrative Region
China

Henry Newman, chairman and CEO of Newman Horizon Development, was in a foul mood. It was seven o'clock in the morning; the sky was low, heavy as lead; and rain seemed imminent. Instead of being pampered by the two flight attendants of his company Gulfstream IV and being halfway through his flight to Ko Samui—an island off the east coast of Thailand where he kept a beach house—for a long weekend of debauchery with friends he hadn't seen in months, Newman had been summoned by Executive Council member Zhang Mo, the Commissioner against Corruption, mere minutes after he'd arrived at the Macau International Airport. It wasn't Newman's first dealing with the commissioner. For the last five years, every four months, like clockwork, the commissioner had expected Newman to show up at his office to pay a special tax.

Special tax, my ass! A damn bribe, that's what it is, Newman fumed.

Though Geng Peiwu had warned Newman that Mo was out of his Red Dragon Triad's reach, he had assured him that despite his important-sounding title, Commissioner against Corruption Zhang Mo was quite harmless.

"But do pay his special tax, Henry," Peiwu had warned. "Mo, too, has masters to please, and we don't want him to be replaced by someone less . . . accommodating."

To keep himself in Peiwu's good graces and to preserve the almost nonstop flow of money coming to him from the Red Dragon Triad leader, Newman had been happy to oblige. At least at the beginning. But in Newman's opinion, Commissioner against Corruption Mo had gotten greedy over the last eight months, and the special tax had gone up by 400 percent and now had to be paid twice as frequently. That couldn't stand. Not because Newman couldn't afford it—he could—but as a matter of principle and respect. If Newman didn't fight back, more members of the Executive Council would try to squeeze him for *their* cut. Still, not wanting to take a course of action that would anger Peiwu, Newman had reached out to the triad leader to hear his thoughts. Peiwu had promised he'd do his best to straighten things out, but with a polite reminder that the commissioner was out of his sphere of influence.

"Go to the meeting, and see what the commissioner wants," Peiwu had said.

Shit!

Newman's friends, business leaders in the tech world, would party on *his* dime, at *his* house, without him being present.

Bastards.

His more expensive bottles of wine were under lock and key in a special display in the library, but knowing how his friends liked to party, there was little doubt in Newman's mind that the two cases of 2005 Château Cheval Blanc Premier Grand Cru Classé he had had delivered directly from the French winery for the occasion would be emptied by the time he made it back to the beach house.

Outside Newman's chauffeured Mercedes S 580, the rain had started. Fat pellets of water stroked the vehicle's roof and windshield with increasing intensity. The early-morning traffic was thick and getting worse, and the cacophony of car horns did nothing to brighten Newman's mood.

"Two minutes, sir," Newman's driver said. "Should I go in with you?"

"That won't be necessary," Newman replied. "Drive around and I'll text you when I'm through."

The driver pulled in next to the headquarters of the Macau government, a two-story pink Pombaline-style building on Avenida da Praia Grande facing the Nam Van Lake. While most visitors found the headquarters to be out of place in the revitalized downtown of Macau, due to its Portuguese influence, Newman liked it. Having lived in Macau for years, he knew the building had been the residence of the governor prior to the handover.

Newman exited the Mercedes sedan and hurried toward the headquarters, briefcase in hand, navigating his way around numerous puddles, unwilling to muddy the waxed alligator skin of his Louis Vuitton shoes.

Upon entering the headquarters, Newman was met by two uniformed police officers he didn't recognize. Newman's identity was verified before he was allowed to walk through a metal detector. One of the officers inspected Newman's briefcase. The man didn't even flinch when he found the secret compartment filled with American dollars. Clearly, he was used to businessmen delivering cash payments to members of the Executive Council. Satisfied Newman hadn't hidden a firearm, the officer closed the briefcase and issued Newman a badge with his name on it.

"Follow me, Mr. Newman," the officer said in English, leading the way toward the elevator.

Coming from the opposite side, a woman was also headed to the elevator, her high-heeled shoes clicking on the polished white marble floor of the foyer. She wore a pair of snug-fitting blue jeans with the cuffs up around her calves and a black long-sleeved turtleneck that clung to every curve. She was strikingly beautiful and walked with the grace of a runway model, her every step radiating confidence and sexual prowess. Newman and the woman reached the elevator at the same time. She smiled, enchanting him with a dimple in her left cheek. Newman graciously smiled back, his pulse quickening. Then the scent of her perfume reached his nose, and Newman went utterly still—its smell, a fragrance of white tea coupled with notes of cedar and vanilla, reminding him of the last woman he had truly loved. This woman, who seemed to notice his discomfort, cocked her head to one side and gave him a long, penetrating look.

"Is everything all right?" she asked in Cantonese.

"My apologies," Newman replied in the same language. "I didn't mean to stare."

When the doors of the elevator parted on the second floor, saving him from additional embarrassment, Newman gestured for the woman to leave first, and he watched her walk confidently down the corridor, surprised to find himself disappointed by the fact that she didn't glance back over her shoulder.

"Mr. Newman," the officer snapped. "This way."

Commissioner Zhang Mo's office was situated in the east wing of the building. As Newman and the officer entered the small waiting room adjacent to the commissioner's private office, they were greeted by a man in his early twenties dressed in a custom-made black business suit. For as long as Newman could remember, Mo's secretary had been a serious-looking middle-aged woman named Li.

"Thank you, Officer, you can return to your post," the young man said. "I'll take it from here."

"Miss Li isn't here this morning?" Newman asked in Cantonese.

"Sick, I'm afraid," the man replied in perfect English. "I've been asked to cover for her."

"Nothing too serious, I hope?"

"Sore throat," the man replied. "Nothing to worry about."

56

Newman was invited to sit in one of four straight, and very uncomfortable, wooden chairs.

"It shouldn't be too long. Commissioner Mo will see you shortly."

Though Newman tried not to judge, the man standing behind what he still considered to be Li's desk looked more like a professional athlete than a secretary or a receptionist. The man was shorter than Newman, but his business suit barely hid his muscular frame or the unmistakable bulge of a pistol over his left hip. He had a dark, devious presence that quickened Newman's pulse.

Something was wrong. There was more to this summons than Newman had originally thought. And he didn't like it. He was about to mumble an excuse and leave when the door to Commissioner Mo's office opened.

"Sorry to keep you waiting," Mo said in Cantonese, his voice weaker than Newman remembered it to be. "Please come in."

Mo's new "secretary" had quietly moved behind Newman, standing in a nonthreatening manner with his hands folded in front of him, but nonetheless blocking Newman's path toward the exit.

Mo, a balding man of medium height and modest build, wore dark-rimmed glasses that were propped halfway down his nose. A veneer of perspiration had formed above Mo's upper lip—another anomaly. The man was nervous; that much was clear. The question was why. Mo was in a position of strength. Newman was in *his* office, and there was enough security around to ensure the commissioner's safety. Not that Newman had any intention of using violence to get out of whatever mess this was.

What am I missing?

Mo stepped aside to let Newman pass, then closed the door and pointed to the two visitors' chairs.

"Have a seat, Mr. Newman," Mo said as he walked around his desk, a large antique made of natural oak that had been restored to a

Simon Gervais

high-gloss finish. A single yellow file folder was positioned squarely in its center, next to a desktop computer.

Newman sat and placed his briefcase on the floor beside him. "What am I doing here, Commissioner Mo?" he asked once the commissioner had sunk into his own chair.

Mo seemed to notice the slight tremor in his hands and tried to steady them by placing his elbows on his desk. Newman noted that Mo's perspiration was no longer limited to his upper lip. It had spread to his eyebrows.

"It has come to my attention that your company is somehow involved with Geng Peiwu," Mo said. "Is that true?"

Alarm bells rang in Newman's head. Mo was aware of his dealings with the Red Dragon Triad leader. Hell, part of why Newman paid Mo was to keep the authorities at bay. What kind of game was the commissioner playing?

"You seem confused by the question, Mr. Newman," Mo said as he flipped open the file folder.

From where he sat, Newman could see the photograph someone had clipped to the cover page. It showed a man in his fifties with an angular face and rather good-humored eyes, whose dark hair and beard showed a touch of gray.

Newman sighed. It was his picture. His file.

"What is it that you want exactly, Commissioner?" Newman asked.

"This file contains information about your involvement with a known and dangerous criminal—"

Before Newman could protest, the door behind him burst open, and the man who was masquerading as Commissioner Mo's new secretary rushed inside the office, a suppressed pistol in his hand. The weapon barked once as Newman was getting up, then once more as he propelled himself at the shooter. Newman's tackle, which he had honed a long time ago playing college football, was perfect. His right shoulder smashed into the man's knee, collapsing its joint. The shooter fell

58

backward, coming down hard on an old coffee table, whose two short front legs snapped under the weight.

Though the shooter was dazed, and probably surprised by the speed at which Newman had reacted, he was still holding on to his gun. Newman, who was on top of the shooter's legs, pushed himself farther toward the man's upper body and punched him twice in the face with all his strength. Both punches caught the man on the nose, which shattered on the second impact. Still, the man didn't quit, and he started to swing his pistol toward Newman, who chopped down at the shooter's forearm with the edge of his hand. The gun clattered to the floor. But while Newman had been focusing on the pistol, the shooter had managed to pull a small knife from a sheath with his other hand and was about to stab Newman between his ribs. Newman tried to intercept the man's wrist but wasn't fast enough. The blade pierced the center of Newman's hand. Newman screamed with pain. Looking for a weapon of his own, Newman grabbed one of the broken coffee table's legs and thrust its sharp tip into the shooter's face several times until he felt something give way and heard a strange suction noise.

Only then did Newman slowly get to his feet. His heart was racing, but his legs were feeble under him. He steadied himself against the wall. His right hand was a bloody mess and felt as if it was on fire. At Newman's feet, the shooter lay dead, the coffee table leg protruding from the man's open mouth.

Shit! What the hell just happened?

CHAPTER TEN

Macau Special Administrative Region
China

Henry Newman had never killed a man before. Truth be told, he had often wondered how he would react if he was one day caught in a situation like this. Again and again, he had concluded that until that scenario happened in real life, he wasn't sure he would be capable of pulling the trigger.

Now he knew, assuming pulling the trigger wasn't more difficult than shoving a piece of wood into someone's mouth deep enough to kill him. Newman was now moving on pure adrenaline. After quickly bandaging his hand with the dead man's tie, Newman picked up the man's pistol, remembering to ensure there was a round in the chamber. It had been years since he'd gone through any sort of weapons training.

Taking a deep breath, Newman gazed over one last time at Commissioner Mo, who was still in his chair, slumped forward with his head resting on top of his polished desk. The shooter's two bullets had done their job and left a single large gaping wound at the back of the corrupt bureaucrat's head.

Despite the suppressor attached to the pistol, the two gunshots had been loud. But had they been loud enough to be heard from outside the waiting area?

Probably. Newman swore out loud. He had to get out of the building. *No. I must get out of Macau! But how?*

He needed help. He reached into the breast pocket of his suit for his phone, keeping an eye on the door leading to the hallway. Were there security officers already stacked on both sides of the door, getting ready to breach the small waiting room? Newman didn't think so. Less than a minute had elapsed since the shooter barged into Mo's office. Newman hesitated between two numbers. In the end, he dialed his chauffeur's cell phone, having a hard time doing so thanks to his injured hand. Looking at the carnage around him, he wondered if calling the other number wouldn't have been a better idea.

No answer. *Damn it!*

Newman looked at his phone, confirmed he had good reception, and was about to dial again when the single window of Mo's office shattered, a flash-bang grenade landing five feet to his right. Newman looked at it in horror. The pin was missing. The grenade exploded a millisecond later in the confined space in a burst of white light and noise such as Newman had never seen—or heard—before. Newman was knocked off his feet, blinded and completely disoriented. He tried to get to his knees, but the next thing he knew, he was shoved face first to the ground.

Hard.

Then both his arms were forced behind his back, and he felt the cold steel of handcuffs as they closed around his wrists. Incapable of seeing, with his ears ringing, Newman didn't feel the sharp sting of a needle entering the side of his neck, but for the second time that day, the subtle smell of white tea mixed with notes of cedar and vanilla reached his nose. As consciousness escaped him and blackness enveloped him, Newman's last coherent thought was of the woman he'd met at the elevator.

CHAPTER ELEVEN

Saint John
US Virgin Islands

Clayton White was laughing so hard his ribs hurt. Veronica had tears running down her cheeks and was clearly having a hard time not spitting out the mouthful of sparkling water she'd just taken.

"And then I shoved the bastard overboard," Emily Moss said.

That sent White and Veronica into another fit of laughter, which garnered their table a few curious, good-natured looks from patrons seated at nearby tables. White apologized with a wave of the hand. He looked at Emily. She had a straight face, but it was evident she was having a rough time keeping a smile off her lips.

"Are you pulling my leg, or you really threw this guy off his own yacht?" Veronica asked.

"I wouldn't lie to you, Vonnie," Emily said, casting a fake frown. "And if you don't believe me, you can always ask your good friend Pierre Sarazin."

"Pierre was at the party?" Veronica asked.

"Of course he was. Pierre goes to all the parties. And he knows everyone in Monaco," Emily said.

These last words spoken by Emily were enough to put a broad smile on White's face. Pierre Sarazin, a former French spy from the Direction Générale de la Sécurité Extérieure—and the biggest wine connoisseur

White knew—had saved his life in Kommetjie, a small town in South Africa, almost two years back. More recently, he'd traveled to England with White for an unsanctioned operation and had been critically injured. But, baffling the medical professionals who treated him, the small Frenchman had rebounded and had decided to return to the French Riviera, or, more precisely, Monaco. Notwithstanding that Pierre was officially retired from the French foreign spy agency, White couldn't help but think that his friend had somehow stayed connected with his former employer. Monaco's extravagant parties, often attended by royals, tech moguls, and Russian oligarchs, were a great place to collect intelligence.

"Good for him," White said. "I'm glad he's enjoying life on the Riviera."

"I'm not kidding, Clayton," Emily said. "Next time you see him, ask him about that party. Everyone that saw what happened will remember the slap of that Russian pig hitting the dark water for a very, very long time."

"Shit, Emily," Veronica said, wiping her tears away with a napkin. "You could have killed the man."

"That's what the police said too," Emily said, then drank the rest of the local beer she'd brought down from her room. "But I'll bet you a round of drinks that man will think twice before he grabs a woman's ass again."

"I'm sure he will," White said, still unsure how much of Emily's story was true.

Their waiter, a tall, beefy man of about fifty, made his way to their table and handed menus all around, opening them as he did so.

"Very nice to see you again, Miss Hammond," he said, "and you too, Mr. White."

"Glad to see you'll be taking care of us again tonight, Gerald," Veronica replied with a charming smile. She gestured toward Emily and said, "And this is Emily Moss, a very dear friend of mine."

"A pleasure, Miss Moss," the waiter said.

"Pleasure is all mine, Gerald," Emily replied.

"Can I offer you anything from the bar?"

Emily ordered a glass of champagne, Veronica said she would stick with sparkling water, and White, who had never cared for the usual island colorful rum punches, settled for a locally made hazy IPA from St. John Brewers.

"We're starving, Gerald," Veronica said. "Is it okay if we order right away?"

"Of course."

"These two haven't stopped raving about the grilled scallops they ordered last night," Emily said. "Are they still available?"

"I'll make sure they are, Miss Moss, even if I have to get into the water and catch them myself."

Emily clapped her hands together. "A true gentleman. Thank you."

"Would you like anything to start? To share with the table maybe?"

"Why don't you bring us an order of fried calamari and a seafood platter," Veronica said, looking at White and Emily, who both nodded with enthusiasm.

"An order of conch fritters, too, please," White added.

"For the main, I'll take one of your Caribbean lobster tails with a side of grilled vegetables," Veronica said.

"A fantastic choice," Gerald said, beaming.

White smiled. He'd be happy, too, if he was in Gerald's shoes. With the automatic 22 percent gratuity added to the bill, Gerald had just made a quick twenty bucks with Veronica's lobster tail.

"I'll have the same," Emily said. "But I'm also keeping the scallops."

"Marvelous!" Gerald exclaimed, his smile getting bigger by the second. Turning to White, he said, "Same for you, sir? I highly recommend the lobster tail. It is su-blime."

Though he already knew he wasn't going to order a one-hundred-dollar piece of shellfish he'd swallow in three bites, White acted as if he was considering it.

"You know what, I'll pass on the lobster tail, Gerald. I'll have the beef burger with fries," White said, closing his menu and handing it back to the waiter, whose smile had melted away.

Once Gerald was gone, Veronica squeezed his hand with hers.

"Gerald really wanted you to get that lobster, baby," she said, not missing a beat. "He would have been so happy if you did."

"I could have ordered the Kobe steak and he would have been even happier," White said with a chuckle.

"Maybe. But a burger? With fries? You just wanted to piss him off."

White looked at his fiancée. His chest clenched.

Stunning. Veronica was stunning. Glowing, really. Her green eyes were sparkling brighter than the real emeralds on the necklace resting against her skin. Her smile, sexy as hell, had always made him weak in the knees, and tonight was no exception. White leaned toward her and kissed her.

The stars were out, and the temperature, although warm, wasn't the brutal heat they'd experienced in the afternoon. Way out across the bay, the lights of Saint Thomas could be seen against the mountainous backdrop. White, like pretty much everyone else on the entire island, hadn't dressed too formally for dinner—a soft white cotton shirt, blue jeans, and brown leather sandals. Even the three members of Veronica's protective detail who were seated a few tables over had ditched their business suits in exchange for more casual clothing befitting the early-evening warmth. The open-air setting of the restaurant created a friendly and relaxed atmosphere, and White was grateful for the slight breeze coming off the ocean, which kept the mosquitoes at bay. On the beach behind them, a string trio of local musicians was setting up on a small platform. Fifty feet to White's left, a large circular bar occupied the space between the eating area and the resort's pool. Behind the counter, two bartenders scrambled around, busy filling drink orders.

It was a perfect evening, the kind that made it easy for White to forget he was here because he had a job to do.

Emily must have said something funny because Veronica was laughing again.

Emily, a young and energetic woman of no more than five foot two, was Veronica's best friend. She had been awarded the prestigious Pulitzer Prize for International Reporting, and four months ago, she had turned down a full-time editorial position with the *New York Times* and opted to continue her career as a freelance journalist, preferring the thrill of the unknown to the guarantee of a steady paycheck at the large newspaper.

"I'll be bored out of my mind if I take this job," Emily had shared with White the day she'd decided to pass on what most reporters would have considered the opportunity of a lifetime. "I'm not made to work in a cubicle."

White understood. He felt the same way. He couldn't picture himself trapped between the four-foot-high gray fabric-covered walls of a cubicle either. He'd go nuts.

"You heard that, Clay?" Veronica asked, bringing White back to the here and now.

"I'm sorry," White said. "What was that?"

"Emily said Angus dropped the engagement ring he bought last week down the elevator shaft of their apartment building."

"No way. Did he get it back?" White asked.

"He eventually will," Emily said, "but since it happened on Saturday and the maintenance company can't come until Monday, he'll spend the night in the lobby of our apartment building until they arrive. I think that's cute."

"I guess I would have done the same if I had dropped a diamond ring down an elevator shaft," White said. "But how did you learn about this if you're here and Angus is in New York? He called you to confess?"

"No, the concierge called me. Angus doesn't know I know."

"Will you ever tell him?" Veronica asked, dropping a wedge of lemon in her glass and pouring herself more of the sparkling water.

"Don't know yet, but enough about me. What's up with you and the little one?" Emily asked, waving her finger toward Veronica's stomach.

Veronica's hands moved to rest over her very pregnant belly. "We've been taking it easy for the last four months. Clay's been doing liaison work for—"

"Liaison work? Taking it easy? Really, Vonnie?" Emily asked, rolling her eyes. "Two months ago, your fiancé, the father of your unborn child, actively participated in a raid against a safe house belonging to the most dangerous cartel in the world, and you're telling me he's been taking it easy?"

Veronica smiled at her friend and took one of her hands into hers. "You done?"

"No, but go ahead. Finish your thought."

"As I was saying, Clay is now working for the White House."

"You mean for your dad, right?"

"Yes. For my father."

A dark cloud passed over Emily's big blue eyes as she turned her attention to White, whose hope to escape Emily's wrath suddenly vanished.

"So, San Diego wasn't a one-off? You're traveling again and leaving my friend and her baby all alone?"

"I . . . I'm rarely away for more than three or four days at a time," White said, knowing he was about to be chastised by his fiancée's best friend.

"It's okay," Veronica said, intervening on his behalf. "He never leaves for long and *always* asks my permission before doing so."

Emily's features relaxed, but only slightly. "Be around," she warned White. "And don't get yourself into any more shoot-outs, got it?"

"Yes, ma'am," White said, meaning it.

He was glad to know Emily had Veronica's back. She was a true friend and very protective of Veronica.

And she isn't wrong either, he thought.

At some point, he'd have to tell the president he could no longer travel overseas. Alexander Hammond wouldn't be happy about it, but he'd keep his opinion to himself. Veronica wouldn't tolerate anything else. Four months ago, Hammond had been thrust into the Oval Office when his predecessor had suffered a heart attack while having dinner aboard a private yacht belonging to Jack Buchanan, a longtime friend and former Alaska senator who had made his fortune in the oil and gas industry.

Minutes prior to the former president's death, Hammond had promised White he was about to publicly announce his resignation, planning to cite that he needed time to properly mourn his wife, who'd been killed by a rogue Iranian intelligence operative.

While it was true Hammond's wife had been murdered, catching the bullet meant for him, this wasn't what had triggered his scheduled resignation.

Far from it.

The two-faced sonofabitch's involvement in my father's death did, White thought.

More precisely, it was the undeniable proof that White had uncovered about Hammond's active—albeit forced—participation in the shooting down of General Maxwell White's chopper in Afghanistan that had frightened him into quitting. White's threat of releasing the irrefutable evidence to his daughter had no doubt accelerated the process. If there was one thing Hammond was afraid of, it was incurring Veronica's wrath.

But with the untimely death of the Oval Office's former occupant—a death in which White still wasn't convinced Hammond hadn't somehow played a role—White had no choice but to let Hammond ascend to the most powerful office on earth. Right now, his country needed stability, not the chaos guaranteed to ensue if White were to release the compromising evidence to the media. With Russia's hegemonic ambitions and Beijing's warships and fighter planes buzzing around Taiwan, the entire world had become a powder keg. Even the slightest show of weakness from the president could give America's enemies the opening they were waiting for. Although the internal divisions within the United States were still worrisome, they were down from the all-time high they had been at when Alexander Hammond assumed the presidency four months ago. White had to give it to the man. Hammond was a liar, a cheat, and a murderer, but he was a gifted politician. With his exemplary military record and his time spent as the commanding officer of the Joint Special Operations Command, Hammond had the absolute trust of the military. He was also the first president in years to successfully, and consistently, reach across political lines to get deals done. It was clear to anyone watching from the outside that Alexander Hammond was firmly in command and that making a move against him, his policies, or the United States' best interests would be foolish.

And potentially dangerous.

It hadn't been easy for White. Heck, he was still struggling daily to let go of his will to get justice for his father. Even if the authorities were right and White's suspicions about Hammond's involvement in the former president's death were incorrect, Alexander Hammond didn't deserve to be sitting in the Oval Office.

He belongs in jail.

But to go after him now would cause irreversible damage to the presidency.

White hadn't mentioned Hammond's role in his father's murder to his fiancée. He didn't see any upside in doing so. The bond between

Hammond and his daughter wasn't as unshakable as it had once been, but it was still there. White didn't want to be the one to shatter it.

When Hammond had asked him why he hadn't shared the details of his involvement with Veronica, White had answered him by speaking the truth.

"I love her more than I hate you," he had said.

And that still holds true today, he thought.

Besides, taking legal action or even leaking Hammond's involvement to the press would tarnish the highest office in the land, not only its current occupant, for a generation. And, in White's opinion, it would have a good chance of fracturing the still-fragile political alliances Hammond had managed to concoct between the two main parties. It would be a selfish act to take down Hammond, and there would be very little to gain from it, apart from White's satisfaction at seeing Hammond held accountable for his role in his dad's assassination.

Just as he'd done with the two main political parties, Hammond had brokered a truce with White. In exchange for White's patience, Hammond had sworn not to run again for office once his term was over. Trying to make amends for his past sins, Hammond had offered White a position in his administration. Though White didn't want to have anything to do with Hammond or his administration—he could barely stand the man in a family setting—he had ended up accepting.

Keep your friends close and your enemies closer, they say, he thought.

And now here he was, the special assistant to the president for the Office of Special Projects. Prior to his being sent to San Diego to link up with the DEA task force, his job had consisted mostly of meeting with foreign heads of state's envoys to convey a specific message too delicate to be handled by an ambassador. The work was certainly not boring, and it gave White a glimpse into how high-level politics was conducted between friendly—and sometimes not so friendly—nations. Excluding the recent event at the border, his new job wasn't as dangerous as his previous ones, and, more often than not, White stayed in lavish five-star hotels. Occasionally, when the threat level was low enough and he thought that the destination would be of interest to Veronica—as was presently the case—White would lengthen his stay and ask his fiancée if she'd like to tag along. Most of the time, Veronica was too busy. A bit too busy for his liking. During their recent visit to Veronica's obstetrician, the doctor had spoken to her about her hectic work schedule. Veronica had assured her doctor that she was going to drastically reduce the number of hours she spent at work and shrink the volume of projects she was involved with by at least 50 percent. Upon their return to Key West, White would ensure she kept her word. With luck, the last few days would have shown her that it was okay to relax.

Three days ago, White and Veronica had landed in Saint Thomas, the chief island of the US Virgin Islands, and had chartered a private boat to bring them to the Westin resort located on the island of Saint John, four miles east of Saint Thomas. White was here for work—at the president's request—but since his confidential meeting with the director of the FBI wasn't scheduled until tomorrow, he and Veronica had spent the first few days of their stay enjoying life on the island. White had cold-called Ian Miller, a former pararescueman he had served with who had opened a dive shop in Cruz Bay after he'd retired from active duty. Though he and Vonnie were both certified scuba divers, White had opted to borrow Miller's Axopar 37 to explore the waters around Saint John instead of booking a dive. Vonnie had pleaded for him to get a few dives in, but White had come to realize that diving into the crystal-clear waters around Saint John—like pretty much everything else in his life—would be exponentially more enjoyable if his fiancée was by his side.

Gerald arrived with their drinks and told them he'd be back shortly with the fried calamari. White took a sip of his IPA, then said, "You guys have any plans for tomorrow?"

"Emily and I were thinking about taking the ferry back to Saint Thomas for an afternoon of shopping," Veronica replied. "Care to join us?"

"I might, but it all depends on how long my meeting lasts," White replied.

"Your hush-hush meeting with the FBI director?" Emily asked, keeping her voice low and giving White a side glance.

"Yeah, that's right," White said.

White wasn't surprised that Veronica had shared with her friend the reason behind their trip to Saint John. He didn't mind. Emily would never publish anything that could compromise him or Veronica. And, after everything they'd been through together in the Florida Keys and then in New York City, White trusted Emily with his life. He also valued her opinion.

"I heard he owns a cool house not too far from here," Emily said, bringing her flute of champagne to her lips.

"It's a nice modern house," Veronica said. "It took a while to build, a couple of years, I think. You can see it from here during daylight. I'll show it to you tomorrow morning if you want. We can take one of the resort's stand-up paddleboards or two-seater kayaks to see it from up close. It's worth it, and it's good exercise anyway."

"I'm in," Emily said, then turned to White. "What's your meeting about, if you don't mind me asking?"

"I don't, as long as this stays between us three, understood?"

Emily nodded.

"What do you know about the Red Dragon Triad?" White asked.

"Quite a lot, actually," Emily said. "Their headquarters is in Hong Kong, but they're active worldwide. It's one of the oldest criminal organizations in China, dating back to the Chinese Civil War, if I'm correct. They count approximately twenty thousand members, but they're split into a multitude of subgroups that often have only loose affiliation to each other. In Asia, if something is illegal, you can bet the Red Dragon

Triad is involved in some way. Drugs, arms, and human trafficking are big-money tickets for them, and to a lesser extent so are money laundering and contract murder. How am I doing?"

"Pretty well. Everything you just said is true, but the Red Dragon Triad is no longer Sinocentric. It's now well entrenched in the United States too," White said.

"Really? I didn't know that."

"I didn't either," White said. "Until San Diego."

"Really? How? I've listened, watched, and read everything I could get my hands on about that raid," Emily said. "I haven't come across anything mentioning the Red Dragon Triad."

"The man I shot in California was a member of the Red Dragon Triad," White said. "I didn't know he was until a senior DEA agent showed me the tattoo marking him as a member."

"A small red-ink dragon tattooed on his wrist, correct?" Veronica said.

"Correct." White wasn't sure if he should be impressed or worried that his future wife knew that. "Anyway, this agent's husband, his name is Don, works in Los Angeles for one of the FBI international corruption squads. She told me Don kept current on everything triad related. So, I linked up with him, and his take on the Red Dragon Triad was interesting."

Veronica opened her mouth for what White expected to be a follow-up question, but he pointed behind her to Gerald, who was exiting the kitchen with the appetizers. Moments later, three steaming platters were on the table. The calamari and the conch fritters looked good, but the seafood platter was something else. It was enormous and contained an assortment of crab legs, mussels, lobster bites, and prawns. On the beach, the trio of musicians began playing soft Caribbean music.

"All right, let's dig in," Emily said, leading the way by dunking a piece of calamari into a small bowl of marinara sauce.

"Tell me, Clay, what is it that your contact at the FBI said about the Red Dragon Triad that intrigued you?" Veronica asked as she cracked a crab leg.

White, who hadn't expected the conch fritters to be *that* spicy, had to wash them down with a long sip from his IPA before he could answer.

Though his mouth was still stinging from the hot pepper he was sure Gerald had hidden in his conch fritters as a punishment for not ordering the overpriced lobster tail, White said, "Don was under the impression that, like most triad societies, the Red Dragon was designed as a loose cartel consisting of autonomous gangs that adopted a parallel organizational structure and ritual to unite their members."

"That's what I thought too," Emily said, opening a mussel with her fingers.

"And so did I," White admitted. "It's possible that it was indeed the case in the past, but it isn't anymore. What this guy discovered was that the Red Dragon Triad is nowadays more or less regulated like a military organization."

"There's a reason why the triads have always preferred a decentralized command structure," Veronica said. "It allows them to operate under the radar more efficiently while keeping their activities separate from the rest of the group. Did your friend say why the Red Dragon would change their organizational chart in such a way?"

"He didn't, but when I spoke to him last week, he believed that during the last twelve months, the Red Dragon Triad has been forging alliances with major gangs in Los Angeles, San Francisco, and even Chicago. And that's not all," White said. "He thinks the triad has recently started to reach out to fringe groups across the United States."

"What kind of fringe groups?" Emily asked.

"I asked. He didn't know."

"How did he come to that conclusion?" Veronica asked as she squeezed another lemon wedge into her glass.

"It's not his conclusion, it's what he believes is happening," White said. "Unfortunately, the guy who gave him the intel is no longer among the living."

Veronica and Emily both stopped chewing and looked at him. "He's dead?" Emily asked.

"Yep. They found him dead in his cell. His name was Shane Brooks. He's the guy Chris Albanese and I arrested in California. Oddly enough, Brooks didn't have a criminal record, but he was a well-known figure within the California anarchist movement."

What White didn't share with the two ladies—he didn't want to ruin their appetite—was that Shane's testicles were in his mouth when they found him hanging in his cell. As for his tongue, the coroner had located it only during the autopsy. Before killing Shane, his assassin had forced him to chew and swallow his own tongue.

"Will the FBI investigate the Red Dragon Triad further?" Emily asked. "Because if they won't, I sure will."

Of course you would, White thought.

Emily was the type of journalist who could sniff a good story from a mile away and who wasn't afraid to go after it, no matter who stood in her way. She had done just that in Syria, and it had almost cost her her life.

"I'll let you know how my meeting with the FBI director goes," White replied. "But there's one thing my new friend at the FBI said that surprised me."

"What's that?" Emily asked.

"When he spoke to the commanding officer of the Gang and Narcotics Division at the LAPD, he was told that investigating the Red Dragon wasn't a priority for the division."

"Which kind of makes sense when you think about it," Veronica said. "Specialized units like Gang and Narcotics are dangerously understaffed and overworked."

"And don't forget their stretched-to-the-limit budget," added Emily.

"Right," Veronica agreed. "With that in mind, I don't think the LAPD has the manpower or the budget to start any kind of new investigation unless loss of life is imminent or public opinion is such that the politicians have no choice but to go ahead and make it a priority."

White knew his fiancée had a point. The LAPD, like most major organizations, public or private, was having a difficult time meeting its staffing goals. Years of police bashing—sometimes justified, sometimes not—had made recruiting new law enforcement officers a bigger challenge than it should have been.

"I get that," White said, "but Don was led to believe that the final decision not to get involved with the Red Dragon Triad had trickled down from the members of the Board of Police Commissioners themselves, which he thought was odd."

Emily's eyes lit up. "You bet that's odd. I'm intrigued," she said. "I'll make a few calls."

"Not yet, please," White hurried to say. "President Hammond is aware of the situation regarding the Red Dragon Triad. I briefed him myself. Apparently, the CIA has known for quite a while that the Red Dragon Triad is increasing its operations in the US. But the CIA doesn't know why and—"

"And my dad is worried about it," Veronica said, cutting in.

"He is, and I can't fault him for it," White said. "He doesn't understand why there's political pressure at the state and city levels against investigating that particular triad."

"And you do?" Emily asked.

"We now know that Russia has funneled over three hundred million dollars through think tanks and shell companies to influence foreign elections," White said. "It isn't a stretch to imagine China is doing the same thing here in the United States, is it?"

Veronica shook her head.

"Anyway, I shared my thoughts with the president," White continued. "And we both agreed that the Chinese MSS is known for collaborating with criminal organizations when it fits its needs."

"You think Chinese influence is what's at play in Los Angeles and the other cities you mentioned?" Veronica asked.

"I don't know," White said with a slight shrug. "But your father wants to know what's happening on American soil under his watch. He spoke in private to Director O'Donnell about the possibility of starting a discreet intelligence operation into the Red Dragon Triad. O'Donnell liked the idea. I'm here to iron out the details with him."

The sound of breaking glass interrupted White and drew his attention toward the bar, where a waitress had dropped her tray on the concrete floor, spilling beer and a bunch of colorful frozen drinks at the feet of nearby customers. For a split second, White made eye contact with a man sitting on a barstool. The man averted his eyes right away, but White didn't.

He had seen this man before. There was something familiar about him.

There were no alarm bells ringing in White's head, but White studied him nonetheless. Muscular, with short-cropped hair and in his early forties, he had a strong, prominent jaw and a serious expression. The man might have had a piña colada in front of him next to a bowl of tortilla chips, but White wasn't duped. The man wasn't here on vacation.

Where have I seen him?

CHAPTER TWELVE

"How long before he comes to?" Peiwu asked Eu-Meh, his niece and trusted asset.

"Any minute now," she replied from the front passenger seat of the armored Maserati Quattroporte S.

They had left the Macau government headquarters thirty minutes ago and were now parked in the underground garage of Peiwu's office tower. To Peiwu's left, seated in the back of the luxury sedan, Newman was motionless, his head leaning against the thick window, the handcuffs Eu-Meh had slapped on him securing his wrists.

Peiwu was still stunned about the unforeseen turn of events at Commissioner Mo's office. The wireless surveillance cameras Eu-Meh had installed inside the corrupt bureaucrat's workplace had allowed Peiwu to witness it all.

The plan had been simple. Foolproof. Or so he had thought.

Red Dragon Triad members, working in collaboration with officers from Director Ma Lin's 4th Bureau, had replaced the regular police officers manning the security checkpoint at the former governor of Macau's residence. Miss Li, Commissioner Mo's longtime secretary, had been asked to stay home for the day. Ma Lin's nephew, an up-and-coming young MSS intelligence officer eager to make a name for himself, had taken her place.

As for the Commissioner against Corruption Zhang Mo, Peiwu had personally briefed him. He'd given the man clear and simple instructions to follow. As far as Mo had been concerned, his only job was to show Henry Newman a file Peiwu had put together. The file implicated Newman in several illicit dealings, all of them punishable by up to thirty years in prison. Then Ma Lin's nephew was supposed to step in, shoot Mo, and neutralize Newman. Ma Lin's 4th Bureau tech geeks and hackers would take it from there. Within an hour, they would have had a deepfake video showing that it was Newman, not the MSS officer, who'd shot and killed Commissioner Mo in anger. Ma Lin had assured Peiwu that the computer-generated video would be indistinguishable from the real thing. The idea behind the whole operation had been that with Newman caught on camera bringing a suitcase full of cash into the government building, then murdering Mo in cold blood, Peiwu would have the leverage he needed to get Newman and O'Donnell to collaborate fully. Director O'Donnell's connection with Newman's organization would probably be enough to force him to resign, but Peiwu had asked Ma Lin to push one step further by creating a trail of recent wire transfers between Newman and O'Donnell's wife. If that didn't work and O'Donnell refused to play ball, there was always plan B.

Peiwu had watched the video a dozen times. The speed at which Newman had reacted was incredible. It was as if he'd known what was about to happen. And where had the American businessman learned to fight like that? Had it been luck? Peiwu couldn't say, but Newman hadn't hesitated the slightest when it came to jabbing that piece of wood deep into Ma Lin's nephew's mouth. Peiwu had never pictured Newman—as ruthless as he was in his business dealings—as the kind of man who'd be capable of killing another man without hesitation. It had caused Peiwu to challenge his opinion of Newman—hence the handcuffs around the American's wrists.

Newman began to stir, then slowly opened his eyes. He blinked a few times.

"Hello, Henry," Peiwu said. "How are you feeling?"

Newman looked at Peiwu; then his eyes moved to Eu-Meh, who waved at him.

"I believe you've already met my niece, Eu-Meh," Peiwu said. "A word of wisdom, Henry. Don't be duped by the look of innocence about her. She's a cold-blooded killer."

Newman's face reddened with anger and confusion, but he remained quiet. Peiwu waited for a moment, expecting Newman to say something, but the American didn't utter a word. Peiwu could tell Newman's brain had gone into overdrive.

Peiwu entered his password into the tablet on his lap, selected the footage he wanted to show Newman, and angled the screen so that the American could see.

"Watch and listen carefully, Henry," Peiwu said. "Your survival depends on it."

Despite the operation not going according to plan, the 4th Bureau techies had been able to doctor the actual footage into something Peiwu could use. The video didn't show Newman killing Commissioner Mo, but it didn't matter. A video recording of Newman ramming a piece of a broken table leg into a man's mouth was sufficient. The fact that Newman was holding the pistol that had fired the two rounds that had killed a high-ranking official of the Macau government was all the evidence the police needed to put him away for a very long time.

"You sonofabitch," Newman said once the video ended.

Peiwu didn't react to the insult. He handed the tablet to his niece.

"So, you're behind this, Geng," Newman said, his voice betraying his anger. "I'm trying to figure out why you'd do such a thing, but I can't find a single valid reason. From where I stand, there's nothing for you to gain from it. Care to enlighten me?"

Peiwu asked Eu-Meh for the key to the handcuffs.

"Are you—" Eu-Meh began to ask.

"Yes," snapped Peiwu. "I'm sure. Now give me the key, and I want you and the driver to leave us alone."

Eu-Meh's face contorted into a deep frown. She wasn't happy about it, that much was clear, but she and the driver climbed out of the Maserati. Once he was alone with Newman, Peiwu unlocked the handcuffs.

"I'm sorry about the theatrics," Peiwu said as Newman massaged his wrists. "But I needed you to truly understand how much trouble you are in."

"Trouble you manufactured. You did this," Newman said, pointing his index finger at Peiwu. "Why? We've been working together for years. Your organization is now more profitable than ever because I've let you use my network. I arranged for your people to get green cards, for heaven's sake."

"I know, my friend," Peiwu said in a conciliary tone. "But I had no choice."

"Don't give me that bullshit. You're Geng Peiwu, for crying out loud, the prince of Macau! Of course you had a choice. You always do."

"No, Henry. Not this time."

CHAPTER THIRTEEN

Macau Special Administrative Region
China

The pain coming from his injured hand played havoc with Newman's ability to concentrate. Any adrenaline that had helped mute the pain had long dissipated. While he'd been unconscious, someone had quickly replaced the tie he'd used to bandage his wound, but Newman doubted they'd taken the time to disinfect it.

Fighting back the throbbing in his hand, Newman focused on Peiwu's choice of words.

No, Henry. Not this time. The words had spiked Newman's interest.

Peiwu was at the very top of the criminal food chain in Macau. There weren't many people who could order him around. In fact, Newman could think of only one.

Ma Lin. The MSS 4th Bureau director. A real asshole Newman had done his best to stay well clear of. Until now, Newman believed he'd done a decent job of staying off the man's radar.

But obviously not good enough, Newman thought. He wondered if Peiwu was going to mention the 4th Bureau director by name or if he'd keep his involvement a secret. Newman didn't scare easily, but there was one thing he was terrified of. One thing that could destroy his entire world.

They don't know, he thought. *Because if they did, they wouldn't have gone to all this trouble to blackmail me. And I wouldn't be sitting in the back seat of a Maserati. I'd be in a reeducation camp in Xinjiang, hunched over a sewing machine, or being tortured in the basement of a secret prison. Nah, they need something from me. Something only I can provide.*

Maybe there was a way he could turn this entire saga to his advantage.

"Do you have pain medicine?" he asked.

"I have something better," Peiwu said, grabbing a small first aid kit from the seat pocket in front of him. "It's not much, but it will do until we drive you to a hospital to get your hand looked at."

Newman accepted the kit. "That means I'm free to go after our little chat?"

"I hope so, but it's entirely up to you. There's a reason why we're having this chat here and not somewhere more . . . unpleasant."

Newman opened the first aid kit. Inside were fresh dressings, disinfectant, a tube of antibiotic cream, two painkiller pills, and a small pair of scissors. A quick look outside confirmed that Peiwu's driver and the woman he'd met at the elevator were standing guard twenty feet away. The driver seemed distracted, but the woman was staring straight at him, her eyes shining with the heat of a challenge.

She's daring me to make a move.

The thought of severing Peiwu's jugular with the scissors, which had briefly crossed his mind, vanished. There was something unsettling about Eu-Meh, a sense of perpetual watchfulness, that Newman found disturbing.

He sighed.

Killing Peiwu wasn't the right move anyway. He had to learn why he was here, why Peiwu—and possibly the MSS—had gone to such lengths to squeeze him into a tight spot. Newman uncapped the bottle of disinfectant.

"All right then, let's have it," he said, pouring some of the liquid onto a cotton ball and pressing it against his wound.

"Patrick O'Donnell," Peiwu said.

Newman's head snapped in the triad leader's direction, his expression frozen in place.

Damn it. Now I get it.

There was no point denying he knew the FBI director. Doing so would only compromise his standing. "I've known him for years, before I even began doing business with your father," Newman said as he wrapped a bandage around his hand. "We played football together in college, and we remained friends. He was an early investor in Newman Horizon Development. He helped me out when I started, and I've made him a multimillionaire. But we had our differences several years ago, and I rarely speak to him nowadays."

"Yes. I know all of this," Peiwu said. "For the record, the thought of you betraying our friendship by talking to the FBI hasn't even crossed my mind."

Yeah, right, Newman thought. *Just like the thought of me thrusting that pair of scissors into your neck hasn't crossed mine.*

"By the speed at which my organization is meeting its objectives in the United States, it is clear to me that you haven't spilled any of our secrets, Henry. And for that, I thank you."

"Then I'm not sure what the problem is," Newman said. "We all benefit from our arrangement."

"Here's the problem, my friend. O'Donnell is presently at his vacation home in the US Virgin Islands," Peiwu said. "Tomorrow morning, he's scheduled to meet with a White House representative to discuss a potential investigation into the Red Dragon Triad's undertakings in America. You're to convince the good director that opening such an investigation would be unwise at this time and that he should refrain from doing so for the next eight to ten months."

"If I refuse?" Newman asked, though he already knew the answer.

"You won't," Peiwu said. "It would be the end of you. To be honest, Henry, I don't think you'd last very long in a forced labor camp."

Newman zipped closed the first aid kit and handed it back to Peiwu, minus the pair of scissors he'd nonchalantly dropped by his left side, out of Peiwu's sight.

"You're probably right, but I'm puzzled, Geng. Since when are you so terrified of the FBI? Even if O'Donnell decided to launch an investigation, would it really be the end of the world? Seems to me like you took a huge gamble for not much reward. I was your trusted partner. Do you really think I'll work with you again after this?" Newman asked.

FBI investigations were often long and complex and not a real deterrent to criminal organizations. Newman didn't think Peiwu would offer an explanation, but it was worth asking the question just to see his reaction.

Newman was rewarded by the sudden, but very brief, flash of anger as it lit Peiwu's face, but it disappeared as Peiwu took an incoming call.

"Is it done? Good," he said, ending the call.

When Peiwu spoke next, his voice brimmed with irritation. "Don't concern yourself with the reasons. As for you and I working together again, I'm under the impression that we will."

"Oh, really? Why in hell would I want to do that?"

"The way I see things, Henry, you have two options. The first one is to spend the rest of your life in a forced labor camp, but we've talked about that already, and we both agreed it wasn't a life for you. The second option, the one I'm hoping you'll choose, is that you'll call Patrick O'Donnell and tell him to leave the Red Dragon Triad alone. If you do, you and I will embark on a new journey with terms that will be even more favorable to you than the ones you have right now. And—I really think you'll be delighted to hear this one—you'll be recognized as the person who took down Commissioner Mo's assassin. Based on that accomplishment alone, I would be shocked if, at the very least, you weren't awarded the Golden Lotus Medal of Honor, though I suspect the Grand Lotus could also be in the cards."

Newman snorted—not a laugh, but close. He couldn't care less about medals and honorary titles, but some people did—people who could unlock doors that were shut to him at the moment.

That could be beneficial.

"All of this sounds lovely, but I'm afraid you're overestimating my influence. I told you already, I barely speak with the man anymore. I doubt he'll even take my call."

Peiwu glanced at his watch, then pulled out Newman's phone from the inside pocket of his jacket.

"Oh, he will. In fact, he's expecting it."

Newman cocked his head, then looked at Peiwu. "What do you mean he's expecting my call?"

Peiwu spent the next couple of minutes answering Newman's question. By the time he was done, Newman's stomach was in a knot.

Peiwu handed Newman the phone, a wry smile twisting his lips.

"Now make the call."

CHAPTER FOURTEEN

Saint John
US Virgin Islands

FBI Director Patrick O'Donnell poured three glasses of his favorite single malt and handed a tumbler to his son Jeremy and another to Daphne, Jeremy's fiancée. Keeping one for himself, O'Donnell settled into his favorite leather armchair, propped his foot on the matching ottoman, and leaned his head back as he exhaled a sigh of sheer pleasure. It had been a perfect day. He'd made love with Michelle—his wife of thirty-five years—first thing in the morning and had spent the entire day on the water. His belly was filled with filet mignon, he'd uncorked two excellent bottles of cabernet from California to go with the steaks, and his wife's crème caramel had been exquisite—as it always was.

"What a day, right?" he said, looking over at his son, who was holding Daphne's hand in his own. "You guys enjoyed it?"

"Of course, Mr. O'Donnell. It was a hoot," Daphne said, a genuine but very tired smile on her lips.

O'Donnell was tired too. It had been a hot day aboard *ToothFerry*—a sixty-foot Viking Convertible—despite the air-conditioning blasting cool air onto the bridge and cockpit. Michelle, the CEO of a medium-size dental support organization that owned over one hundred dental practices across five states, had bought him the boat as a gift for their thirtieth wedding anniversary. Though he loved driving his own yacht, O'Donnell had hired a skipper for the day—a friend of his who was a former LAPD homicide detective who'd retired in the US Virgin Islands at the end of his twenty-five-year career—since he wanted to be on the deck to fish with Michelle, his son, and Daphne. Two FBI agents assigned to his protective detail had accompanied him to the Virgin Islands, but he'd given them the morning and afternoon off. He hadn't needed them on the boat.

After they'd left the dock, O'Donnell had asked the skipper to head to the North Drop, which was located about twenty miles north of Saint Thomas. For generations of fishermen, the Virgin Islands had been a worldwide hot spot for big-game anglers, but the North Drop was its true mecca. A ten-mile stretch where the Puerto Rico Trench— the deepest oceanic trench in the Atlantic—took a ninety-degree turn to the north, the North Drop reached down to depths of twenty-nine thousand feet. The cool, swift-moving Atlantic currents drove up from the ocean floor nutrient-rich water and masses of baitfish, which in turn attracted some of the world's largest game fish. For a woman who claimed to have never fished offshore before, Daphne had handled herself like a pro, managing to bring in a 375-pound blue marlin with very little help. Daphne had even impressed his wife—a difficult thing to do.

"I'm delighted you had the chance to catch a marlin," O'Donnell said. "It's something else, isn't it?"

"My arms are so tired I can barely lift them," Daphne said, chuckling. "But the heart-racing, spine-tingling sensation I got when the outrigger clip snapped open, and you shouted—"

"Fish on! Blue marlin on!" O'Donnell yelled, exactly as he'd done on the battlewagon earlier that day.

Daphne laughed while Jeremy smiled at his dad, shaking his head.

"Well . . . catching that fish was one of the most exhilarating things I've done in my life. So, thank you, Mr. O'Donnell." Daphne took a sip of the single malt. "Any chance we can go back out tomorrow?"

"I'm afraid tomorrow is out of the question," he said. "The weather is supposed to turn in the afternoon, and I have a meeting in the morning."

"Yes, of course. I remember now. Jeremy told me about it. You're meeting with Clayton White, right? Veronica Hammond's fiancé? I'm a big fan of her. You know, women's empowerment and all that?"

"Yes, that's him," O'Donnell confirmed, forcing a smile while he glanced over at his son, wondering why Jeremy would have shared such a detail with Daphne.

It wasn't a big deal, but O'Donnell liked to keep things compartmentalized. He'd have to talk to his son about that. Now wasn't the right time, but he made a mental note of it. Jeremy should have known better, especially since he'd recently joined the Bureau himself. Jeremy would have to get used to not sharing everything about his job with his future wife. Working for the FBI wasn't like being a cook at a restaurant. Not that there was anything wrong with being a cook. Heck, his dad had forced him to work in a kitchen when he'd turned sixteen, so he knew precisely how freaking hard cooks worked for their money. But FBI special agents were held to a higher standard. As federal law enforcement officers, they often came across files that were confidential, and in this business, keeping your mouth shut was as important as knowing how to shoot your service pistol. O'Donnell recognized it was an uphill battle, not only for his son but for all Jeremy's generation, a generation that was accustomed to sharing the tiniest details on social media.

"Anyhow, I'll let you two catch up properly," Daphne said as she looked at her watch. "My mom's due to call anytime now. I'll wait for her upstairs."

Jeremy kissed his fiancée on the forehead as she rose to her feet.

"It might take a while for me to get back," Daphne warned. "My mom and her younger sister, who's my favorite auntie, just flew back from a seven-night cruise in northern Europe, and I know she'll want to tell me all about it."

O'Donnell chuckled. "I'm sure she does. Sounds like a fun trip, though," he said.

"Take your time, baby," Jeremy said. "And please say hello to your mom for me and remind her that I can't wait to meet her."

"I will," Daphne replied with a smile.

O'Donnell looked at the departing figure of Daphne and playfully punched his twenty-nine-year-old son on the shoulder.

"Well done, son. Well done," he said, touching the rim of his glass of single malt Scotch whisky with Jeremy's. "She's fantastic."

"I know, Dad," Jeremy said. "That's why I put a ring on her finger after two months. Didn't want to miss my chance."

"Well, I've got to say that your mom and I were a bit worried about that, to be honest," O'Donnell said. "Two months isn't a lot of time, son. You know how long I dated your mother before I—"

"Dad, stop," Jeremy said, interrupting his father. "I know what I'm doing. She's the one, okay? Can you please be happy for me?"

O'Donnell took a deep breath, then said, "I am happy for you. And I'm glad you brought her here, allowing us to meet her and know her a little better."

"Thank you for that. I know this was an important step."

"When are you going to Vermont to meet Daphne's mother?"

"Sometime next month. The dates aren't finalized yet."

O'Donnell indulged himself with a long sip of whisky and took a moment to savor the rich, smoky taste of the sixteen-year-old Lagavulin. O'Donnell was glad his son had the palate to enjoy what was his favorite brand of whisky. One of O'Donnell's neighbors had given him the bottle as a thank-you gift after O'Donnell had taken him and his family on the boat for an afternoon of offshore fishing. That same night, O'Donnell had opened the bottle during a poker game he had hosted at his house and had been disappointed, and frankly quite surprised, that not a single one of his guests had enjoyed the single malt. The common excuse had seemed to be its smokiness. Some had even gone as far as saying that it tasted like an ashtray.

To each his own, he thought, taking another sip.

"I have to leave the day after tomorrow, but your mom will stay for another week," O'Donnell said. "If you and Daphne feel like it, you're welcome to extend your trip for a few more days."

"Thanks for the offer, but Daphne has to fly to Miami to show a boat she represents to a big client who's coming in from Dubai with his broker," Jeremy said.

"Cool job she has there."

"She thinks so, but it's a high-risk, high-reward kind of job," Jeremy replied. "She's spending her own money to fly to Miami, and she'll probably spend a small fortune on wining and dining the client and his broker without any guarantee of a sale."

"If the guy is flying in from Dubai, he's definitely serious about the yacht," O'Donnell said.

"He's serious about buying *a* boat, but not necessarily this one, Dad. There's no way to tell if his broker from Dubai has made appointments with other local yacht brokers to see other boats."

"Got it, son, but on a two-mil yacht, her commission is what? Like two hundred grand? It's worth spending a few bucks to get that kind of return on investment."

"That's what I thought, too, at first, but the truth is that even if the commission rate is at ten percent, she splits it with the other broker, and she then splits it again with her agency," Jeremy said. "I'm not saying it isn't good money, but it isn't as lucrative as you might think."

"Good thing you have a good and stable job, then," O'Donnell said. "You told her about your trust fund?"

His son looked down at the glass of whisky in his hand before answering O'Donnell's question.

"I did, but only a few days before we arrived in Saint John. I needed to, Dad. This house is a bit different than our second-floor condo in Hollywood Beach. I didn't want her to think I was hiding something from her. It's kind of a big deal, not something I wanted her to find out once she was here, you know?"

O'Donnell understood. His FBI director's salary wouldn't even be enough to pay for *ToothFerry*'s annual maintenance and fuel burn. His vacation home in Saint John was worth close to $7 million. O'Donnell's parents had passed away while he was in college, leaving him an almost million-dollar inheritance. Henry Newman, a friend of O'Donnell with whom he had played football, was endowed with a sharp entrepreneur's mind. During their third year, Newman had wanted to buy two dozen vacant lots and was looking for investors to partner with. O'Donnell had given Newman $500,000 with the understanding that the money was to buy into Newman Horizon Development, Newman's newly incorporated company, not just the vacant lots. Hands were shaken, and a legal contract was signed. Fifteen years later, just before Newman Horizon Development became public, O'Donnell's $500,000 investment had turned into a $40 million fortune.

"I get it, Jeremy. And you're absolutely sure she's the one?" O'Donnell asked, regretting the question as soon as it came out.

Jeremy looked over his shoulder, then leaned forward. "Are you deaf?" he asked, keeping his voice low, his eyes as angry as O'Donnell ever remembered having seen them. "I just told you she was. Do you think I would have spent so much money on a diamond ring if I wasn't?"

What O'Donnell wanted to say was *Love will make you do crazy things,* but what he said instead was, "You're right, Jeremy." He raised his left hand in surrender. "Stupid question."

"What stupid question?" Michelle O'Donnell asked, stepping into the living room and taking a seat next to her son, a golden retriever following a few feet behind her. "Please tell me he didn't ask you if Daphne was the one, because your father explicitly told me he wouldn't."

O'Donnell swallowed hard and refused to meet his wife's gaze.

"It's okay, Mom. I think it was the booze asking," Jeremy said, as the golden retriever sat in front of him, its big brown eyes looking at him lovingly.

"Hey, Maya, how you doing, girl?"

The golden retriever replied by thrusting her nose into Jeremy's free hand and pushing it upward. Jeremy placed his drink on the table so that he could pet Maya with both hands.

O'Donnell chanced a quick look at his wife, to see if she was still upset with him for asking the one question he'd promised not to. She was, so O'Donnell threw an olive branch to his son.

"Would you and Daphne be interested in spending Christmas week here with us on the islands?"

"I'm not even sure I'll get a day off this year," Jeremy said. "I'm the new guy, remember? Anyway, Daphne changed brokerage firms four months ago, so she'll probably have to work Christmas too. Sorry, guys, but I don't think we'll make it."

"That's too bad, honey," Michelle said. "It would have been so nice to have you over for the holidays."

"You never mentioned she changed agencies before," O'Donnell said. "What was the name of the brokerage firm she used to work for before she moved to this one?"

"She never mentioned it to me, but I once saw a business card with her name on it. If I remember correctly, the firm's called Silver Yachts," Jeremy said. "A boutique agency in the Pacific Northwest. Why?"

Silver Yachts. For some reason, the name rang a bell, but too much fine wine and single malt had fogged his mind.

"You know your father, Jeremy," O'Donnell heard his wife say. "He's always looking at boats online."

When he'd first learned that his son's fiancée was a yacht broker, O'Donnell had checked her online footprint, curious to see what kind of yachts she represented. Everything had seemed legit, and a quick look through the federal database hadn't raised any red flags either.

O'Donnell felt his personal phone vibrate against his thigh. Annoyed, he fished it out of his pocket. A string of texts had come in, accompanied by a series of disturbing photos and a short video. The video automatically began to play after he had scrolled through the pictures.

"What the hell?" he muttered.

"What's that, honey?" his wife asked.

But O'Donnell didn't reply, shocked by what he was seeing on his screen. He tried to stop the video but couldn't. Someone had hacked into his phone. He gasped as he witnessed Henry Newman stab a man in the mouth with a piece of wood.

My God. Is this real?

When the video ended, two additional texts came in. The first was a bank account statement showing a bunch of wire transfers his wife had supposedly received in an account she kept in the Bahamas.

That can't be.

The second text contained only five words:

TAKE THE CALL, MR. O'DONNELL.

O'Donnell felt the blood drain from his face.

"Dad," his son said. "Are you okay? You look like you're gonna be sick."

Then O'Donnell's phone rang, and Maya began to bark.

CHAPTER FIFTEEN

Macau Special Administrative Region
China

The phone felt heavy in Newman's hand. His mind was in overdrive, trying to find a way out of the morass he found himself in.

"Just make the damn call, Henry!" Peiwu snapped. "And you better be persuasive. O'Donnell's life depends on it."

Newman didn't know what to make of the triad leader's last statement. It wasn't like Peiwu to bluff or to utter a threat he wasn't ready to see through. The Red Dragon Triad might have gotten bigger and stronger in the United States during the last year, but Newman suspected the triad was in no position to threaten the life of a sitting FBI director.

Or am I missing something? And if so, what is it that I'm not seeing? There's more at play here than meets the eye, I'm sure of it. Whatever this is, it's big.

Newman grabbed the phone and dialed Patrick O'Donnell's number.

"Put it on speaker," Peiwu ordered.

The FBI director picked up on the first ring.

"Who's this?" O'Donnell barked into the phone.

"It's me, Patrick. Henry."

"What the fuck have you gotten yourself into?" O'Donnell asked, his voice tense and lacking any kind of compassion. "I just watched a video of you stabbing a man to death."

"I'm aware," Newman said. "It was self-defense. I know how it looks, but—"

"Really? You know how it looks? You must be out of your goddamn mind! What about the Macau commissioner you shot and killed? I've seen the photos. Are you claiming that killing an unarmed high-ranking Macau government official was done in self-defense? Save me your bullshit, Henry. There's a reason why I distanced myself from you years ago. You're toxic!"

Newman counted to two, then said, "Are you done, Patrick?"

"Listen to me very carefully, you low-life piece of shit," O'Donnell said, almost screaming. "I don't know what's going on with you, or what you've got yourself involved in, but if you think I'm gonna raise even a finger to help you get out of the hole you dug for yourself, you're even more insane than I thought."

"I haven't even asked you what I want yet," Newman reminded O'Donnell. "You have no idea why I'm calling you."

"Whatever it is, my answer's no."

"Have you looked at the statement that was issued by Michelle's bank in the Bahamas? Your wife is involved in some shady shit, old friend. You should keep an eye on her."

"Michelle doesn't have an account in the Bahamas. And neither do I."

"I have documents here that say otherwise. But I hear you, you don't want to help, so I guess I'll just let ICIJ figure out what's true and what's not. Goodbye, Patrick," Newman said, but he didn't terminate the call.

Peiwu's mouth dropped open in disbelief, but Newman gestured for him to be patient. He could still hear O'Donnell's breathing at the other end of the line. The ICIJ, or International Consortium of Investigative

Journalists, was a network bent on exposing corruption at the highest level. The ICIJ was the organization that had published—among other things—the Panama Papers, which had exposed in meticulous detail an industry that had blossomed in the gaps and loopholes of international finance and its laws, more specifically the offshore banking system and its tax havens.

"You wouldn't do that," O'Donnell said after a long pause. "I couldn't care less what happens to me. I'm retiring next year anyway. But you would really destroy everything my wife has built over the last two decades?"

"You're right. I wouldn't do that to Michelle, but my associates won't hesitate."

"Your associates? Shit, Henry, I told you years ago to get out of Macau. You should have listened to me."

"It's a bit late for that now, isn't it? But since you're thinking about retiring, maybe you won't mind what I'm about to ask you."

"I should just hang up right now," O'Donnell said, but Newman heard the resignation in the other man's voice.

"I think you love your wife too much to take a chance," Newman said. "Honestly, Patrick, it's not much of an ask."

"Stop messing around and tell me what it is that you want."

"I have it on good authority that you're about to meet a White House representative about a possible investigation into the Red Dragon Triad—" Newman started but was interrupted by O'Donnell.

"Stop right there! Who told you that? Who told you about this meeting?" O'Donnell snapped.

"I'm not going to answer that, Patrick, and what I'm asking here is to delay such an investigation into this specific triad for eight months, maybe ten at most. Convince the DC official that's coming to visit you tomorrow that this is the best course of action. I don't think this is such a big ask, am I right? And ten months from now, you can do as you see fit. Retire; open an investigation. I don't care."

O'Donnell's reply was immediate and exactly as Newman had expected.

"Go to hell, Henry. And you can shove your request up your ass."

"Wait, Patrick, don't do anything stupid now," Newman warned. "Patrick, did you hear what I just said?"

But the line was dead. The FBI director had hung up.

"Damn it! I had him." Newman could feel Peiwu's eyes on him. "What?"

"I think he was playing with you," Peiwu said in Cantonese, dialing a number on his phone.

No shit, Newman thought, knowing O'Donnell was too smart to fall for such a ploy. The call had been a balancing act between being credible enough to convince Peiwu he was playing ball with him and whoever else had orchestrated this whole charade and making sure that O'Donnell got the warning.

"We will need to move to plan B," Peiwu said into his phone; then there was a long pause, and Newman knew his fate was being decided, wondering if it was Director Ma Lin at the other end of the line.

Newman's fingers closed around the scissors, ready to plunge its blades into Peiwu's neck.

"No, I believe he did what he could, but he's not ready. Soon, maybe. We will see."

And with that, Peiwu ended the call, and Newman knew he had won. He would live to see another day.

CHAPTER SIXTEEN

Saint John
US Virgin Islands

O'Donnell felt a tightness in his chest. He didn't know what had happened to Newman, but there had been a subtext in his delivery. Newman hadn't called to threaten him; he had called to warn him. They might not have been the best of friends anymore, but Newman would never have turned against him and Michelle like that. Of that O'Donnell was sure.

He looked at his wife and said, "I don't know what's going on, Michelle, but I swear to you I'll get to the bottom of this."

"It's okay, hon," she said, placing a hand on his shoulder. "I'm not worried."

O'Donnell squeezed her hand and refrained from telling his wife that she should indeed be worried. Newman wasn't someone who was easily manipulated. Whoever had gotten to him had vast resources at their disposal, the kind of resources only dangerous people possessed.

O'Donnell looked at his bodyguard, a tall, heavyset FBI special agent with chiseled features and short blond hair.

"You got the whole thing, Nestor?"

"Yes, sir. I recorded the entire conversation. I'm glad you had the presence of mind to put the call on speaker right away."

"I might be old, but I'm not dumb," O'Donnell said.

"I thought you would have kept him on the line a bit longer, Dad," Jeremy said. "We might have learned more about whatever it is he's planning to do."

O'Donnell rubbed the corners of his eyes with his fingers. "No, I think he said everything he wanted to."

"That was my feeling too," Nestor said.

"Okay, so we need to figure out two things," O'Donnell said, then stopped, realizing that his second bodyguard wasn't there. "Where's Mitch? I'd like his input on this."

"I'll fill him in later, sir. He went outside with Maya when she began to bark."

"Understood. As I was saying, we need to figure out two things. The first, how did Henry, or whoever else was on that call with him, learn about my meeting with Clayton White tomorrow?"

"He said you were meeting with a White House representative; he didn't mention Clayton White by name," Jeremy said.

"Good point," O'Donnell conceded. "And the second?"

Jeremy didn't hesitate. "It concerns the Red Dragon Triad. Unless I misunderstood what he was saying, Henry wants you to back off, but not forever, only for eight to ten months. Why is that?"

"Exactly," O'Donnell agreed. "Whatever it is that the Red Dragon Triad is planning to do in the next months is of special importance for whoever is pulling the strings in Macau—"

"Or in China," cut in Nestor.

Right. China.

Several loud barks coming from outside the house pulled O'Donnell's attention toward the four-panel sliding door at the other end of the living room. It was Maya. She barked again, a loud, heartrending bark; then she pressed her black nose against the glass. O'Donnell moved across the living room and slid the door open.

"Come in, girl. Come in," he said, but the dog refused to move.

That was when O'Donnell realized that Maya was still on the leash, but Mitch wasn't at the other end of it.

CHAPTER SEVENTEEN

Saint John
US Virgin Islands

Clayton White kept his eyes glued to the man's head, almost daring him to look in his direction. But the man seated at the bar didn't, not even a side glance. Despite his best efforts, White couldn't remember where or when he'd seen the man before. He considered asking one of Veronica's Secret Service bodyguards to go check the man out, but if White was mistaken, it could potentially create a scene. Furthermore, the man at the bar hadn't done anything to justify an intervention.

Still, White couldn't let it go. Something was gnawing at the back of his mind, trying to crawl to the surface.

Or I'm just being my paranoid self, he thought.

"What's wrong, Clay?" Veronica asked. His fiancée always knew when something bothered him.

"Don't look right away, but there's a man at the bar who seems vaguely familiar. Blond hair, midforties, wearing a pair of black shorts and a loose-fitting white shirt. But I can't place him."

Because Emily only had to turn her head a few degrees to look at the bar, she was the first to reply.

"I see him," she said. "Never seen this guy before."

The man, who hadn't looked in White's direction since the waitress had dropped the drinks tray, pulled a cell phone from his pocket and took a call. A few seconds later, he signaled the bartender for his check, which was odd since he had barely touched his piña colada. Then, for an instant, White thought he had seen the man make a slight head gesture to someone seated at the opposite end of the bar, but he couldn't be sure since his view was blocked by rows of liquor bottles and polished martini glasses.

"He looks like the type of guy you used to work with, Clay," Veronica said after glancing over her shoulder. "But his face doesn't ring a bell for me either."

Veronica was right. The man did look like he could have been a pararescueman, but there was something off about him that told White the man hadn't served with him as a PJ or when he was with the 24th Special Tactics Squadron—the Tier One unit of the Air Force Special Operations Command.

"You know what, maybe you're right, Vonnie," White said, careful to keep his tone jovial and light. "I'm gonna go say hi. What if I did work with him? Maybe he recognized me and he's too shy to come to our table to introduce himself. That wouldn't be the first time that happened, right?"

"Because of me?" Veronica asked.

"Who knows? You've become quite the celebrity, my dear," White said, giving her a wink before rising to his feet. As a reflex, White's right hand moved to the small of his back to confirm the Glock 45 and the spare magazine he kept concealed in a waistband holster under his shirt were still there.

Tom Doyle, the lead Secret Service agent assigned to Veronica's protective detail, looked at White for directions. White shook his head and signaled Doyle to stay back. Instead of heading directly toward the man at the bar, White looped right, hoping to get an overall picture of the comings and goings around the bar area and see who else was seated at its counter.

At the bar, as if sensing White approaching, the man with the black shorts got up from his stool. He was much taller than White had thought, towering a good five inches above White's own six-foot height. White suddenly felt like a fool. He had never seen this man before. He would have remembered someone that tall. White's eyes scanned the length of the man's body, looking for clues that would indicate that he was armed, doing so more as a reflex than because he believed the man was carrying a weapon. Like White's, the man's shirt was loose, and a pistol could easily have been concealed beneath it. White's gaze moved to the other patrons seated at the bar. The first two, a young couple drinking shots, were of no interest to White. The third, a good-looking woman in her late twenties, wasn't either. But the fourth, a man with black hair and a large black mustache, wearing a gray T-shirt, was. Very much so.

It was Ian Miller, White's former colleague, from whom he'd borrowed the Axopar 37 earlier that week.

Miller's eyes widened in recognition when he saw White, his right hand moving to his side and under the bar, out of White's view. At the same moment, the man wearing the loose-fitting white shirt pivoted toward White.

And then the first two shots rang out, breaking the peace of what had been until then a quiet and very, very pleasant evening.

CHAPTER EIGHTEEN

Saint John
US Virgin Islands

Hans Roth watched the FBI director from his observation post, a thirty-five-foot sailing boat secured to a mooring ball in the middle of the Great Cruz Bay. The small yacht was one of many vessels moored there because of the good holding ground of the bay's ocean floor and the protection from the prevailing winds the surrounding hills offered. The night was still, the winds calm, with only a gentle breeze brushing against the rolled-up sail of the main mast. To his left, the water glittered under the lights from the Westin resort at the end of the bay. A three-person band was set up on the beach, playing soft island music for the restaurant's patrons. Every now and then, Hans would get a whiff of sizzling onions mixed with the sweet, peppery aroma from someone grilling marinated steaks in a nearby yard. Hans did his best to ignore the mouthwatering smell, but his stomach wasn't cooperating and kept rumbling.

Compared to a marina where liveaboards were plenty, Hans hadn't seen a single vessel with its interior lights turned on among those tied to a mooring ball. Hans had spotted this timeworn sailboat during his reconnaissance. He'd recognized right away its potential. It had a direct and unrestricted view of the FBI director's house. A small dinghy, which appeared to be much newer and in better condition than the sailboat, was rigged with a small electric motor and mounted on the stern of the vessel. Hans had written down the boat's registration number and asked one of his associates to find out who and where the owners were. It turned out that the boat was registered to an elderly couple in their early eighties who lived in Baton Rouge, Louisiana. A quick call made from a burner phone had confirmed that the couple was home and that they were in no way interested in an extended warranty for their aging Buick.

Pointing his range finder at the FBI director, who was still standing in the doorway between his living room and the wooden deck, Hans confirmed the distance.

Two hundred and ten meters.

An easy shot with Hans's night vision–equipped Austrian-built Steyr SSG 69, a weapon he had used the world over to fulfill his contracts. A simple pull of the trigger and it would all be finished, but Hans was disciplined, and his finger didn't move from the trigger guard. He wouldn't kill the FBI director until he received the final authorization to execute, even if that meant the assassination would be more difficult. His handler for this mission, a woman he'd never actually met in person but who had given him and his team half a dozen lucrative jobs in the last three years, was yet to give him the green light to proceed.

Hans's earpiece came alive with the voice of one of his men, who, like Hans, was a former Austrian armed forces Jagdkommando who'd been kicked out of the elite unit over an incident in Mali dating back to 2016.

"Retro-One from Retro-Two, the bodyguard is done picking up the dog's poop. He's heading back toward the house."

"Good copy, Retro-Two."

Over the last four days, Hans's team had identified eight different people coming and going from the FBI director's lavish vacation home. In addition to O'Donnell, his wife, and his son Jeremy, Hans had counted two bodyguards, one chef, one housekeeper, and Daphne, Jeremy's squeeze. She was an attractive woman, fit, maybe five foot eight or a little more, with natural honey-blonde hair and a nice tan. If Hans had to guess, he'd say she was a little older than O'Donnell's son.

Though he tried not to think about it, Hans was beginning to wonder if they would ever get the authorization to proceed. It had taken him two weeks to prepare the logistics for the operation and to insert himself and his two men in the US Virgin Islands clandestinely. The night before, using the cover of darkness, he and his team had scouted the property grounds and pinpointed the location of the backup diesel generator. Hans had disabled it and rigged the pole-mounted distribution transformer he'd located on the main road off O'Donnell's property with a small explosive charge. Hans's assault plan called for cutting the power sixty seconds before the beginning of the attack, and he wanted to make sure the generator wouldn't kick in.

Hans expected the actual attack to last no more than two minutes and to be long over by the time the local police made it to the residence—if they were called at all—but he was glad he'd also prepared a surprise for the officers in case the assault took a bit longer.

Never had there been so many moving parts forced upon him for an operation. Then again, he'd never been asked to kill someone of Patrick O'Donnell's stature before. Hans had assassinated his share of local terrorist leaders in Africa and corrupt bureaucrats from former Soviet republics, but this was his first time operating on US soil. Being asked to work with another team of operators for the exfil had also thrown him off. Hans had never been a fan of interagency cooperation. It always seemed to add multiple levels of bullshit. That had been true when he was an officer in the Jagdkommando and it hadn't changed one bit when he'd founded G9S Security Solutions five years ago. Every single time he'd had to collaborate with an outside group on an operation, it had heightened the degree of difficulty. The way this mission had come together was also something that weighed on Hans's mind. He wasn't in the habit of going after targets he considered "good guys," but the ridiculous amount of money he had been offered for this operation had forced him to reconsider his moralities. The way Hans saw it, with what he'd done in Mali back in 2016, he was going straight to hell anyway.

His handler interrupted his thoughts. "Retro-One, this is Home Plate, over."

At last.

"Go ahead from Retro-One."

"I'm sending you a photo," his handler said. "This is coming from our employer. I just got it myself. Before I can give you the green light to move to the objective, it is imperative that you acknowledge receipt of the picture and the instructions below it. You'll do that by reading back to me the five-digit code at the end of the message."

The phone in his tactical vest pulsed twice, indicating an incoming message.

"Stand by, Home Plate, let me look at it."

Hans rolled to his side so that he could get to the phone. He opened the attachment and studied the photo his handler had sent him. Then he read the message.

Hans cursed. Twice. In a matter of a few clicks, the job had become exponentially more difficult to pull off.

I knew this was going to happen.

"Home Plate, this is Retro-One. I acknowledge receipt. The five-digit code is four-nine-two-three-four. I'll pass this along to my guys. I'm not happy about this."

The handler's reply came fast, and it was sharp and unyielding. "Like you, they'll do what they're told. You're not getting paid to be *happy*, Retro-One."

Hans sighed. She was right, of course. But a change of this magnitude to the operational plan so late in the game was dangerous. Still, it was too late to quit now. That time had come and gone once he'd cashed that first check. Hans would adapt to the new rules, and he would overcome the difficulties, just as he'd done so many times before, in and out of uniform.

"Copy that, Home Plate."

"Glad we're back on the same page, Retro-One. Your ride out of there is nearby. You can reach the team leader on his mobile, and he'll need five to six minutes to make his way to you once you call him. Good luck. And good hunting."

Finally. Hans was anxious to get started. He pushed the transmit button and updated his team, telling them about the new rules of engagement and the additional task their employer had dumped on them.

"Retro-Two and Three, I sent you the photo and the written instructions," Hans said.

Once both men had acknowledged receipt and Hans had confirmed with them that they didn't have any questions, he told them the good news. "We have a green light. When I reach the shore, this will be your cue to cut the power, Retro-Three."

Hans grabbed his rifle and the single M72 he had been able to get his hands on. The M72 LAW—light antiarmor weapon—was a portable one-shot rocket launcher that could be used against any kind of lightly armored vehicle, including cars, boats, and even low-flying, slow-moving helicopters. It took Hans less than one minute to board the seven-foot dinghy. He started the electric motor, which was virtually silent, though not powerful, and started navigating toward the shore. He was halfway there when one of his men came over the air with a sitrep.

"Retro-One, this is Two. The bodyguard that was out with the dog is coming back, and he's heading in my direction with a flashlight," his man whispered, his voice amplified by the comms system. "Shit! The dog is on its way, too, and so is the main target's son. I have maybe ten, twelve seconds at most before the dog or the bodyguard reaches me."

Hans's jaw tightened. "If you think you're about to be made, take him. Take them. But be quiet. We can't afford to spook the main target."

CHAPTER NINETEEN

Saint John
US Virgin Islands

As she waited in the second-floor bedroom for the call, Daphne figured the odds were that she would never see Jeremy alive again.

Her cell phone buzzed. "Hello," Daphne said into her phone as she closed the bedroom door.

There was a series of clicks on the line; then a woman's voice came through. "Can you talk?"

"I can. Is it about to start?" Daphne asked as she looked at the time on her Omega watch.

"Yes. I've just given the last-minute instructions to the assault team. As I told you they would, they bitched when I shared with them that they had to extract you, but they'll do what they must. Like you, they're very good at what they do."

"How much do they know?" Daphne asked.

"Very little. You'll understand your uncle isn't taking any chances with this operation. If all goes well, it will be up to you to brief them. But wait until you're out of harm's way."

"Is the exfil team nearby?"

"Yes. Everything is ready. I'm sending the team leader's contact information to your phone now."

"Is that all?" Daphne asked.

"For now. Be careful, Ulyana Volkova."

There was another click, and the line went dead.

Ulyana Volkova. A wave of excitement washed through her. It had been years since anyone had called her by her birth name. Did it mean she was done with Daphne the yacht broker, the identity she'd assumed for the last five years? Was she being pulled out and reassigned somewhere else?

Surely. But it would have to be outside of the United States. With what was about to happen, there was no other choice. She'd be burned. Then again, she'd thought the same thing four months ago, after the operation on Jack Buchanan's yacht had turned into a major disaster. The former president of the United States might not have been Ulyana's target, but he was the one who had ended up dead all the same.

An honest mistake, she thought, smiling.

Ulyana, who'd been a yacht manager with Silver Yachts at the time, still had palpitations thinking about how it had all gone down. She'd been sitting behind her desk at the Silver Yachts office, watching the twelve live feeds coming in from the security cameras installed inside Buchanan's yacht, when she had witnessed the sommelier picking two bottles—one red, one white—from the wine fridge in the galley. What the sommelier couldn't have known was that the pinot noir he had selected was part of a lot of four bottles Ulyana had tampered with. Using a very thin hypodermic needle, she had injected a hard-to-detect synthetic poison through the wine cork that would remain potent in an unopened bottle for up to two weeks, or about thirty minutes once uncorked. While the president had drunk the red and died, Buchanan's decision to go with a chardonnay had saved his life.

When Ulyana had been given the task of spying on the former Alaska senator in an effort to undermine him, she'd spent some time studying his life. She'd quickly discovered his taste for fine, expensive wines and his playboy lifestyle—which had given her great hope. Alas for Ulyana and her employer, Jack Buchanan had built a solid company and had done so within the established rules and without breaking any laws. Even more unfortunate, Buchanan had never crossed the line when it came to his interactions with women—she'd watched plenty of those *interactions* from her office's computer. With nothing of significance to use against him, and with Buchanan's unwillingness to resume the sale of his company's advanced drilling technology to Russian oil and gas firms, a decision had been made. Senator Buchanan had had to die before the end of the month, prior to his trip to Kuwait, where he was scheduled to meet the minister of foreign affairs with an American coalition of oil and gas businessmen. Knowing how many bottles of wine Buchanan drank in a week while on his yacht, Ulyana had figured that poisoning him was the best option. It wasn't messy, and this technique left very few clues for the investigators. Buchanan had already experienced a heart attack three years ago. He would suffer another one.

That had been the plan, anyway.

How was she supposed to know that the president of the United States would show up unannounced? Ulyana guessed that she could have stopped the sommelier from pouring the wine if she had truly wanted to. A simple call to the sommelier—who Ulyana had befriended, as she'd done with the rest of Buchanan's yacht crew—would have done the trick.

But she had opted not to do so. It had been enthralling to see the most powerful man in the world drink the poisoned wine.

Ulyana sighed. How many people on the entire planet could say they were responsible for the death of a sitting United States president? Ulyana smiled at the thought. She knew the answer to that.

I'm the only one.

The warm and fuzzy feeling that knowledge gave her—well, it was better than sex. It was the achievement of a lifetime. Or at least that's what she had believed until her handler had threatened to have her eliminated for her ineptitude. Apparently not everyone back home had been thrilled to learn about the former president's death.

"Do you realize who will take over his administration, you dumb bitch?" the handler had asked her, raising her voice for the first time in their business relationship. Ulyana had thought the woman sounded as if she was about to have a heart attack. "You have no idea what you've done. Our network could potentially become exposed because of you. And if this happens, we'll have to put a stop to ongoing operations that are critical to the safety of our nation."

"How was I supposed to know this would happen? And I'll remind you that it was you who authorized the initial plan."

"Don't you dare blame me for this," her handler had hissed. "It is you, not me, who might have single-handedly destroyed the most significant network we've ever established in the United States."

Three weeks later, once the dust had settled and her superiors were confident her cover was still holding, she'd received new orders.

"We don't care how you do it, but find a way to seduce Jeremy O'Donnell," the handler had said. "And no more slipups, because next time, I'm not sure even your uncle Yuri will be able to save you."

Now, a few short months later, the final page of this mission was about to be written.

The truth was, there wasn't much she liked about Jeremy. He was cute enough, but he was far from being great in bed. And it wasn't like he had a brilliant mind to compensate for what he lacked in ingenuity in the bedroom.

Quite the contrary.

The night before, Jeremy's mother, who admittedly could have been a bit tipsy at the time, had confided in Daphne that Jeremy had almost flunked out of the FBI Academy. It had been her opinion that if her husband hadn't been the director, her son would have never made it to graduation day.

"Jeremy's good with people," his mom had said. "He should have been a real estate agent, just like his brother."

Though she hadn't said so, Daphne had agreed with her wholeheartedly.

Ulyana opened the night table drawer in which she had seen Jeremy drop his Glock 19. She pulled it out of its holster, verified there was a round in the chamber, then checked the magazine. Satisfied, she placed the pistol in her handbag.

Then she sat on the bed and waited for the show to begin.

CHAPTER TWENTY

Saint John
US Virgin Islands

Jeremy O'Donnell walked around his father, who was still standing at the door, and stepped onto the wooden deck. Maya was wagging her tail, happy that she had managed to get another human outside to play with her.

"Where's Mitch?" his father asked him.

"Probably picking up Maya's poop. Unless he stepped in it," he said. "Wouldn't be the first time. I'll help him out. Could you please turn on the outdoor lights?"

His dad nodded and went back inside.

"What do you want, old girl?" Jeremy asked, turning his attention to his eleven-year-old golden retriever. "You wanna play? Is that it? Is that it?"

Jeremy unclipped the leash from Maya's collar. The dog immediately ran down the four steps leading to the backyard and dashed across a gravel pathway before making a sharp turn to the right and disappearing into the thick foliage.

"Maya, wait!"

Silly dog, Jeremy thought. There was no way he was going to run after her at night. She'd probably sniffed out a mongoose or a deer. Old girl or not, Maya was a hunting dog, and a good one at that. From the corner of his eye, Jeremy picked up the beam of a flashlight.

"Mitch, what are you doing back there?" Jeremy said as he got closer.

"After I picked up after Maya, I thought I saw something over there," the bodyguard said, sending the beam a few feet into the greenery. "A small flash of light, like a phone screen, you know? But it was probably just a firefly."

Jeremy followed the beam with his eyes. Then the beam stopped moving, and for a moment he couldn't make out exactly what it was that the flashlight was shining its light on. By the time the gears in Jeremy's brain clicked into place and concluded that what his eyes were seeing was in fact the darkened silhouette of a man in tactical gear holding a rifle, Mitch already had his pistol out. Then there were two bright flashes, followed by two gunshots coming from Mitch's pistol, which caused Jeremy to jerk involuntarily. To his left, Mitch was shoved back, as if he was a quarterback who had just been sacked by a charging defensive lineman. Jeremy's hand instinctively moved to his holster.

Nothing. The holster wasn't there.

Jeremy experienced a moment of panic as he visualized his holster, along with his Glock 19, which he had left in the nightstand drawer next to the bed he was sharing with Daphne.

Daphne. The idea that he was the last line of defense between his fiancée and whoever this asshole was jolted him back to reality, and he sprang into action. But, as he was about to launch himself at the shooter, he realized he wasn't going to make it. The shooter had already swung the barrel of his rifle toward Jeremy's chest. Just then, when he thought his life was over, a light-colored shadow leaped into the air and struck the shooter sideways at full speed just as he fired. The round missed Jeremy's right arm by inches.

Maya!

Between the weight of the dog and its momentum, the shooter was knocked off his feet, but Maya held on tight, her teeth sunk deep into the man's arm. Jeremy reached him in two flying steps and landed on top of him just as the shooter was about to stab Maya in the neck. Jeremy felt a sharp jab in his side and exhaled painfully, conscious he'd caught the knife meant for his dog. The shooter screamed in agony as Maya's teeth shredded through his bicep muscle, forcing him to let go of the knife, which was still embedded between two of Jeremy's ribs. The searing pain of the wound was almost unbearable, but Jeremy didn't dare quit, not with his fiancée's life on the line. Conscious that it would worsen the severity of his wound, Jeremy gripped the knife by its handle and pulled the blade from his side, nearly passing out from the pain. He thrust the tip of the knife into the shooter's neck once, then a second and a third time. The man stopped screaming as air hissed and gurgled through two of the neck wounds, arterial blood spurting in waves from the third.

Multiple pistol shots coming from the house, followed by several muffled bursts from suppressed automatic weapons, told Jeremy the assailant he'd killed hadn't come alone. The fight wasn't over yet. Jeremy was confident that the moment Nestor heard the first shots, he would have brought his mom and Daphne to the safe room. His mom had never fired a gun in her life, and he knew that Daphne was terrified of firearms. His dad wouldn't go down quietly, though; Jeremy was convinced of that. He and Nestor were going to fight back.

Jeremy rolled off the man he had killed and looked for Maya. She was gone. He hoped she was okay. She had saved his life.

Brave girl.

He touched his side and felt the blood flowing out of his body. It was surreal. Life was draining out of him.

Fast.

CHAPTER TWENTY-ONE

Saint John
US Virgin Islands

White was aware that the two gunshots had come from far away, but they had been loud enough to be heard by everyone seated at the bar or at the eating area. Most of the patrons had simply stopped moving, like deer caught in headlights. Even the trio of musicians on the beach had stopped playing. But out of the dozens of people in his field of vision, only two reacted like trained soldiers. The tall man with the loose-fitting white shirt who'd been seated at the bar, and Ian Miller.

White drew the pistol holstered at his back in one fluid motion and set its sights on the tall man, who'd sidestepped to his left and grabbed a teenager walking by the moment the shots had rung out. His left arm was curled around the teenager's neck like a python constricting its prey. The man was so tall that in order to shield his vital organs, he had to lift the teenager off the ground. The teenager's feet were now a good six inches off the floor, and her legs were thrashing madly in the air.

"Police! Let her go!" White shouted, identifying himself as a law enforcement officer, not caring one bit that it wasn't true any longer.

The man wasn't impressed, and White could tell this wasn't the first time he had had a gun pointed at him. Instead of releasing the girl, he jammed a small pistol against the side of her head, his finger coiled around the trigger. There wasn't a doubt in White's mind that the three

Secret Service agents of Veronica's protective detail were already on the move, but he hoped that shouting the word *police* would draw their attention to the threat he had identified. Realizing that their lovely outings had turned into a hostage-taking situation, the rest of the customers panicked and began to run in different directions, like cockroaches suddenly exposed to daylight.

Keeping his pistol pointed at the hostage taker, White chanced a quick look to where he'd last seen Miller. He was gone. But where? Miller was a man of action. There was no way he'd just leave without giving White a hand, especially given that from the position he had occupied, Miller would have had a clear shot at the bastard who was holding the girl.

Unless he isn't armed.

Then again, as he remembered the sequence of events, hadn't the hostage taker looked in Miller's direction? Was it possible Miller was in on this?

No way. Miller was a former air force PJ. *These Things We Do, That Others May Live.* For PJs, that motto was sacred. At least it was for White.

"Coming to your left, Clay. To your left," White heard Tom Doyle say as the experienced Secret Service agent pushed through the mass of frightened people running for their lives to take position five meters to White's left.

"We have a problem, Clay," Doyle said.

"I can see that, Tom," White replied while doing his best to get a clear shot. But the prick was moving too much, and, with the teenage girl in his arm, White wasn't ready to chance it.

Not yet.

"We just received a distress call. The FBI director's house is under attack," Doyle said. "Multiple assailants."

White almost asked Doyle to repeat what he'd just said, it sounded so implausible, but he knew he'd heard correctly.

Damn. And this thing here is quickly turning into a major shit show.

"Back off, gentlemen, or she dies," the tall man said, slowly backing away while scanning left, right, and behind him. His voice was cold, dispassionate, but not cruel or distressed, which alarmed White even more. The hostage taker remained calm while most criminals would have already pissed their pants. His body language showed he wasn't taking pleasure in what he was doing either. That was good and bad at the same time. He wouldn't kill just for the sake of inflicting death, but he wouldn't shy away from murdering the teenage girl, either, if it became necessary.

In the distance, a firefight was raging, its echoes bouncing off the hills surrounding the bay.

Next to White, Tom Doyle was giving instructions to the two Secret Service special agents who'd remained with Flower, the code name the Secret Service had given Veronica. "Tell me the moment Flower is in the safe room," White heard him say.

In the tall man's arm, the teenage girl had stopped battering her aggressor's shins with her heels. Her eyes were closed, her body shutting down due to the lack of oxygen. White figured he had a minute, maybe less, to bring this situation to an end before the teenage girl was too far gone. White quieted down his breathing and allowed himself to focus entirely on calculating all the environmental factors that might affect the shot he knew he had to take. At this distance, there weren't many. It wasn't as if he was about to take a shot at a target three hundred meters away with a sniper rifle. White was nine, maybe ten meters from his target—a man choking the life out of a young girl—but it didn't mean it was an easy shot. The man was moving a lot, swinging the teenager's limp body from left to right as he moved and scanned. Behind him, frightened tourists ran by, making it even more challenging for White by adding another level of stress. White knew it wasn't tactically sound to have tunnel vision, but with the young woman's life in his hands, he didn't see any other way.

Sight picture. Trigger pull.

"Leave the girl," White warned, his weapon steady in a two-hand grip. "You have nowhere to go."

"Don't come any closer, Clayton," the man said, using White's name. If his objective had been to unsettle White, it didn't work. With all the media coverage he and Veronica had been subjected to during the last year, White knew his face had become recognizable. He didn't care if the man knew who he was.

"Same goes for you, big boy," the man said to Doyle as White's finger started to work the trigger.

Sight picture. Trigger pull.

The man was shouting now, which wasn't a good sign.

"You guys want her to live? Drop your weapons! If you want her death on your conscience—"

Then there was the crack of a single gunshot, and the man's head snapped to the side, and his legs collapsed from under him. He fell backward, and the teenage girl landed on top of him. For a moment, White thought it was he who'd fired the shot, since it seemed that the round had struck exactly where he'd been aiming. The appearance of Ian Miller, who had stepped out from behind the activity hut twenty meters away with his hands high above his head but still holding a pistol, changed that narrative. White pivoted in Miller's direction, his pistol leading the way.

"Stop right there, Ian!" White ordered him.

Miller obeyed, but White could tell the former PJ wasn't happy about it.

Keeping Miller in sight, White said to Doyle, "Go check on the girl."

"Her parents are by her side, and my guys have already called in local law enforcement and EMS," Doyle said; then his eyes stopped on Miller. "Clay, isn't that your friend Ian Miller?"

"I'm not a threat, Clay," Miller shouted before White could reply. "I'm here to help, but something messed up is going on."

White moved behind cover—one of the posts that supported the rooftop of the restaurant—and told Miller to slowly put his weapon on the ground.

"My team just confirmed Veronica and Emily are in the safe room," Doyle said. "They're unhurt."

White nodded, feeling as if a huge weight had been lifted off his shoulders. The first shot that had started this mayhem had been fired less than ninety seconds ago.

"I'll cover you, Tom. Handcuff Ian," White said.

"You got it," Doyle replied.

Miller eyed White as Doyle approached him. "Really, Clay? I just saved this girl's life. We're losing time."

"Just do as you're told and everything will be fine, Ian," White said.

Once Miller's hands were cuffed behind his back, White holstered his pistol and picked up Miller's weapon—a SIG Sauer P320—before rendering it safe. He looked around and was relieved to see that the teenage girl had regained consciousness. Two adults who White assumed were the girl's parents were holding her in their arms and escorting her away, hopefully to safety. In the distance, the firefight hadn't died down. Quite the contrary.

"Clay!" Miller snapped at him.

White looked at Doyle and said, "I've got this, Tom. Secure the perp's weapon before someone gets an idea."

Staying low, Doyle raced to where the man had dropped his pistol.

"What the hell's going on, Ian?"

"I'm not sure, brother," Ian said. "I was asked to show up here and meet with a customer who wanted to rent my boat for two days without a skipper."

"A customer?"

"Yeah, Clay. A customer. I run a business; you remember that, don't you? Anyway, I was texted a time and place where I needed to be. The only thing I was told was that I was going to meet a man with a white short-sleeved shirt who'd be seated at the bar drinking a piña colada. Details are on my phone. Front pocket."

White fished the phone out of Miller's pocket and positioned the phone in front of the former PJ's face, unlocking it.

"Go to my text messages. Should be the first or second from the top, I think."

It was the first. Miller wasn't lying. "What else can you tell me?" White asked.

"The man knew who I was, or at least what I looked like, because he nodded to me the moment I sat down at the bar. I watched him gesture for his bill, and then you showed up. You know the rest."

"Where's your boat?" White asked.

"It's right there at the resort dock," Miller said, nodding toward the water.

Doyle, who'd returned with the dead man's pistol, pressed a hand against his ear.

"Got it," Doyle said. "I'll let Clayton know my intentions."

"What is it?" White asked.

"A member of the FBI director's security detail was able to call in the assault. They're outgunned and outmanned, and they're quickly running out of ammo. The rest of my team is staying with Veronica, and you should, too, Clay, but I'm heading over there now."

"You and me both, Tom," White said without the need to think about it. There was no way he could sit this one out. If he was in the shoes of the FBI special agent who had called in the attack, he'd be happy to have two guys on their way to help him.

Vonnie won't be happy, but she'll understand, White told himself.

"I can help, Clayton," Miller said. "Take the damn handcuffs off."

Doyle said, "Did I miss something?"

"Take them off, Tom. I trust him."

"Good enough for me. And by the way, I grabbed the dead man's cell phone," Doyle said as he unlocked the cuffs around Miller's wrists.

"Let me see," White said.

Doyle handed him the phone.

"Were you able to unlock it?"

"No. His face was too messed up by the bullet he caught," Doyle said.

White pocketed the phone. There was no point leaving it at an unsecured scene. He'd give it to whichever agency ended up in charge of the investigation. He didn't think it would be the US Virgin Islands Police Department.

White realized that it had been quiet for almost a full minute. The firefight had ended the same way it had started.

Abruptly.

White handed Miller his SIG Sauer back.

"I'm familiar with the director's house," White told them. "We can access it by following the beach. We'll come across a rocky portion once we leave the resort's grounds, so be careful not to sprain an ankle, but it shouldn't take us more than three or four minutes to reach the objective."

"Tracking," Miller said, loading a new magazine into his pistol.

"Did you receive any additional intel?" White asked, looking at Doyle.

"Negative."

"Okay then. Let's go," White said. "Once we're there, follow my lead."

CHAPTER TWENTY-TWO

Saint John
US Virgin Islands

Ulyana hadn't expected to hear two unmuffled gunshots coming from outside the residence. It had sounded like a pistol.

And the power hasn't been cut.

Something was wrong. She could feel it. Moments later, she was proved right. A full-fledged gun battle had begun downstairs.

Time to improvise.

Ulyana got up from the bed and headed for the door, her hand around the grip of Jeremy's pistol. Before she could reach it, the door flung open, and Jeremy's mother barged in. She was breathing hard and fast, but panic hadn't yet set in.

"Daphne! Thank God, you're all right. Follow me, dear, we need to get to the safe room. Come on! Come on!"

"What's going on, Michelle? What's all that noise? Fireworks?" Ulyana asked as they raced out of the bedroom.

"No. It's . . . they're not firecrackers. We're being attacked," Michelle replied, making a beeline toward the master bedroom where Ulyana knew the safe room was located.

"What? Attacked? Why? By whom?"

"I . . . I don't know," Michelle replied. "Just . . . follow me."

Ulyana stayed three steps behind Michelle until they reached the master bedroom. Michelle pushed a full-size mirror out of the way. A heavy door appeared behind it. Michelle's hands were shaking as she began to punch in the access code. After four failed attempts, she began to weep.

Ulyana had had enough. She would have preferred to do it inside the safe room, but what the heck.

"Hey, Michelle," Ulyana said. "Look here."

Michelle turned toward Ulyana, who was already swinging Jeremy's gun in front of her from left to right. The butt of the pistol struck Michelle on her right temple, steel against bone, and blood spilled onto the light-colored hardwood floor as Michelle fell. Her body spasmed, then went limp.

One down.

Ulyana heard someone screaming downstairs. It was Patrick O'Donnell. He'd been shot. Nestor, his bodyguard, was yelling for him to get to the safe room, but O'Donnell didn't want to hear it. He wanted to go out to look for his son.

Then there was another yelp, followed by a groan and the sound of a falling body.

Ulyana ran to the staircase and began to climb down the steps. When she reached the quarter-turn landing, she could see the living room, where O'Donnell and Nestor were making their stand. O'Donnell, who'd taken a round to the leg, was trying to get back up behind the partial cover the bar afforded. There was a large and very bloody laceration on his left cheek where another bullet had grazed him.

"I'm almost out," Nestor shouted as he fired three rounds in the direction of the sliding doors.

Then a volley of suppressed shots forced him to dive for cover next to O'Donnell. As he did so, his eyes met hers. Ulyana had the feeling that Nestor never had the chance to grasp what his eyes had seen before it was too late.

Ulyana fired the Glock twice, both her rounds finding their target. Nestor was slammed against the lower cabinets of the bar, hit twice in the chest. Remembering Nestor was wearing a bulletproof vest under his shirt, Ulyana squeezed the trigger one more time, putting a bullet into the bodyguard's open mouth, killing him.

O'Donnell, alerted by the sound of Ulyana's pistol, turned toward her but fell on his ass as he did so, his wounded leg no longer strong enough to support him. She shot him in the stomach. O'Donnell looked down at his gut, then back at Ulyana. A stunned, almost quizzical look was plastered on his face.

"Yuri Makarov sends his regards," she said, then pulled the trigger one second before two black-clad operators entered the room through the sliding doors.

CHAPTER TWENTY-THREE

Saint John
US Virgin Islands

Light-headed, Jeremy understood he had no choice but to stop the bleeding if he wanted to survive. He considered spending whatever energy he had left looking for the trauma kit the assailant had surely carried on him, but the intense gunfire told him there was no time for that.

His dizzy mind had a hard time understanding what was happening, but his family needed him. His own wound would have to wait.

Gathering his forces, Jeremy painfully got to his knees and relieved the dead man of his rifle. There was just enough illumination coming from the outdoor lights of the backyard for Jeremy to realize he didn't recognize the type of rifle. He wasn't familiar with it at all. It looked very different from the MP5 submachine gun or the M4 he'd learned to shoot at the FBI Academy.

Shit. Think, Jeremy. Think.

Then it came to him, and guilt washed over him at the realization that he'd all but forgotten about Mitch. One hand pressing hard against his side in a futile attempt to slow down the bleeding, and with wobbly legs, Jeremy made it to where Mitch had fallen. There was so much blood. Two rounds had struck the FBI agent. One had caught his vest, but the second round had hit him in the face.

Jeremy picked up Mitch's Glock 19 and confirmed there was a round in the chamber. He scanned his surroundings but didn't see or hear anything that would indicate the presence of another attacker in his immediate vicinity. He made it to the house as fast as he could, doing his best to employ the tactics he'd learned at the academy, but he didn't seem to remember any of them. Everything was happening so damn fast. Jeremy stopped before the four steps leading to the wooden deck and noticed that the sliding doors to the living room were open. He heard a woman's voice. Did it belong to Daphne?

Yes. That's hers.

But the voice was harsh, different from how she usually sounded. It was almost as if she was barking commands. Then he understood.

She's under duress. She's about to be taken.

Jeremy brought his pistol up and placed his right foot onto the first step. *Hold on, Daphne. I'm coming.*

The sole of Jeremy's shoe failed to grip the wood due to the slick pool of blood at his feet, and he lost his balance, pitching forward. Jeremy faltered and found himself sitting on the second step, his back resting against the outside wall of the house.

C'mon. Get up! Get up! They need you. Daphne needs you.

Wincing with pain, his shirt soaked with blood, Jeremy got to one knee. Then, like an angel, Daphne walked out of the house.

Thank God. She's okay.

For a moment, all was right with the world. Everything was going to be fine. This moment of bliss was quickly replaced by sheer terror when two men dressed in black combat fatigues, wearing goggles and balaclavas and toting the same strange assault rifles as the man he had killed, exited the house behind Daphne. Jeremy tried to warn her, but he was out of breath, and no words came out. The pistol in his hand was much heavier than it should have been, and he managed to lift it by only a few inches. Her eyes met his, but he didn't recognize them. Gone was the love. Gone was the tenderness. Only a blank, emotionless stare.

She had a gun in her hand. A gun very similar to his.

I don't understand.

Then Daphne raised the pistol and shot him in the face.

CHAPTER TWENTY-FOUR

Saint John
US Virgin Islands

White, Tom Doyle, and Ian Miller had made good progress, moving swiftly toward O'Donnell's vacation home in a combat crouch, their pistols up and ready. In less than two minutes, they had covered more than three-quarters of the distance that separated the Westin resort from their objective.

The gunfire had completely stopped now. There had been a final gunshot when they had crossed the Westin property line, but it had been quiet since then. White was beginning to think they would make it to the house without getting into a shoot-out when three explosions rocked the beach, sending the three men diving to the ground.

The blasts had come from their left, but higher up the hill. The first two had been smaller than the third one, which had followed half a second later. For thirty seconds, White didn't move. He listened and watched. Then, signaling Doyle and Miller to cover him, White dashed into the shadow of a palm tree a few meters away. One at a time, Doyle and Miller joined him.

"Any idea what those explosions were about?" White asked.

"First two sounded like small charges of C-4," Miller replied. "Hard to say for sure."

White agreed with him.

"I know the detonations didn't originate from inside the house," Doyle said. "I think they blew up something, but I have no idea what it could be. There's nothing in these forests but a few houses and the access road."

"Tom, when was the last time you checked in with the FBI guys?" White asked, getting down on one knee.

"I didn't get any update since we left the resort," the Secret Service agent said. "It's my dispatch who relayed the intel. I didn't communicate directly with the agents inside the director's residence. Local police are on their way."

If there was one thing White feared, it was a blue-on-blue confrontation. Without comms, there was a good chance of that happening. He needed to find a way to let the FBI agents inside the house know that he was coming with reinforcements. He didn't want him, Doyle, or Miller to be mistaken for bad guys and be shot at by the agents defending O'Donnell's vacation home. There were scenarios that called for charging ahead without announcing one's presence, but this wasn't one of them.

"Try to get ahold of your dispatch, Tom," White said. "We need to figure out a way to let them know we're coming."

Doyle pointed a finger to his ear, then gestured for White to wait for a moment.

"Dispatch is already on the air, letting me know they're unable to reach the agent who called it in," Doyle said.

White cursed under his breath.

"And that's not all," Doyle continued. "The explosions we heard earlier, seems like someone blew up a bunch of trees and a Jeep Wrangler. The only road up to O'Donnell's house is now impassable. USVI PD officers are continuing on foot, but they won't breach inside the house until SWAT gets there, which may take another twenty to thirty minutes."

"Damn it." This wasn't what White had wanted to hear.

"What do you want to do, Clay?" Miller asked.

White heard a muffled ding. It took him a moment to understand that the sound had come from the phone in his pocket—the phone he'd taken from the man Miller had shot dead. White pulled the phone out and looked at the screen. Since the phone was locked, he could read only the first two lines, but it was enough to send a chill through his bones.

Where R U? Where's the boat? Need to X-fil now!

White showed the message to Miller and Doyle. By the looks on their faces, they had reached the same conclusion he had. The message confirmed what White had suspected from the get-go. The dead man by the bar had been involved in the assault on the FBI director's house.

"Shit," Miller whispered. "Ten bucks it's my boat they're talking about."

"Yeah, and now we know why dispatch hasn't been able to talk to anyone inside the house. They're all dead," Doyle said.

"We don't know that," White said, testier than he had intended to be. "Listen, guys, for all we know, there are still friendlies alive inside the house. At the very least, this message tells us that the chances of us being fired upon by the good guys have drastically gone down, right?"

Both men nodded.

"All right. The way I see it, these assholes are hunkered down in place until their ride arrives. We don't have the manpower or the gear to launch a counterassault on the house, so we need to level the playing field. We have to draw them out into the open," White said.

Miller smiled. "I know where you're going with this, Clay, and I like it," he said. "They're waiting for a boat, so we'll give them a boat, right?"

White gave him a fist bump. "You got it, brother."

CHAPTER TWENTY-FIVE

Saint John
US Virgin Islands

Ulyana didn't know why the speedboat she'd been promised hadn't shown up, but now wasn't the time to cry about it. She, Hans, and the other commando had to leave the island. Now. She raced back inside the house, heading straight to O'Donnell's office. She opened the top left drawer of his work desk and grabbed the keys to *ToothFerry*, O'Donnell's sixty-foot yacht. Keys in hand, Ulyana hurried back to the living room, walked past the dead bodies of the FBI director and his bodyguard, and exited the house through the sliding doors.

Hans's plan to slow down the inbound police vehicles seemed to have worked since none of them had made it to the house yet. Hans had told her he and his team had been on the island conducting reconnaissance for days and that his team's job had been to prepare for such an eventuality, hence the rigged trees and Jeep. Ulyana's first impression of Hans was that he was the kind of guy who spent the better part of his life outdoors, fishing and hunting. He was tall and lean, but by no means lanky, and in his late thirties or early forties. He spoke English with a light Central European accent she found *very* sexy.

"You find them?" Hans asked.

She showed him the keys to the boat and noticed Hans was carrying three rifles—a Steyr SSG 69 sniper rifle slung on his back, and one Steyr AUG assault rifle in each hand.

All Austrian made, she thought. *That explains the accent.*

"And you know how to drive it, yes?" Hans asked.

She nodded. She had watched O'Donnell attentively and taken mental notes of the battery switch's location. Though she'd never owned her own boat, she had been working in the yachting industry since she'd first moved to the United States years ago. She'd manage driving the damn boat.

"Your shot placement on the two dead guys tells me you know how to shoot a pistol," Hans said, extending a Steyr AUG in her direction. "But what about this one?"

Ulyana accepted the assault rifle, taking a moment to examine it. It had been almost a decade, but she remembered firing it in training. She set her eyes on Hans and said, "Conventional gas-piston-operated action that fires 5.56 mm rounds from a closed bolt, and this one is equipped with a 1.5X telescopic sight. Satisfied?"

A surprisingly charismatic smile appeared on Hans's lips. "I like you."

To her left, a figure emerged from the shadows. It was Josef, Hans's colleague. Josef had scooped up their downed comrade in a fireman's carry and was making his way to them.

"I'll lead the way and cover our left flank," Hans said. "Josef will follow, and you'll close ranks, Ulyana. You keep your eyes glued to our right flank, understood?"

"I understand," she said.

"Good. The pathway to the beach is narrow, but it isn't too steep," Hans reminded them. "I want you to hold at the beach, Ulyana. Don't cross over to the pier right away. Wait for me to catch up, and we'll clear the area together. Only then, once we know it's clear, will we continue to the pier and board the vessel. Questions?"

Ulyana shook her head, her heartbeat spiking in anticipation. She did as Hans instructed and held short of the end of the pathway, then got down on one knee and waited for Hans. A text came in on her phone, and she contemplated not looking at it. But what if it was her handler trying to reach her with an update on the Axopar? O'Donnell's boat was nice and comfortable even in rough seas, but, unlike the Axopar, it was incapable of reaching speeds in excess of fifty-five miles per hour.

And right now, we need speed, not comfort, she thought.

They were already well behind schedule, and she wasn't sure the mother ship waiting for them just off the coast of the Dominican Republic, 190 nautical miles away, would wait past the agreed-upon window. It was a four-hour boat ride with the Axopar, but if they were to do the trip aboard O'Donnell's beefy ninety-one-thousand-pound Viking Convertible, it would take twice as long. In the end, she decided to read the message.

It was the right call. The handler had a new set of instructions for her.

When Hans arrived, she told him she'd received new orders.

"Yes. I did get something too," he said.

"Okay. What did yours say?" she asked, though she already knew the answer.

"To follow your lead," he replied.

Good. She was pleased with Hans's honesty. And who knew? Maybe this could be the start of a mutually beneficial relationship. Ulyana shared with Hans and Josef the new plan, and, as if on cue, she spotted the navigation lights of a boat approaching the pier at idle speed, its twin four-hundred-horsepower Mercury Verado outboards humming in low gear.

"All right," she said. "Let's do this, shall we?"

CHAPTER TWENTY-SIX

Saint John
US Virgin Islands

White and Doyle had set up their firing position two feet into the foliage and ninety feet east of the sandy pathway linking the beach and O'Donnell's vacation home. The beach off O'Donnell's property was only twenty feet wide, so it would take the assailants barely two or three seconds to reach the pier once they stepped out from the trail.

The one bit of good news they'd received since Miller had raced back to his boat was that the USVI Police Department had launched a spotlight-equipped helicopter from their headquarters in Saint Thomas. With a bit of luck, it would be there in time to provide White and Doyle much-needed air support.

The low grunt of the Axopar's outboards told White that Miller was on his way. Sixty meters from the shoreline, almost parallel to White's position, the Axopar's double-stepped hull cut across the calm surface of the bay, a small wake fanning out behind it. Despite the boat's extended hardtop, which blocked the moonlight from entering the helm station, the helm's twin twelve-inch Simrad multifunction displays provided enough light for White to see Miller standing behind the wheel.

Thank goodness O'Donnell's boat is docked on the opposite side of the pier, White thought, watching Miller maneuver the Axopar along the thirty-meter pier but keeping it far enough away that he could back out at a moment's notice. If O'Donnell's vessel had been docked on the other side of the pier, White would have lost sight of the Axopar as it disappeared behind the bigger, taller yacht.

Off in the distance, White saw a fast-moving light. The chopper was coming. A few seconds later, the thunder of the helicopter's rotors reverberated off the hills. White looked again at the Axopar.

What the hell was Miller doing? He had brought the Axopar way too close to the pier. Less than two feet separated it from the boat. Miller had to back the boat out of there! Now!

"Clay! I see them!"

White turned his head back toward the beach. He had missed the first few strides of the lead attacker as a small group of three sprinted across the narrow beach. White adjusted his aim, but he didn't fire. A woman dressed in civilian clothing was leading the group, an assault rifle pointed in Miller's direction. He had no choice but to raise his hands above his head.

It was too dark for White to see the woman's features, but he could clearly make out the shape of a man on the shoulders of a second assailant as the group continued to move toward the Axopar.

Shit.

"What do we do, Clay?" Doyle asked.

Friend or foe? White didn't know. He couldn't simply open fire on them without knowing the answer.

And then, stunning White, the woman fired two shots at Miller. White could only watch in horror as his friend was thrown back against the gunwale. Miller began to slide down to the deck, and the woman fired one more shot at him as she prepared to jump into the boat.

Having witnessed Miller being shot while his hands were up, White was no longer debating which side the people on the pier were on. He fired once at the woman just as her feet left the pier, but at this distance, and with reduced lighting, hitting a moving target was virtually impossible. The woman crashed into the boat, leaving White wondering if he had aimed true or not. Next to him, crouched behind the trunk of a palm tree, Doyle squeezed off a few shots, which were immediately answered by short, accurate bursts of rifle fire from the third assailant. Rounds snapped overhead, shredding tree limbs and foliage. White rolled to his right, finding refuge in a small crevice as more bullets slammed into the beach, sending geysers of sand in all directions.

As soon as there was a lull in the incoming fire, White raised his head and took aim at the second assailant, who was making a dash toward the boat while still carrying someone over his shoulders. While White had been busy burying his head in the wet soil, the USVI PD chopper had switched on its powerful spotlight, and its beam swept the pier as it hovered about five hundred feet above the water. With the additional light coming from the chopper, White had much better visibility, but he had time to pull the trigger only twice before being reengaged by the third shooter and having to flatten himself in the crevice again. This time, though, White was sure of it: one of his rounds had found its target. He'd seen the second assailant spin, then crash onto the pier, dropping the body hoisted on his shoulders into the water.

Unfortunately, White wasn't the only one who had hit his target. His back resting against the palm tree he had used for cover, Doyle was holding his left knee, looking at White and shouting something. The helicopter was making too much noise for White to understand what Doyle was saying verbatim, but the Secret Service agent's eyes, wide with shock and pain, conveyed everything White needed to know. Doyle's gun battle was over. He was out of the fight. On the pier, the second assailant was on his feet again, helped by the third man, who was firing wildly in White's direction, trying to keep him pinned down.

And it worked. It had been a poor idea to get into a long-range gun battle against people wielding assault rifles while he and Doyle only had pistols.

And now Miller's dead, Tom's knee is a mess, and I'm probably about to catch a round in the head.

But he was still in the fight, and when the rounds stopped zipping by his position, White rolled out of the small depression and aimed his pistol at the closest threat. There was only one assailant left on the pier. The man was limping, but he was mere meters away from reaching the boat. It was the man who had carried his injured colleague. White fired at the same time a muzzle flash appeared from the open side door of the helicopter, which had moved farther away to allow the sniper to angle his shot properly. The assailant collapsed, hit by either White's or the sniper's round. A second later, a bright flash lit up the Axopar, and, for an instant, White thought one of the outboards had somehow caught fire, but a thick white trail of smoke streaking toward the helicopter told another story. An RPG was arrowing straight for it.

My God! No!

A heartbeat before impact, the chopper banked hard left, but it was too late. The rocket struck below the cockpit and detonated. The scene in front of White was surreal. The entire front half of the helicopter had disintegrated, the tail end of the chopper spinning wildly out of control. White followed it with his eyes, praying that he would see a survivor jumping out of the burning wreck. But no one did, and the helicopter crashed into the bay, missing an anchored power catamaran by less than fifty feet.

At the pier, the Axopar had backed away and was now heading toward the open sea, the whine of its powerful outboards quickly fading away into the night.

CHAPTER TWENTY-SEVEN

Sir Francis Drake Channel
British Virgin Islands

Ian Miller, who was still on the deck of the Axopar, closed his eyes just as the woman fired the M72. From this distance—the helicopter was less than six hundred feet away—she wasn't going to miss. The explosion turned the night into day, and its shock wave rocked the boat violently. When the initial flash of light was gone, Miller opened his eyes. The police helicopter was transformed into a lethal fireball that was peppering the water around them with burning debris, some of them landing on the Axopar's hardtop.

Miller got to his feet and saw that the man wearing black combat fatigues was about to jump back onto the pier, one leg already atop the gunwale. Miller grabbed him by his tactical vest and shoved him back into the boat.

"What do you think you're doing?" Miller shouted as he moved behind the helm.

"Josef is—"

"Your friend's dead! Leave him be or we'll never get out of here."

Miller pushed the throttles fully forward as soon as the Axopar's bow had cleared the pier, and the twin Mercury Verados came alive. The Axopar shot forward, and the man had to hold on to one of the posts supporting the hardtop in order not to be thrown overboard by the sudden acceleration. To his right, the woman was using one of the seats as support and was sending short bursts toward the beach. Miller hoped that White had found some cover, but knowing his former colleague, the man was probably sprinting toward O'Donnell's house to check for any survivors.

Exiting the bay, Miller made a sharp left and headed east toward the British Virgin Islands, instead of turning right in the direction of Saint Thomas, as he'd been instructed. He wondered if the woman was going to challenge him. Miller didn't look at her, but he could feel her eyes on him. After a while she looked away and sat next to him.

The man hadn't said a word either. He looked lost in thought, his eyes unfocused. Miller didn't blame him. The operation had turned into a major blunder, and the man, who Miller had pegged as the leader, had lost two members of his team. He was probably replaying the whole ordeal in his mind, trying to figure out what he could have done better.

Miller could relate.

He didn't know who the woman sitting next to him was, but she'd just shot down a police helicopter. It made Miller sick to his stomach to think that he'd had a hand in killing American police officers. There would be hell to pay for that.

Heads will roll, and mine will be the first to fall into the basket, he thought.

———

Two weeks ago, Miller had received a call from Carlos, his main contact with the Jalisco New Generation Cartel and one of the cartel leader's top lieutenants, with an uncanny job request. Would Miller be willing to provide transportation for five people from Saint John to the Dominican Republic? Carlos had even mentioned that the request had come from the jefe himself. Carlos had promised the job wouldn't last more than ten hours but had assured Miller he would get paid twice his regular fee nonetheless.

"And you'll get the jefe's gratitude, Ian," Carlos had reminded him. "He'd like to invite you to Mexico to personally brief you. He thinks it would be the perfect occasion to finally meet you. What do you say?"

It was nice of Carlos to ask, but they both knew it wasn't as if Miller had a choice in the matter.

Miller had been running drugs in the Caribbean for the JNGC for four years, and never before had he been invited to the jefe's lavish compound in Mexico. He'd heard rumors about the parties at the jefe's house, but the level of debauchery he would encounter there was beyond what he could have imagined.

Apparently, receiving such an invitation was a huge honor, if Miller was to believe Carlos. Only those who had been found worthy—whatever that meant—were ever invited to the jefe's residence. Though Miller got only two minutes of face-to-face time with the big boss before being rushed out of his office, he had spent three days at the man's humongous estate with some of the biggest names in the drug trafficking business. It had been the wildest, and the most dangerous, party Miller had ever attended. With everyone either drunk or high, Miller had learned more about the JNGC's leadership structure and operations in three days than he had in the four years he'd been working with them.

Loose lips sink ships, Miller had thought.

On the morning he was supposed to depart the jefe's compound, five armed cartel members, one of them Carlos, had entered his room, holding him at gunpoint. Expecting a bullet in the head—or worse, since the JNGC had the reputation of torturing their victims for days before killing them—Miller had been relieved when Carlos had asked him to take off all his clothes and to hand him his phone. Though Miller couldn't say he had enjoyed the search—it had been particularly thorough—he knew they wouldn't find anything on his person. Carlos had checked the phone for any photos, notes, or recordings Miller had taken during his stay. Not to worry, he hadn't taken any. When Carlos hadn't ordered him to hand over his phone prior to his arrival at the jefe's compound, Miller had seen it for what it was. A test. He was being vetted. But for what?

Upon his return to Saint John, a man in his fifties had been waiting for him in his apartment. Though the man had been casually dressed in a simple black T-shirt, with white Bermuda shorts and a pair of powder blue flip-flops, Miller hadn't been fooled. This wasn't someone to take lightly, and not only because there was a suppressed pistol on the table next to him. The man was fit to the extreme, his muscles lean and hard. His eyes, dark blue, were bright and alert. Miller had served with men like him before. There was no mistake about it. The man was an operator.

"Who are you, and what do you want?"

"Hello, Ian. My friend in Mexico tells me you can be trusted. Is that true?"

"Wouldn't I be dead if it wasn't?"

The man had seemed satisfied with that answer.

"I've been keeping an eye on you, you know?"

"Oh yeah? Since when?"

"Since your parents introduced me to you. I'm your friend from Russia."

Miller's heartbeat had quickened, but not overly so. He had been waiting for this moment his entire professional life and had started to doubt it would ever happen.

"You didn't tell me your name."

"Yuri Makarov, and I'm here to talk about the trip you're about to make to the Dominican Republic."

Miller had smiled. "Would you like a beer, Mr. Makarov?"

The light chop was hardly noticeable as the Axopar sliced through the two- to three-foot waves like a much bigger boat, with no pounding whatsoever. Wanting to keep as low a profile as he could, Miller had turned off the vessel's navigation and running lights as well as the two multifunction displays. He knew the area well, and he didn't need the GPS to get to where he was going. At this time of night, there would be no police or Royal Navy vessels on duty, so the odds of being picked up by a thermal-imaging sweep were minimal. At the speed they were traveling, it didn't take long to reach the edge of Tortola—the largest and most populated of the British Virgin Islands. Miller cut the Axopar's speed by half as he tried to pinpoint the entry to the narrow channel he was looking for. Using the island's topology as his guide, Miller steered the boat carefully. Wanting to diminish the speed further, Miller reached for the throttles, but the woman already had her hands on them. She brought the throttles to neutral, then shut the engines down before taking two steps back.

A gun was in her hand, and it was pointed at his chest. He glanced over his shoulder. The assailant was there, but he had taken a position that would keep him out of the woman's line of fire. Miller was happy to see that the man's sidearm was still holstered.

Miller shook his head. "What are you doing? The current will drive us onto the rocks."

"Then I suggest you answer my questions rapidly," she replied.

This wasn't a surprise. Miller had known this was coming. It was totally understandable. The only surprise was that it had taken her so long to stop the boat. Miller would have done it much sooner.

"Okay. Shoot," Miller said. "Your questions, I mean. Not the gun."

His attempt at humor fell flat. He'd have to work harder on his stand-up skills.

"What's your name?"

"Ian Miller. At your service."

"Why did you head east instead of west? The instructions were to travel west toward the Dominican Republic."

"That was before you got into a gunfight half of the freaking island heard," Miller said. "But clearly this wasn't enough fireworks for you, was it? You had to blow a police chopper out of the sky. For God's sake! Do you really think we could have made it to the Dominican Republic? There's no way we could have made it past Puerto Rico, and that's if we were lucky. Odds were, we would have been intercepted, and sunk, way before we even made it to international waters."

"What happened back there?"

"Where? What do you mean by *back there*? Can you be more precise?" he asked nonchalantly, as if having a gun pointed at him was no big deal. Which wasn't entirely accurate.

She looked at him, seemingly puzzled that he had replied with a question of his own.

"What happened at the Westin?"

"Someone screwed up, that's for sure," he said.

"I think you're the one who screwed up."

"Nah, lady. I'm the one who saved your ass," Miller said.

The woman's face darkened, and she aimed her pistol at his right knee. "Be condescending like this one more time and I'll blow your knee out. Who told you to pick us up?"

"Whoever's paying me," he said.

Miller deduced that she hadn't liked this answer, either, because the point of her shoe hit him solidly in the testicles. The air whooshed out of him and he doubled over, falling to his knees while clutching his balls, his breath failing him.

The woman repeated her question. "Who told you to pick us up?"

Groaning, with tears in his eyes, Miller got to his feet, slowly.

"Listen," he said once he'd regained his breath. "The only thing I know was that I was supposed to meet a guy named Aleksei at the bar at the Westin resort. I just got there, didn't even have the time to order a margarita, when two shots rang out. I didn't know what was going on, but now I guess it was you guys, right?"

"I ask the questions. You don't. What happened next?"

Miller shrugged. "The guy I was supposed to meet with panicked."

There was enough moonlight for Miller to see a shadow of suspicion cross the woman's face, and he knew he had to be careful.

"Panicked? How?" she asked. "You're not making any sense."

"I can only tell you what I witnessed with my own eyes, okay? I think your friend Aleksei got spooked by a man named Clayton White—"

"Clayton White? White was at the Westin bar?" she asked, her face reflecting considerable shock.

"He was. His fiancée, Veronica Ham—"

"I know who White's fiancée is," the woman snapped at him. "Who else was there?"

"I can't say for sure. I didn't get a good look at their table, but there was at least one Secret Service agent."

"Why did you say Aleksei was spooked?"

"Because after the two shots were fired, he jammed a pistol into the side of a teenage girl's head," Miller said. "That wasn't cool, let me tell you that much. Very scary shit."

"Why would he do that?" the woman asked, but Miller had the feeling the question wasn't directed at him, so he kept his mouth shut.

The next question came from the man behind him. "Where's Aleksei now?"

"He's dead. I had to shoot him," Miller said without looking back. The man's voice had been enough to tell Miller where the man had moved to and the approximate distance at which he was standing from him.

"You . . . you had to shoot him?" the woman growled, her eyes blazing with anger.

"Yes, that's what I just said. Weren't you listening?"

This time, Miller was ready for the kick to his balls, and he blocked it by deflecting her foot away with a quick, powerful swipe of his leg. Not expecting to encounter resistance, the woman lost her balance, and Miller moved in, grabbing her pistol with two hands and twisting it clockwise, forcing the woman to release it. Taking advantage of the moment of surprise he'd created, Miller moved behind her just in time to see the man draw his pistol.

Ah shit!

Miller extended his arm and fired, sending two rounds square into the man's tactical vest. The man dropped, but Miller knew he had made himself vulnerable by extending his arm. As he'd feared she would, the woman pivoted and delivered a mighty elbow strike into his exposed armpit. The blow delivered an electric shock into Miller's arm, and the pistol clattered on the deck. The woman, who was clearly enraged, continued into her swing and telegraphed a left hook Miller easily ducked beneath. As he came up, Miller grabbed the woman, one hand on her belt and the other gripping her hair, lifted her up, and threw her over the gunwale and into the black, ominous water.

CHAPTER TWENTY-EIGHT

Saint John
US Virgin Islands

The incoming rounds fired in his direction by a retreating shooter aboard the Axopar kept White pinned down longer than he would have wished. When the bullets stopped flying, White quickly moved to Doyle's side and offered his assistance, but the Secret Service agent waved him away.

"I'll be fine," Doyle said, handing White a small flashlight. "Go check the house."

A cursory look at Doyle's leg confirmed he had stopped the bleeding. Doyle would probably never walk without a limp again, but he would live.

"Advise the local cops I'm on my way to the house," White said. "Give them my description and tell them not to wait for the SWAT team. There's no need."

White sprinted to the pier, wanting to secure the assailant and his weapon. Midway to the pier, he remembered he wasn't carrying any handcuffs or zip ties. It turned out he didn't need them. The assailant had caught a round at the top of his head. The bullet had gone through the front part of his brain and exited under his chin. A rifle White recognized as a Steyr AUG lay next to the dead man. White picked it up, released the magazine, emptied the chamber, and disassembled the weapon. He dropped the rifle into the thick foliage on his way to O'Donnell's house but pocketed the firing pin.

With his pistol and newly acquired flashlight in hand, White followed the pathway to the FBI director's house. He stepped off the trail and sent the beam of his flashlight around the residence's backyard. At the edge of the yard, no more than three feet before the heavy vegetation began, a man was sprawled on his back. Not knowing who the man was, White kept the beam of his light on him as he approached. As he got closer, White spotted the FBI badge clipped to the man's belt.

Ah shit.

White squatted next to the FBI agent and checked for a pulse. None. Struggling to keep his anger in check, White followed a gravel pathway that led him to a wooden deck. Another dead body. This one slumped halfway up the stairs leading to the deck. The man had been shot in the face at close range and it took White a moment to identify him, but when he did, his heart sank.

Jeremy O'Donnell. The director's son. A newly minted FBI special agent, if White remembered correctly. *What a damn shame.*

White entered the living room by the sliding doors and found O'Donnell's body behind the bar. He'd been hit at least four times, with the kill shot being a bullet to the heart. Next to O'Donnell, another FBI agent lay dead, shot in the head, though White saw that the agent had also been on the receiving end of at least two more gunshots, both bullets catching him in the vest. White examined the scene. The way the blood and brain matter were splattered on the lower cabinets of the bar behind the FBI agent meant that whoever had fired the shots had been standing . . . there.

The staircase landing.

How was that possible? So far, all the indications had pointed to an assault originating from the backyard, including the dozens of spent 5.56 mm shell casings White had found on the wooden deck. He was yet to find one in the living room. All the casings he'd seen inside the house had been 9 mm.

They were caught off guard. Whoever had killed the FBI director and the other special agent had come from upstairs. As White moved toward the stairs, he heard a deep, low growl coming from the second floor. White began to climb the stairs one at a time. The growl grew louder as he continued to ascend. White stopped at the top of the stairs. At the end of the hallway, a golden retriever was standing in the doorframe, blocking the entry, and showing serious teeth too. The dog didn't make any move toward White, but it didn't stop growling either.

It was protecting something, or someone.

White holstered his pistol and gently approached the dog, showing open hands. He didn't back away when the golden began to bark. Instead, he started talking in a measured tone.

"Hey, buddy, I'm not here for you, okay? Are you gonna let me through? The last thing I want to do is hurt you."

His words didn't seem to appease the golden one bit. Clearly the dog couldn't care less about what he was saying and continued baring its teeth. Its growl had a renewed intensity. It kept its eyes fixed on White, with saliva dripping from its mouth. White had the sinking feeling that the golden was about to attack. Reluctantly, he pulled out his pistol again as he backed away a few steps.

"Please don't force me to hurt you. Please," White heard himself beg.

Then, as if by magic, the dog stopped growling and seemed to reassess the situation. The golden turned its back to White and retreated into the bedroom. White followed, staying as nonthreatening as he could. He noticed the woman as soon as he entered the bedroom. She was on the hardwood floor, sprawled on her back, one hand touching one of the front paws of the golden retriever.

Sweet Jesus. Michelle O'Donnell.

Michelle had an enormous gash on the side of her head, and there was so much blood pooled around her that White didn't comprehend how she could still be alive. The golden looked at White with big, sad, sensitive eyes. It was as if the dog knew something terrible had happened to its family and was now asking White for his help.

"I'll take care of her," White said, kneeling next to the FBI director's wife. "I promise."

Michelle slowly turned her head toward White, and her eyes fluttered open, glassy and unfocused. She tried to speak, but only a quiet moan emerged from her lips.

"It's okay," White said. "I'm here to help."

The woman suddenly grabbed White's wrist with surprising force and pulled it toward her, forcing White to get lower.

"Da . . . Da . . . Daphne . . . Co . . . Cook," she managed to slur out.

"Daphne Cook?" White asked. He had heard the name before but couldn't remember where. "What about her?"

Michelle shuddered. White felt the pressure around his wrist lessen as she released her grip on him and moved her hand back on top of her golden retriever's paw. Then she closed her eyes and took her last breath.

Downstairs, help had finally arrived.

CHAPTER TWENTY-NINE

Sir Francis Drake Channel, South of Road Town
British Virgin Islands

Ulyana was suspended in the air for a split second, and then she hit the water headfirst. Complete darkness enveloped her, and she felt as if the ocean current had taken hold of her clothes and was pulling her down, farther away from the boat and the surface. She didn't know which way was up. She kicked her legs but didn't seem to make any headway. She couldn't breathe, and panic began to stir inside her. Her lungs were about to burst from the physical effort, but she refused to quit and fought with everything she had. The only thing she knew was that giving up meant death. And she wasn't yet ready for that. With a desperate force born of sheer terror, she swam with all her might, and, just as she felt she could go no farther, a beam of light appeared in front of her. Digging into the last vestiges of her energy, she kicked her legs twice more and propelled herself with her arms, taking a lungful of water as she broke the surface.

She coughed violently and almost went under again. Then someone shone a light in her eyes.

"Grab the ring," she heard Miller shout. "It's right there."

The beam of light swung to her left where a white ring was floating five feet from her.

She swam for it, half expecting Miller to pull it away from her, but he didn't. She grabbed it, then wrapped her arms around it. She let him pull her toward the boat. At the swim platform, he helped her transition onto the boat; then her legs gave out, and she fell onto the deck. She lay there, panting and too weak to move. At some point—it might have been seconds or minutes later; she couldn't say—Miller helped her to her feet. She didn't have the strength to resist. He guided her to the aft bench, where she sat next to Hans, who was no longer wearing his tactical vest. She was surprised to see him alive, though he seemed to be very much in pain. His hands were zip-tied behind his back, and Miller had rolled heavy-duty duct tape around his ankles. Miller had also shut him up by slapping several pieces of duct tape over his mouth. Miller used a pair of zip ties to secure her right hand to one of the aft bench posts but somehow didn't feel the need to secure her ankles or tape her mouth shut. Her clothes, wet and cold, clung to her body, and she began to shiver.

Miller looked at her and sighed, then threw her a towel and took his place behind the helm seat.

"Get dry," he said as he started the Axopar's engines. "Then we'll talk."

———

Twenty minutes later, Ulyana watched Miller tie the Axopar to a cement dock next to a small bungalow alongside a canal. Clouds had moved in, partially obscuring the moon. The lights inside the boat were off, but there was a faint glimmer emanating from the bungalow that allowed her to see. It had taken her longer than she had thought to dry up and regain all her senses. She still wasn't sure how Miller had managed to neutralize both her and Hans, but one thing was clear: he was no Jeremy O'Donnell. She had badly underestimated Miller, and she was embarrassed by it.

She knew Hans was antsy to take some sort of action, and he had kept looking at her when Miller had his back turned to them while driving the boat, but she had ignored him. Hans's pride had taken a hit, but he'd get over it. Ian Miller wasn't someone she wanted to toy with. Not anymore. Ulyana felt like she should be angry at Miller for what he had done to her, but she found herself intrigued by him instead.

Which confused her.

As he stood in front of her, holding a suppressed pistol in his right hand, half of Miller's face was in the dim light provided by the bungalow. He had sharp, serious eyes, and he had a great mustache going on.

"Shooting Aleksei was the only way I could keep my cover," Miller said without preamble. "Clayton White and I served in the military together. He got out and joined the Secret Service. I didn't."

"What did you do?" she asked.

"I chose another path," Miller said. "More lucrative, and a lot less boring, if you ask me."

"Boat chartering?"

Miller smiled, then continued. "Anyway, I was pretty sure White had already seen Aleksei nod in my direction. And let me tell you, Clayton White is no dummy. If I hadn't shot Aleksei, White would have assumed I was working with him, and I would have lost control of the narrative."

"He would have found a way out," she said, although she doubted that very much. Aleksei had been the newest addition to her team, the guy responsible for the logistics. Saint John had been his first assignment with her.

Miller laughed. "Didn't you tell me you knew who Clayton White was?"

"What's your point?"

"I don't think you know him at all. Your friend Aleksei was dead the moment he decided to take a teenage girl hostage. In fact, I'm almost certain White was about to pull the trigger when I killed Aleksei."

Ulyana considered everything Miller had shared with her. There were still a few things that weren't adding up. The message she had received from her handler had mentioned that the boat was on its way. It had also stated that it wouldn't be Aleksei driving it but a new player named Ian Miller, and that it was essential that Ulyana pretended to kill him prior to boarding the boat. She was curious about how that had come to be.

"How did you know you had to pick us up at O'Donnell's house or how to reach my handler?"

Miller smiled at her. "Two things," he said, holding up two fingers. "The first is that I received your text. The one you sent Aleksei when you realized the Axopar wasn't there. I had taken his phone after I killed him."

"Can I have it?"

"What? His phone? No, it's at the bottom of the ocean, I'm afraid. It slipped out of my pocket when I helped you out of the water."

She knew it was bullshit, but she didn't push the issue. Her handler would wipe it clean remotely.

"And what's the second?"

"When I realized how screwed up the situation was, I called the man who hired me in the first place."

She shot Miller a quizzical look. Then she swallowed hard, coming to terms with what he had just said. Who was Miller really working for? Was he an American agent? Were she and Hans about to be shot? Miller looked like the type who wouldn't think twice about doing it. Next to her, Hans was struggling to get out of his restraints. He, too, had read the room perfectly and knew what was coming next.

"What now?" she asked.

"I don't know. It's not up to me," he said.

She watched him dial a number on his phone.

"It's me," Miller said.

Then there was a short pause, during which he looked at her.

"Yeah, it's bad," he said. "But she's fine, and so is Hans. The others are dead, but I had already told you about Aleksei."

There was another pause, this one longer than the previous one.

"It's entirely up to you," Miller finally said. "I couldn't care less one way or the other. Just say the word."

Ulyana began to feel an edge of panic. She took a deep breath through her nose, willing her heartbeat to slow. She had to think. She had to find a way out.

"You're sure? Okay."

Miller raised his gun.

Shit. She was out of options and out of time.

Miller's gun spat once, and Hans's head snapped back, a neat hole in the center of his forehead.

I'm next, Ulyana thought. *Let's be done with it.*

She looked into Miller's eyes, unwilling to give him the satisfaction of knowing how scared she was.

But instead of aiming his pistol at her, Miller lowered it.

"Here," he said, handing her the phone. "Someone wants to talk with you."

Stunned to be alive, she took the phone with her free hand and pressed it against her ear.

"Da?" she said, not even realizing she'd spoken in Russian.

But it was okay, because the person at the other end spoke Russian too.

"Hello, Ulyana. This is Yuri."

CHAPTER THIRTY

Macau Special Administrative Region
China

Geng Peiwu stood by one of the floor-to-ceiling windows of his thirty-eighth-floor office with Yuri Makarov by his side. The twenty-four FIM-92 Stinger surface-to-air missiles Yuri had promised had been delivered to the port of Macau by a Russian-flagged vessel. Peiwu and Yuri had spent the last two days at the docks supervising the loading of the missiles into the three cargo ships Peiwu had selected. The three ship captains, and a good part of their crew, were on Peiwu's payroll in one way or another. But with such an important payload, Peiwu had dispatched two four-man teams of heavily armed Red Dragon Triad members to each ship.

"To be on the safe side," he'd said to Yuri.

The three ships were all taking different routes to get to their objective. The first ship would travel northward through the Sea of Japan once it had passed through the East China Sea before finally entering the North Pacific Ocean. From there, it would steam ahead to Los Angeles, where longshoremen working with Red Dragon Triad members would be waiting. The second would speed across the Indian Ocean before rotating north toward Miami once it had sailed past South Africa's Cape of Good Hope. The third, the smallest of the three vessels, wouldn't go to the United States like the others. Instead, it was headed to the

Mediterranean, where it would be met by a private yacht owned by an associate of Yuri—a last-minute change that had been approved by Director Ma Lin. Peiwu had warned both Yuri and Ma Lin that unlike at the ports of Miami and Los Angeles, he was in no position to provide any kind of assistance in ports located on the Mediterranean, Marseille being the only exception.

"Thank you for your input, Mr. Peiwu," Ma Lin had told him. "Our friend Yuri will take care of the rest."

Peiwu didn't ask, but it wouldn't have surprised him to learn that the request for the change had come directly from the office of the president of the Russian Federation. Moscow was out for blood. They had still not recovered from the embarrassing debacle that Russian forces were involved in in Ukraine, as well as the still-unresolved assassination of one of the Russian president's closest friends by a Ukrainian-led hit team. Peiwu didn't rule out an attack on European soil. While he didn't believe the Russians would do it themselves, there were plenty of fringe groups in Europe that Moscow could use as proxies.

Though the Chinese government stayed well clear of professing such an outrageous idea publicly, Peiwu was aware that an attack in Europe would make the Chinese leadership very happy. For the likes of Ma Lin and the other fools in Beijing who fantasized about the "great reunification" with Taiwan and claimed that it should be fulfilled at any cost, the more chaos on the European continent, the better.

Peiwu didn't believe so. Not only did he have family in Taiwan, but he had also worked hard to get a solid foothold in Taiwan. Now that he had it, and now that his business was finally thriving, he wasn't ready to let it go so easily.

Peiwu took a pack of cigarettes from his jacket and offered one to Yuri. The Russian accepted and Peiwu leaned over, giving him a light. Peiwu took one for himself, lit it, and inhaled deeply. After a count of three, he let the smoke seep out of his mouth and nose very slowly, enjoying the infusion of nicotine into his blood.

"I'm told that Henry Newman has done well for us," Yuri said. "I'm glad this worked out."

"He always comes through."

And it was the truth. It hadn't been a week yet since Peiwu had talked with Newman in the back seat of his Maserati. O'Donnell had failed to listen to Newman's warning, but Peiwu had heard the conversation. Newman had played his part. He had done exactly what Peiwu had requested of him. As a test run, the MSS had sent two junior covert operatives to the United States using the pipeline Newman had established. There had been no problem, and Ma Lin had been thrilled with the initial results.

From where they stood by the window, Peiwu and Yuri could see one of their three cargo ships, the one set to go to Europe. The two others were hidden by nearby office towers. Despite the early hour, the port was humming with activity. Colossal cranes could be seen swinging left and right, loading and unloading containers from the hulls of the cargo ships. Around the vessels, a small army of longshoremen kept themselves busy manning forklifts, driving trucks, and transporting cargo to and from warehouses.

Peiwu grabbed two pairs of high-powered binoculars from a nearby cabinet and gave one to Yuri. Peiwu pointed toward the port.

"One of ours just left the port," he said as he looked through the lenses. "You see it?"

Peiwu focused on a large ship with a green hull churning its way through the narrow channel. Its deck was loaded with multicolored containers that were stacked eight high.

"I do," Yuri said. "I've always been fascinated by the sheer size of these ships and how they can float with so much cargo."

Peiwu was tempted to explain to Yuri the simple physics behind it but decided against doing so when he couldn't find a way to do it without sounding condescending.

"Have you heard anything from the Virgin Islands?" Peiwu asked.

"Relax, my friend," Yuri chuckled. "Do not worry. There's nothing in Saint John that could lead back to you or your triad. My asset made sure of that. Apart from my people, every contractor who participated in the assault has been dealt with."

"Permanently, I hope?" Peiwu asked.

"Yes. That's always the best way, isn't it?" Yuri said, taking a drag from his cigarette. "I'd be lying if I said that I'm pleased with how the operation in the Virgin Islands unfolded. It is far from being optimal, but the critical objective was met."

Yuri was right. Though the raid hadn't been pretty and had attracted exponentially more attention than Peiwu had wanted, the massive investigation into the assault on Patrick O'Donnell's vacation home and his subsequent death would consume the FBI and the media for weeks to come. Peiwu agreed that for the foreseeable future, there would be little to no appetite within the FBI for anything other than finding the people responsible.

And dead people can't talk.

"What about *your* people, Yuri? What's the plan for them?"

"My team is in Santo Domingo for a few more days while new passports are being prepared. Then they'll make their way to Monaco. That's where I'll meet them."

Peiwu took one last look at the departing cargo ship, then turned to face Yuri. "Monaco, you said?"

Yuri handed back his binoculars to Peiwu.

"I'm done here, Mr. Peiwu. My job was to safely deliver the missiles to you, which I've done. The operation in the Virgin Islands wasn't as clean as we'd hoped, but the objective was fulfilled. I now have other duties to attend to."

Peiwu didn't press further. Although convinced it was no coincidence that the third ship would soon sail to the Mediterranean, Peiwu had too much on his plate to worry about what Yuri and his crew had in mind for Monaco.

It would take up to four weeks for the two cargo ships headed to the United States to reach their respective ports. Once the missiles were off-loaded, Peiwu's triad would see to their transfer to ten different prearranged safe houses across the continental United States, with two missiles per location, and would provide the necessary security until MSS operatives took over. Peiwu wondered when that would be. Ma Lin had remained vague about the exact timing, and Peiwu assumed it was possible the 4th Bureau director didn't have the answer either. How long would it take the MSS to find the right proxies in the United States? Or did Chinese intelligence already have its eyes on some prospects? Finding and training domestic terrorists willing to shoot down airliners in America would have been difficult ten years ago.

But now? Maybe not so much.

CHAPTER THIRTY-ONE

Executive Residence of the President of the United States
Washington, DC

Clayton White stretched out on the comfortable king-size bed, his head on the pillow with his arms folded beneath it, his eyes fixed on the ceiling. The bedroom, situated on the third floor of the Executive Residence between the billiards room and the passage leading to the solarium, was painted in royal blue and meadow green, colors White wasn't particularly fond of. At the foot of the bed was a small sitting area where two rose-tinted love seats faced each other. A panoply of beaded multicolor throw pillows, which did nothing to make the sofas look more inviting, completed the simple, yet very weird, decor.

At least the sheets are soft, White thought, looking at the white Egyptian cotton sheet bunched around his waist. What was supposed to have been an afternoon nap had quickly rolled into a lovemaking session, and both he and Veronica had fallen soundly asleep afterward. Living with Veronica and exploring life with her had taken him to places he had never known existed. And, with their baby growing inside her, she had shown him the true meaning of life. It had taken him a while, probably longer than it should have, but he finally understood that there was more to look forward to than the next mission or the next adrenaline rush.

As Veronica lay curled against him, the warm skin of her naked bottom resting against his right hip, White had a hard time not thinking about the slaughter of Patrick O'Donnell's family in Saint John the week before. He kept replaying the gun battle in his mind, trying to figure out what had gone wrong. Was there something he could have done that would have prevented the O'Donnells' deaths? Could the shooting down of the police helicopter have been avoided? And what about Ian Miller? Why had he moved so damn close to the pier? White didn't have the answers.

In White's line of work, risks were unavoidable. He understood that. But Miller had pulled the plug years ago, hadn't he? He'd been at the bar sipping his drink, hoping to meet with a client interested in renting his boat for a few days. Then all hell had broken loose, and White had pulled Miller right back in by allowing the former PJ to join him and Doyle in White's poorly planned rescue. White's sloppiness had been costly.

His friend Ian Miller was gone.

Following the slaughter at Patrick O'Donnell's vacation home, a government jet had flown Veronica, Clayton, Emily, and the two Secret Service special agents assigned to Vonnie's protective detail back to Washington. The president had insisted that Veronica remain at the White House until the Secret Service could determine whether her life was still in danger. Tom Doyle was still in the Virgin Islands, recuperating from a series of surgeries he'd undergone to repair his knee. Doyle had been lucky.

And so was I, White thought. *Life is so damn fragile. I could have lost her. I could have lost everything.*

Careful not to wake Veronica, White rolled to his right and hugged his fiancée tightly against him. Hours before the shoot-out, as he and Vonnie were getting ready for their dinner with Emily, White had wondered out loud if life could get any better. He'd said to Veronica that he didn't remember a time when he'd been so happy.

That wasn't true any longer.

Saint John had shaken him like no other firefight had done before. He had so much more to lose now. Veronica hadn't come out of it unscathed either. Physically, she was fine. She hadn't been injured, nor had Emily. But seeing him—the father of the child who was growing inside her—running half-cocked toward the sound of the guns had scared her.

She had told him that much. And more.

When he'd finally returned to the resort, she'd almost bitten his head off. It was hard to blame her. Heading to O'Donnell's house armed with a pistol hadn't been his wisest tactical decision. But how could he have done otherwise, knowing people needed him? It had been a lose-lose situation from the start.

White felt Veronica's breathing change. He looked over at the clock on the night table. It was almost time for dinner.

In fifteen minutes, Alexander Hammond would be waiting for them in the president's dining room, an intimate setting on the second floor of the White House with a view of the North Lawn. For White, it was a constant struggle to live under the same roof as the man he blamed for his father's death, but after Veronica's mother's brutal murder, who was he to deprive Veronica of her father's affection? White would never forgive Hammond for what he had done. His betrayal of White's dad, General Maxwell White, was criminal, and unpardonable.

But it was somewhat understandable.

Hammond had been forced into a corner, though in good part due to his own poor decisions, and he had felt as though giving up his friend Maxwell was his only way out of an awfully difficult position. Tortured by his conscience, Maxwell White had tried to contact several investigative journalists to denounce Hammond's involvement, as well as his own, in the sinking of a cargo ship that had in fact been an illegal detention center for prisoners of war. When Hammond's coconspirators had learned about Maxwell's intentions, they'd given Hammond a choice. Give us Maxwell White, or we'll butcher your daughter and your wife.

And then there was the matter of Hammond's predecessor. White didn't know what to make of the official report concluding that the former president had died of natural causes.

A heart attack? Really?

White had a hard time accepting the idea that Hammond hadn't had a hand in the president's death, despite being given the autopsy report and the entire investigative file. Even his friend Chris Albanese had told him there was nothing there and that White should let it go.

But Albanese didn't know everything White knew about Hammond. Like most Americans, Albanese's opinion of Hammond was that he was an incorruptible man who had served the American people all his life, oftentimes at his own peril. It made White sick.

Exasperated, White let out a long sigh and felt Veronica wiggle a little. A moment later, she pushed herself deeper into his side. She lifted his hand to her lips and kissed it.

"Hey, baby," he whispered in her ear.

"Hey. What time is it?" she asked, stretching and rubbing her back against him.

"About time we get ready for dinner. Are you hungry?"

"I'm starving. I'm always starving."

He cupped her belly with his hand. "That's because of this little guy," he said. "Blame it on him."

She slapped his hand away. "Little guy? Really? You're clairvoyant now, Clayton White?"

He could hear the amusement in her voice, but she was right. In the end, they had asked the obstetrician not to disclose their baby's sex. Frankly, White didn't care. A boy, a girl, it didn't matter. He just felt blessed that life had given him the opportunity to become a father.

He'd have to find a way not to mess this up.

CHAPTER THIRTY-TWO

Executive Residence of the President of the United States
Washington, DC

Following a dinner of perfectly cooked roast beef, grilled vegetables, scalloped tomatoes, and garlic mashed potatoes, White had been surprised when the president had asked him if he cared to return to the third floor for a few games of eight-ball.

Cognizant that Hammond wanted to talk, White had followed him up, curious. Veronica had promised to join them later, saying she had one more call to make with her work group at SkyCU Technology before calling it a day.

The billiards room was a cross between a library and a game room. Floor-to-ceiling bookcases lined one wall. Two dark leather armchairs, a glass-top coffee table, and one sofa formed a small sitting area. A corner bar with a granite counter held an impressive collection of liquor bottles. A dartboard hung on the wall next to it. The pool table, ornately carved from Brazilian cherrywood, sat at the center of the room.

"I've been told Tom Doyle will be back stateside early next week," Hammond said as he placed a tablet computer on the coffee table.

"Good news. He's a good man."

"Maybe so, but he'll never serve on a protection detail again."

"I know," White said, grabbing the wooden triangle from under the pool table.

"He shouldn't have followed you up the beach," Hammond said. "His job was to protect Vonnie, not the director of the FBI. That's all I'll say on the matter."

It was hard for White to argue. The president was right. But Doyle had done what he thought was right at the time and had followed his own threat assessment.

"Your break," Hammond said, handing White a cue stick.

———

White was finishing racking up the balls for the fifth time when Veronica walked into the billiards room, a laptop tucked under one arm and a mug of hot water in her opposite hand. She took a seat in one of the leather armchairs.

"Who's winning?" she asked.

Instead of replying, White carefully examined the tightness of the rack before lifting the wooden triangle off the table's gray felt. At the opposite end of the table, President Alexander Hammond leaned over, lining up his shot.

"What are we at, Clayton?" Hammond said. "It's 4–0, right?"

White wasn't much of a pool player. He had played a few games in his teenage years and again at the officers' mess during his time in the military, but he had quickly lost interest.

"This shouldn't take too long," Hammond said, sliding his cue stick back and forth between his thumb and forefinger.

White grabbed the chalk off the table's polished wood as Hammond hit the white ball. The balls scattered across the table, with two stripes and one solid falling into pockets. Hammond surveyed his work as he rubbed chalk against the end of his cue stick.

"Now that you're both here, I can share with you that, as Clayton and I suspected, the Secret Service found no evidence that the raiding party knew about Veronica's presence on the island," Hammond said.

"With the video of Clayton's knife fight in New York City still getting hundreds of thousands of new views every month, we couldn't rule out a potential connection to Iran."

White had indeed suspected this would be the findings, but it was a relief to get it confirmed by the Secret Service.

"That's great to hear," White said. "You heard that, Vonnie?"

"What does that mean for us, Dad?" she asked. "Are we free to go?"

Hammond looked at his daughter. "It isn't like you were in prison, Veronica," he said. "And you have to admit the food is pretty good."

"I need to get back to SkyCU," Veronica said. "There's only so much I can do from here to prepare for Davos."

What Veronica meant by Davos was the flagship event of the World Economic Forum—or WEF—an annual meeting taking place in the Alpine resort town of Davos, Switzerland. For the second year in a row, Veronica had been invited to speak at the invitation-only event, where chief executive officers of multibillion-dollar companies, select politicians, religious leaders, and representatives from different research groups and nongovernmental organizations met to discuss pressing issues facing the globe, such as climate change, international conflicts, and globalization.

Veronica's previous year's exposé on Drain2, a mobile application she had developed in partnership with SkyCU Technology that could potentially help corporations and governments make better decisions about how to combat climate change by using high-resolution satellite imagery, had been a major hit with the attendees. For the upcoming summit, she had been working almost nonstop on a presentation about a new mobile application she and her colleagues at SkyCU were about to launch. The application, which would be free to download, would warn people about forthcoming disasters such as tsunamis, heat waves, hurricanes, et cetera, using data from open-source government databases. Usually held in winter, this year's event would take place in the fall for the first time. White had been looking forward to it. He had visited Switzerland several times, but he'd missed last year's event and had never been to Switzerland in that season. White had always found the landlocked country in the heart of Europe to be a feast for the eyes and other senses.

"About Davos," Hammond said, leaving his cue stick on the table. "There's something I'd like to share with you."

Hammond took a seat across from his daughter and motioned White to do the same.

"What is it?" Veronica asked dryly. "But before you say anything, let me tell you something real quick, Dad: if you think you can prevent me from going, you're dead wrong. So don't try. You'll only make me angry."

The president's face clouded, and White could see that Hammond was serious. "It's not that, Veronica," he said. "Quite the contrary."

"Okay. Then what?"

"As I mentioned when you came in, the Secret Service has deemed neither you nor Clayton were the intended target in Saint John, and that the presence of Aleksei Manturov at the Westin was purely coincidental," Hammond started.

"What do we know about Aleksei Manturov?" White jumped in before the president could continue.

"Very little. There was nothing of value on his phone, including the text message you received when you were making your way by the beach to O'Donnell's residence. That tells us that the phone was wiped remotely. The NSA is looking at it, but they aren't hopeful. We ran his fingerprints through all our databases, and we got nothing."

"Where is he from?" Veronica asked.

"His passport is from the Dominican Republic, and their National Police confirmed Manturov owns a house in Santo Domingo. He supposedly lives there with his wife and three children."

White shook his head. "We can't trust anything the Dominican Republic National Police tells us," he said. "Organized crime organizations have enough police officers on their payrolls that the Dominican Republic's entire security apparatus is unreliable. We'll need to send our own guys to verify the information."

Hammond nodded. "Agreed and done. I'll let you know if anything comes out of it. I have a hunch it will."

"O-kay? Why?" Veronica asked.

"Because Aleksei Manturov owns a small yacht brokerage firm in Santo Domingo."

"Daphne Cook was a yacht broker too," Veronica said. "I'll be damned."

"So, it was Daphne I saw running on the pier and shooting Ian," White said, angry he hadn't taken his shot earlier. If he had, his friend could have still been alive. "Shit."

"And it's not all I have to say about her, or whatever her real name is, 'cause it's sure not Daphne Cook," Hammond warned. "But before I get back to her, I want you to know that we've positively identified the two dead shooters. Both are former Austrian Jagdkommandos."

"Austrian? What the hell?" White said, leaning forward, his head spinning. "You said former. They turned mercenaries?"

"Yes, both working for a tiny private military company named G9S Security Solutions. That PMC was founded five years ago by Hans Roth, a former Jagdkommando officer, following his dishonorable discharge from the Austrian army due to an incident in Mali. CIA is looking into it, but for now we don't know what kind of incident it was, though we suspect it was quite serious since it warranted Roth losing his job. And the same applied to the two dead assailants, by the way. They were with Roth in Mali."

White ran a hand through his hair. "One of them escaped," he said. "The woman, who we can now assume with almost complete certainty was Daphne Cook, led the way onto the pier. She was followed by a man in tactical gear who had a similarly dressed man on his shoulders. A third assailant closed ranks. It could have been Hans Roth."

"CIA thinks, and DOD confirmed, that G9S Security Solutions is a three-person company," Hammond said. "So yes, I think it's fair to assume Hans Roth was the one who got away."

"Let's suppose G9S was hired for the job. Who would want to kill Patrick O'Donnell? And why?" Veronica asked.

"I'd love to get my hands on Hans Roth and ask the bastard," White said angrily, his thoughts once again going to his friend Ian. "He seemed pretty buddy-buddy with that cockroach Daphne."

"Maybe. Maybe not," Hammond said, powering on the tablet computer he'd brought with him.

The screen flicked to life, and Hammond scrolled through several apps White didn't recognize. Once he'd found the one he was searching for, Hammond tapped on it and angled the screen toward White and Veronica.

"This recording was found on the phone of Special Agent Nestor West, one of the two FBI agents assigned to O'Donnell's protective detail."

"Was the phone tampered with?" Veronica asked.

"It wasn't. Before falling, West made a call to FBI dispatch to notify them of the attack. He then hid the phone under a seat cushion in the living room and kept the line open."

"That explains why we weren't able to reach him," White said. "Doyle told me the Secret Service tried to reconnect with him but couldn't."

"Are we able to hear what happened inside the house following his call?" Veronica asked.

"NSA is working on that, too, and we should learn more very soon. They're not confident. Except for the sound of several gunshots, the thick cushion did a good job muffling voices."

"Why wouldn't he have kept his phone with him?" White wondered out loud. "It doesn't make sense, especially since it was his only comm device."

Hammond nodded. "Good question, but I think West realized there was a good chance he'd be overrun, so he concealed the phone hoping we would find it."

"Right. But you said we can't hear anything," Veronica said.

"We can't hear what they're saying during the firefight, but I don't think it was what West wanted us to find," Hammond said. "What you're about to listen to is what I believe pushed West to discard his phone at great personal risk."

The president pushed a button on his tablet, and a recording of the phone call between the FBI director and Henry Newman began to play.

CHAPTER THIRTY-THREE

Executive Residence of the President of the United States
Washington, DC

Veronica studied her fiancé's face as they listened to the recording. Clearly Clayton had no idea who Henry Newman was.

She did.

Newman, a successful real estate developer, was the chairman and CEO of Newman Horizon Development. Newman's holdings in the United States—mostly office towers in New York City, beachfront hotels in Miami, and casino resorts in Las Vegas—were worth billions of dollars. But Newman also had significant assets in Macau, where he seemed to reside full time.

The year before, following SkyCU's board of directors' decision to remain private and not sell to one of the big tech corporations that wanted to acquire the start-up, Newman had personally reached out to her. Apparently, he had been wowed by SkyCU's refusal to sell out and wanted to let her know he thought it was the right call. He had also heard her plea on social media about the need for big, powerful corporations to do more about climate change and had offered $10 million toward one of her pet projects with NOAA. A week later, the funds had shown up.

As far as she was concerned, Henry Newman was a class act.

A man who puts his money where his mouth is.

So it had been with shock and disbelief that she listened to Newman's conversation with Patrick O'Donnell. Barely veiled death threats, extortion, and an association with the Red Dragon Triad? Was she leaving something out?

My God.

It took only a moment for her to realize that by accepting Newman's large donation, she had jeopardized all the groups and associations she had distributed the funds to while threatening the livelihood of everyone employed by them.

Veronica felt sick to her stomach. She'd been caught off guard, completely blindsided. She'd looked over the due diligence, and there had been no red flags.

None!

"I . . . I don't know what to think," she said, her hands shaking. "It's hard for me to believe this conversation really happened. Everything I know about this man paints such a different portrait."

Her dad leaned forward and squeezed her leg. "I know you've had dealings with him," he said. "I'll do what I can to minimize the impact this will have on you and your work."

"No," Veronica snapped back. "Absolutely not. You will not sweep this under the rug. Goddamn it, Dad! You'll only make this worse."

Her father leaned back in his armchair, lifting his hands in surrender. Veronica felt Clayton's eyes on her. "What dealings, Vonnie?"

She told him everything she knew about Newman, leaving nothing out, and concluded by saying, "That recording, that conversation, it's completely out of character for him. I'm so sorry, I really thought I—"

"Whoa, baby," Clayton said. "None of this is your fault. There's no way you could have foreseen this."

"That's not what the media will think," she said, her mind racing to find solutions. "Guilt by association. And they're not wrong."

Damn you, Henry Newman. Damn you!

"I'll have to get ahead of this," she said to no one in particular. "I'll write a—"

"No!" Hammond barked with enough force to make her jump in her seat. "You want to hang yourself with this, Veronica, you'll have the chance to do it. But not now."

"You're not—"

"Goddamn it, Vonnie, listen to me," her father said. "As much as I hate the situation you find yourself in, there are bigger things at play here."

"Your dad's right," Clayton said.

She shot her fiancé a wild look. She couldn't remember the last time Clayton had been in any sort of agreement with her father, and from the pained look on his face, it had been a difficult thing for him to say. Her father, whose head had snapped in Clayton's direction, also seemed dumbfounded. Not an expression she had seen often on her father.

"What do you mean?"

"I admire what you want to do here, Vonnie, but it would be counterproductive at this time. We can't let Newman know we're onto him. The way I see this going," Clayton said, his gaze on her dad, "is your father will send a team of operators to snatch Henry's sorry ass in Macau and bring him back to the United States so that he can face trial. Am I right?"

That makes sense, Veronica thought. She should have come to the same conclusion sooner, but she'd been blind with rage and had missed the obvious. Her father shifted in his seat, clearly a sign that he was uncomfortable with what he was about to say.

"What Clayton said is valid, and, in normal circumstances, I might consider going ahead with what he suggested," he said, "but this is far from normal. It's not as straightforward as it seems."

"Then why don't you enlighten us?" Clayton said, his tone telling Veronica her fiancé was running out of patience.

Her dad nodded. "This is where I circle back to Daphne Cook," he said, his eyes fixed on White. "Just like Aleksei Manturov, we know very little about her."

"Didn't the FBI perform a background check on her?" Clayton asked. "She was the director's son's girlfriend, for God's sake."

"The FBI isn't in the habit of conducting background checks on the boyfriend or girlfriend of a director's kid, Clayton. The FBI director's family doesn't get the same treatment the president's family does."

"What is it you want us to know about her?" Veronica asked.

"Daphne Cook was one of the employees of the now-defunct yacht brokerage firm Silver Yachts."

"You have to be kidding me," Clayton said slowly. Turning toward her, Clayton explained, "Silver Yachts was the agency hired by Jack Buchanan to manage his yacht, including his crew."

Veronica might have been tired and her brain foggy with righteous anger, but she understood the implications right away. "Oh shit."

She looked at her dad. "You think she's involved in the president's death? How? The FBI, the Secret Service, and the coroner all claimed he died of a heart attack."

"Honestly, Vonnie, nobody knows if she's involved or not," her father said. "It's hard to see this as coincidence."

"I don't remember seeing her name in the investigative report," Clayton said. "Why's that?"

"She wasn't in the final report you and I read, but her name was mentioned in one of the drafts. After what happened in Saint John, and you mentioning her name, the FBI did a deep dive on her. Her name popped up. It was later removed from the final version of the report because Daphne Cook wasn't anywhere near Buchanan's yacht when he died."

"What else did the FBI find?" Clayton asked.

"For now, not much. But let's just say there's a renewed energy at the FBI to find out who this woman is. They can't find anything on her before 2018, when she got her California driver's license. Trust me when I say I'm putting a lot of pressure on the FBI to find out everything there is about her."

Veronica swallowed hard. It was even worse than she'd first imagined. Henry Newman hadn't only stabbed her in the back; he might also be involved in the assassination of the former president of the United States.

"I'm . . . I'm sorry," she said, rising to her feet and running toward the door. "I'm gonna be sick."

———

An hour later, White joined Hammond, who was still in the billiards room.

"How is she?" he asked with quiet concern.

"She's sleeping," White said, taking a seat in a leather armchair.

"I know what you think of me, Clayton," Hammond said. "You've been quite forthcoming about this. But it still pained me to know you thought I had something to do with my predecessor's death."

"You threw my father to the wolves," White said through clenched teeth. "It doesn't take a huge leap forward to think you wouldn't do the same to the president."

Hammond let out a low, deliberate sigh. "I understand why you would think that. You once told me I took the easy way out when it came to Maxwell. I didn't want to believe it at the time, but I've had the chance to reflect on it since we had that discussion. And you were right. There are things, a lot of them, that I could have handled better, but none more so than what I did to my friend. To your dad."

Hammond wasn't tearing up, far from it, but White felt the president was being genuine. It was nice to hear Hammond admit his sins, but it didn't change the fact that White wanted to see him go to prison for what he had done.

"It was always my intention to keep my word to you," Hammond continued. "I never intended to become president. I hope you'll finally believe me when I say I had nothing to do with the murder of the man who occupied the Oval Office before me."

White rubbed his eyes. "So, we're talking about murder now?"

Hammond shrugged. "Another thing you were right about, I guess. I'm not sure we'll ever be able to prove it in a court of law, but we both know that bitch is responsible."

"Yeah. We do."

If White was honest with himself, he didn't think bringing Daphne Cook in front of a court of law was the best course of action. If she was working for a foreign power, assassinating an American president would be a declaration of war. And as strong as the US military was, White wasn't sure now was the time to go to war with anyone.

No. This was the kind of scenario that called for covert action.

It's a good thing the man sitting in front of me is the former commanding officer of JSOC.

Hammond had the know-how and the power to get things done.

"What do you have in mind?" White asked.

Hammond tipped his head at White. "Let's discuss this tomorrow," he said. "I want Veronica's input on this. Then I'll tell you about Davos."

PART THREE

Two Weeks Later

CHAPTER THIRTY-FOUR

Larvotto Beach
Monaco

Ulyana eased herself into the protected water of the bay. The cold water shocked her nerves, taking her breath away instantly. But she enjoyed the sensation. It never failed to take her mind off things. When she couldn't take it any longer, she counted to ten, then dipped entirely underwater for a count of thirty before she hurried back to shore. Her hair, which she had dyed black and had shortened by ten inches while in Santo Domingo, was plastered to her head. She grabbed a towel, dried herself, then returned to her lounge chair. The beach itself, which had been recently renovated by the principality, was deserted, though there were plenty of customers seated at the numerous terraces bordering the beach. Older people looked at her strangely, probably wondering who that crazy woman swimming in the bay was, while the younger crowd looked at her very differently. Most men had their eyes shielded behind sunglasses, but she knew they were looking at her, admiring her fine physical attributes. As for the women, well, they were jealous of her. Like they always were. That's why she'd never truly bond with another woman. She found them . . . boring. Even now, as she watched them drink expensive bottles of French champagne, she pitied them. They lived luxurious lives, but none of them had real influence on world events. Not like she did. They spent their time getting drunk, gossiping among themselves about unimportant matters. She wondered how many among them had killed before. One? Maybe two? And if so, had they done it themselves?

Probably not.

Ulyana saw them more as the type who would hire professionals to kill their rich, old husbands or, which would actually be funny, convince their young lovers to do it for them.

She slipped on a pair of sunglasses and lowered herself onto the lounge chair. Two hundred meters away, a superyacht was slowly navigating toward the exclusive Monaco Yacht Club.

In Ulyana's opinion, Monaco was a gazillion times better than Santo Domingo. But it wasn't a fair comparison. The Dominican Republic did have some spectacular white sandy beaches, but none of them were walking distance from Santo Domingo, the country's capital city, which three million people called home. Near and around Santo Domingo, the ocean was contaminated by garbage, plastics, and wastewater bleeding from the city's poorly maintained sewer system, the fetid smell often reaching deep into the city. Santo Domingo was everything Monaco was not: dirty, chaotic, and riddled with crime.

But thanks to Ian Miller, she had still managed to have a good time in the Dominican Republic. She knew Ian Miller wasn't his real name, and she'd been slightly taken aback when he'd refused to admit it, but it hadn't kept her from sleeping with him more times than she could remember.

What can I say? He's intriguing.

Nothing wrong with that, right? After two months of boring sex with that wimp Jeremy, it was nice to finally get it on for real. Just thinking about what he'd done to her that very morning tickled her in all the right places. She wished they could repeat the experience the next morning, but their little three-night escapade in the principality was coming to an end. Yuri was on his way to Monaco with a new assignment.

"You hungry?"

She opened her eyes. Miller was standing over her, blocking the sun's rays. She hadn't heard him approach. Miller had changed his appearance by shaving his black hair down to the scalp. He'd also shaved his mustache, which was a downer.

"What do you have in mind?" she asked with a mischievous smile.

He glanced at his watch. "I heard one of the places here has good pad thai," he said. "Because we don't have time for what *you* seem to have in mind. Yuri will be here in less than an hour."

"Too bad. I guess pad thai will do."

CHAPTER THIRTY-FIVE

Monaco Yacht Club
Monaco

In Miller's honest-to-God opinion, the pad thai he'd shared with Ulyana hadn't been worth the hype. If he had known he would be boarding a superyacht later that same afternoon, he would have skipped lunch. Miller had been on many yachts in his life, especially since he'd moved to the US Virgin Islands, but he'd never set foot on a superyacht like this one. Absolutely everything about the boat sparkled—from the polished stainless steel cleats to its navy blue hull and the two silver stripes that ran just above the waterline for the entire length of the two-hundred-foot yacht. Two decks rose above the main one, and Miller had spotted a small helipad on the bow.

As he followed Yuri Makarov onto the passerelle, Miller estimated that there were over one hundred people drinking, dancing, and shouting on the deck while enjoying the warm afternoon rays of a fall sun. Waitresses dressed like Las Vegas showgirls walked around the crowd with silver trays of elegant canapés and flutes of champagne. Yuri led the way through the throng, with Miller and Ulyana in tow. Many tried to get Yuri's attention, but he shrugged them all off, heading straight to the bar, which was full of guests leaning against it, drinking wine and eating olives and salted peanuts. The bar was manned by two good-looking women, one of them speaking French with a guest, a small but impeccably dressed man. Yuri elbowed his way in, and the bartender stopped talking when she recognized who was standing in front of her.

Yuri didn't speak to her but showed her three fingers. The bartender nodded before disappearing behind the counter. The well-dressed man, who by the deferential look on his face had also recognized Yuri, offered his hand, but the Russian didn't even acknowledge his presence. The bartender handed Yuri three bottles of Dom Pérignon.

"Follow me," Yuri said.

Miller followed Yuri and walked through an automatic—and heavily tinted—oversize sliding door that led into the interior living space of the yacht. Whoever had designed it had done so to impress. And it worked. It was bright and airy and looked more like a five-star hotel than a boat. Walking across the tastefully decorated indoor space, Miller assumed the interior of the vessel was off limits for the guests because the only people he saw inside were uniformed crew.

It seemed like Yuri Makarov had done quite well since he had left the GRU—the foreign military intelligence agency of the General Staff of the Armed Forces of the Russian Federation—where he'd overseen the illegal spy program. Miller, whose birth name was Sascha Babanin, had been one of Yuri's recruits, though not one of his most successful ones. Miller's military activities in the air force hadn't been conducive to great intelligence gathering. He had forwarded a few tidbits here and there, but nothing that could truly benefit Russia. Miller's superiors at the GRU had ordered him to request a transfer out of the air force PJ program, which Miller had done, but he had been turned down every time. After five years of providing little actionable intelligence, Miller had stopped receiving any messages from the GRU. Then, just as his military contract was about to end, he had been contacted by someone who had claimed to be an associate of Yuri Makarov. Apparently, Miller had been transferred to FiveSeas, Makarov's civilian intelligence organization, without his knowledge or consent. In theory, FiveSeas was a separate entity and didn't belong to or do the bidding of the Russian government.

But that was all bullshit.

The whole reason for FiveSeas' existence was to give the Russian government plausible deniability of certain intelligence operations. FiveSeas was to the GRU what the Wagner Group was to the Russian Ministry of Defense.

If Miller had kept track correctly, they were now two decks below the main deck. The level of luxury was definitely not the same as he'd seen on the other decks, but everything was still nice and shiny. Almost at the end of the well-lit hallway, two men in black fatigues and black body armor stared down the hall in Yuri's direction. Across their chests, MP5 submachine guns hung at the ready.

"Go get them and bring them here," Yuri said to the tallest guard while the other unlocked the door they had been guarding.

"What do you think? Pretty nice, yes?" Yuri asked as he gestured Miller and Ulyana into what looked like an office.

The space had two large portholes, three computer stations, and two flat-screen televisions hung on the wall. A medium-size table with a built-in digital monitor occupied the middle of the room.

"I kind of preferred the vibe of the main deck, to be honest," Ulyana said. "But if you open these bottles of champagne, you could change my mind."

Yuri flashed her a smile.

"Life's been good to you, Yuri," Miller said.

With practiced dexterity, Yuri uncorked the three bottles of champagne. He offered the first one to Ulyana, then gave one to Miller.

"And it's about to get even better," Yuri said. "Now we drink."

They each took several long pulls. Miller didn't remember having drunk champagne so fast before, certainly not Dom Pérignon, or directly from the bottle.

Guess there's a first time for everything.

"Have you told her your real name?" Yuri asked with a malicious grin.

He'd had a feeling it would come to that eventually. It wasn't like there was any chance he'd go back to his Ian Miller identity anyway. So why not share his true name with Ulyana? Why was he so reticent about it?

"Sascha Babanin," he said.

She batted her eyes at him, a pouty smile on her lips. "Very nice to finally meet you, Sascha."

There was a polite knock at the door; then it swung open. The guard Yuri had sent away rolled in a cart with two wooden crates on it.

Yuri thanked the guard, and the man returned to his post, closing the door behind him.

Miller read what was written on the side of the crate. *Ah shit.* "Are these what I think they are?" he asked.

To his right, Ulyana had the opposite reaction. Her eyes had lit up as if she was about to have an orgasm.

Yuri tore the lid off the top wooden crate. "Is that what you expected?" he asked.

Sascha stepped forward and peeked.

Damn!

"FIM-92 Stinger surface-to-air missiles," he said, then remembered to smile. "American made."

"Where did you get these beauties?" Ulyana asked, running her hand against the length of the plastic launcher.

"Where I got them is no concern of yours, my friends," Yuri said, between two pulls of champagne. "But I can tell you where you two are going with them. Davos."

CHAPTER THIRTY-SIX

Monaco Yacht Club
Monaco

Yuri Makarov observed his two assets with interest. Sascha seemed uncertain about the whole thing, while Ulyana could barely contain her excitement. Yuri attributed the disparity in their reactions to the different life experiences his assets had gone through. Though Ulyana had by far been the more productive of the two in terms of raw intelligence gathering, the firefight in Saint John had been her first, outside of a training scenario. She'd performed well and hadn't been hurt, so Yuri was convinced that in her adrenaline-fueled mind, she was looking forward to the next time she would have to use a weapon. On the other side of the spectrum, you had Sascha Babanin, a decorated combat veteran who'd been in plenty of gunfights and knew that it was only a question of time before someone got the better of him. He was understandably wary about Yuri's proposition. The strategy Yuri had laid out for them was indeed dangerous, but with high risks came high rewards. Shooting down the plane carrying the American delegation out of Davos would be such a reward.

Sascha didn't have to like it; he just had to do it.

The president of the Russian Federation was breathing down Yuri's neck to get it done, and, by God, he'd get it done. Yuri was under no illusions. His head was on the chopping block. Many of his former colleagues had already lost theirs due to their inability to give the president the military victories he demanded. Danger was coming from within too. With the realization that the battlefield losses Ukraine claimed to have inflicted on Russian forces were a reality, not merely Western propaganda, more and more of his compatriots became skeptical of the president's strategy.

Why had Yuri's country, a formidable military power, struggled so hard against Ukraine, a piece of land not even worthy of a separate national identity?

Because of the Americans and the high-tech weaponry they keep sending to the Ukrainian regime.

The United States and its Western allies needed to be taught a lesson. In Yuri's opinion, it was about time that the president went all in against them.

Time to take the gloves off.

Yuri had pushed the president to move faster, but he'd been dismissed. With the economic sanctions imposed on Russia continuing to hurt the economy, Yuri was beginning to see some cracks in his president's facade, a first since his rise to power more than two decades ago. And with the president's humiliation at not having been invited to the World Economic Forum in Davos still stinging, Yuri couldn't wait to execute his leader's vengeance on the Americans and the pricks at the WEF.

"We'll review everything tomorrow morning in more detail," Yuri said to his two assets. "If you don't have any pressing questions, one of the guards will show you to your staterooms."

"I do have questions," Sascha said. "You told us we'd both be in charge of a team, but you haven't said who would be in these teams. Are they trained soldiers, or locals sympathetic to our cause?"

"They aren't locals," Yuri said. "My operatives in Switzerland have been working for months with known activists and protesters to make sure they will take more active measures during the meeting in Davos, but it would be counterproductive to ask them to help us. Most of them are intellectuals who, if given a weapon, would shoot themselves in the foot."

"Then who?" Sascha asked. "GRU special forces?"

Yuri shook his head. "Absolutely not. Moscow doesn't want conventional or special forces in Switzerland. That's why FiveSeas was contracted for this mission. So, in order to ensure success, I've allocated four members of my own security detail to each of your team."

"What kind of experience do they have?" Ulyana asked.

"They're former Wagner mercenaries who've seen combat in Syria and Libya."

Yuri was pleased to see Sascha tip his head in appreciation.

"When will we know which target to strike?" Ulyana asked.

"I have agents in the field probing. We know the tail number of the plane carrying the American delegation, but although it landed at the Samedan Airport due to its proximity to Davos, we probably won't know for sure whether they'll fly out of Samedan or Zurich until six to eight hours prior to departure. Due to its altitude and its lack of ILS, Samedan Airport's arrivals and departures are unreliable. Weather conditions often don't meet the VFR requirements," Yuri explained.

"That's not a lot of time to get ready," Sascha said.

Yuri agreed, but they would have to adapt. "That's why I want you and Ulyana to travel to Switzerland tomorrow afternoon. I want you to familiarize yourself with the two locations. Tomorrow morning we'll go over this again, and I'll hand you your new phones. Now go to bed, go party on the upper deck. I don't care. But I want you back right here sober and rested at first light."

CHAPTER THIRTY-SEVEN

Davos
Switzerland

The lights of the auditorium came on, and Veronica walked off the podium with a big smile on her face. Her presentation had gone well, and no one had tried to be a wiseass during the Q&A portion at the end. She waved at Clayton, who was in discussion with FBI Special Agent Sarah Wong. Wong, a petite woman with short black hair that framed highly intelligent eyes and a slightly crooked nose, was the woman in charge of the three-man fly team that had flown into Switzerland with her and Clayton to Davos four days ago. The two other FBI agents were undercover, acting as journalists, and were keeping an eye on Henry Newman.

Unfortunately, unless things had changed during the last two hours while she was doing her presentation about SkyCU's new disaster management app, the two agents had seen Newman only twice since the beginning of the conference, both times when he'd participated in a panel. They had covertly taken pictures of the people they had seen interacting with him, but they were yet to get the results back from Quantico, where they had sent the photos for analysis.

Veronica's two Secret Service bodyguards, one of them Chris Albanese, were leaning against the back wall, clearly unhappy about her request they stay as far away from her as possible. Though Albanese was assigned to her father's protective detail, Clayton had requested him by name so that Albanese could accompany her to Davos. Veronica knew Albanese and his colleague were slowly reducing the gap between them and her as she mingled among the small groups of attendees congregating outside the auditorium, but she let them be. Their job was hard enough as it was.

Everyone she encountered conveyed how much they had liked her presentation and that they were in total agreement that if a mobile application like the one she had pitched had been up and running during the last hurricane season, many lives could have been saved. Veronica smiled and nodded politely to the attendees she was not familiar with but reserved sincere handshakes and a few words of gratitude for the people she had previously met and recognized.

"Excuse me, Miss Hammond?"

Veronica glanced behind her. A young man holding a camera was looking at her. A badge identifying him as a member of the press hung around his neck.

"Can I take a few photos?" he asked.

Before she could reply, the three near strangers with whom she'd been speaking gathered around her, eager to have their picture taken with the great Veronica Hammond. One of them reached out, trying to put an arm around her waist, but he stopped just short of her black dress, his fingers less than an inch from her, as if he'd suddenly frozen in place.

Then she saw her fiancé, and she guessed the creep had too.

Clayton had appeared next to the photographer, his eyes unblinking, his gaze fixed on the man who had just seconds ago wanted to put an arm around his fiancée's waist. The man took a hesitant step back, then took off before the photographer could snap the first picture. Clayton wore a satisfied smile. From the corner of her eye, she spotted Special Agent Albanese, who was on a vector to intercept the man.

Veronica almost felt sorry for him. *Almost* being the key word.

The photographer took a few pictures, then pulled a small white envelope out of his pocket. "A gentleman asked me to give you this envelope, Miss Hammond."

"A gentleman? You have a name?" Clayton asked, snatching the envelope from the man's fingers.

"No, I'm sorry. But he's one of the attendees."

Veronica thanked the photographer and edged closer to Clayton. Her fiancé opened the envelope and slid a handwritten note out of it. The note was simple but to the point. It contained a phone number, a time, and the signature of Henry Newman.

CHAPTER THIRTY-EIGHT

Davos
Switzerland

Veronica entered her room and headed straight to the minibar, from which she took a sachet of mini Oreos and a bottle of orange juice. She sat on the couch, opened the Oreos, then kicked off her heels.

"My back's killing me," she said.

"You don't have to wear those, you know," Clayton said. "If I were you, I'd wear slippers."

She looked at him as she popped two small cookies into her mouth. *He's serious.*

"Well, I'm glad you said that because from now on that's what I'll do," she said, selecting another cookie. "Who cares what people think?"

She handed Clayton her orange juice. "Can you open that for me?"

He twisted the cap off, took a sip, and handed the bottle back to her.

Clayton's phone chirped twice, signaling an incoming call. "It's Pierre," he said.

"Put him on speaker," Veronica said.

White nodded and accepted the call.

"Pierre, you're on speaker," White said.

"With whom?" the Frenchman asked, his tone serious.

This isn't a casual phone call, Veronica thought, immediately worried that Pierre's medical condition had taken a turn for the worse.

"Veronica. That's it."

"Okay, take me off speaker if someone else joins in," Pierre said.

"You got it, Pierre," Veronica said. "Are you all right?"

"Me? Why? Yes. Yes, I'm fine, Vonnie. Listen, this might be nothing, but I'd like to share something with you."

"Shoot," Clayton said.

"A two-hundred-foot superyacht named *Lancer* entered the Monaco Yacht Club five days ago. Since the yacht was designed by a Monegasque naval architecture firm and it was *Lancer*'s first time at the yacht club since its official launch two years ago, the firm, with the captain's permission, threw a big party aboard the yacht."

"A party to which I assume you were invited?" Veronica said.

"Of course I was invited," Pierre said. "The top designer and I have become good pals. Anyway, I will not bore you with the details, but when I was on the yacht, I thought I recognized someone. And it turned out that I was right."

"Who was it?" Clayton asked as Veronica tapped a finger on her watch to remind him of the time.

"Yuri Makarov. You know the name?"

"Yeah, I know the name."

"I do too," Veronica said. "He's the owner and founder of FiveSeas, a private intelligence company whose main client is the Russian government."

"I'd go as far as saying that its main client is the president of the Russian Federation himself," Pierre said.

"Do you know what he's doing in Monaco?" Clayton asked.

"No, I don't, but I learned this morning that Makarov is the actual owner of *Lancer*."

"This Yuri guy has a lot of guts docking his multimillion-dollar yacht in Monaco," Clayton said. "Isn't he aware of the sanctions? The local authorities in Monaco haven't been shy about seizing assets belonging to Russian oligarchs, have they?"

"No, they aren't shy, and they don't hesitate either," Pierre said. "But even my friend at the naval architecture firm doesn't know Makarov is the actual owner. The number of shell companies that were used to build and then own the vessel is something like I've never seen before. It's impossible to see through the legal bullshit."

"But still, you managed to do it," Veronica said.

"Only because my friends at la piscine helped me," Pierre admitted.

La piscine? For a moment, the French words threw Veronica off, but then she remembered they meant *swimming pool.* Pierre had once explained to them that the French foreign intelligence service's headquarters was in Paris's twentieth arrondissement near the piscine des Tourelles, which was part of the French Swimming Federation.

"Thanks for letting us know, Pierre," Clayton said.

"That's not all, my friend. I heard one of the crew mention that a van was leaving the next day for Davos. That's what made me think about you guys. I wouldn't even have brought this up with you if it hadn't been for Yuri Makarov. I'm telling you, Clay, this guy is bad news."

"Understood," Clayton said.

"Enjoy the rest of your time in Switzerland. Any chance you could make a quick stop by Monaco on your way back? It would be nice to see you both."

"We'll definitely try," Veronica said.

"Hope to see you real soon," Pierre said. "And Clay, I'll send you the link for the video I was able to capture with my button camera. You could get a few good still shots from it. The resolution isn't the best, but it's not catastrophic either."

Clayton thanked his friend one more time before hanging up.

"That was interesting," Veronica said. "You think this has anything to do with us?"

"I doubt it. I just don't see the link. I'll look at the video later, but now we need to decide what's our next step regarding Newman. Two o'clock is in fifteen minutes. How do you want to handle it?"

Veronica propped her foot on the glass-top coffee table and thought about her answer. She had tried to reach Newman by calling and texting him half a dozen times since she had arrived in Davos, but he was yet to get back to her. She had attended the two panels he'd been on, but both times he had been ushered out of the room by his associates before she could get close to him. He'd made eye contact with her at least three times, so she knew he'd seen her.

So why wasn't he taking her calls or at least replying to her texts? What kind of game was Henry Newman playing? Did he suspect they were onto him? And what about that handwritten note?

Clayton's phone vibrated on the table where he had put it to charge. "It's Special Agent Wong," he said as he read the text. "The FBI has identified one of Newman's associates as a possible MSS intelligence officer."

Why would a suspected MSS officer hang around Newman?

"What about the others?" she asked. "There was more than one associate steering Newman away after his panels."

"Nothing yet," Clayton said. "That's all Wong has for now. She'll loop back if something else comes up."

Veronica finished the last of her cookies and threw the empty bag on the coffee table. Everything her father had shared with her about Henry Newman differed from the opinion she had formed about the man. It was so out of character. She didn't doubt the call between Newman and Patrick O'Donnell had happened, but was there an angle they weren't seeing? A good man could be corrupted, but would he betray his country too? Would Newman sell out to the Chinese government?

Possible. But unlikely.

She had a gut feeling that it wasn't the case with Newman.

Or maybe it is.

Shit. She didn't know anymore. There was only one way to move forward. She had to talk to him.

"Clay, could you please text Special Agent Wong and tell her to come here? I'd like her here when I make the call."

Her fiancé had his eyes glued to his phone.

"What is it?" she asked.

He stared at her for a moment, looking as if he'd just seen a ghost— or worse.

Clayton took a seat next to her and showed her a still image from the video their friend Pierre had forwarded him. It was the picture of a man in his fifties with a chiseled jawline, blond hair, and dark blue eyes.

"That's Yuri Makarov," she said.

White shook his head and used his fingers to enlarge the picture. "Look at the person behind him. Here, you can see her face better now."

Veronica studied the picture. It took her a short moment to recognize the person standing behind Makarov. But when she did, she gasped, goose bumps prickling her arms.

"Oh. My. God. That's Daphne Cook."

Clayton nodded, but her fiancé wasn't done yet. He swiped left twice, then zoomed again, this time focusing on a man. "Do you recognize this one too?" he asked her.

She looked at the new picture. "The face is familiar."

"Yeah. Add a mustache. And black hair."

"Holy shit, Clay."

No wonder Clayton had looked like he'd seen a ghost. He had actually seen one.

CHAPTER THIRTY-NINE

Macau Special Administrative Region
China

Thalia Magallanes picked up the remaining plates, bowls, and wineglasses from the table and brought them to the sink. It had been a long day, and she was glad to see Mrs. Peiwu's guests finally leave the swanky, six-thousand-square-foot penthouse. Thalia liked Mrs. Peiwu. She was nice and had always treated her with respect. She was a demanding woman, but fair, and not cruel like her husband.

Not for the first time, Thalia wondered if Mrs. Peiwu knew about her husband's infidelities. She had to. She lived with the pig. And what about all the other awful things her husband did to other human beings? Did she know about those? Thalia didn't think she did. Well, maybe she did, but only about *some* of them, the smaller ones, like the money laundering and the illegal gambling. But Thalia refused to believe Mrs. Peiwu knew anything about the drug trafficking and the weapons-smuggling rings her husband oversaw. As sickening as the drugs and weapons were, what had truly made Thalia recoil in horror was the human trafficking operation Peiwu had orchestrated where young, attractive Filipinos—like Thalia had once been—were exchanged or sold like pieces of meat.

How could a nice, polite lady like Mrs. Peiwu be attracted to such a man?

———

Thalia had started working for Geng Peiwu fifteen years ago as a house-keeper. She had been only eighteen at the time and had just arrived from Manila. The promise of good pay and three meals per day had been enough to convince her to leave her family and friends behind and to take a leap of faith.

In retrospect, she wished she'd never seen the online ad.

Was that fair, though? If she hadn't seen it, she would have never met Henry Newman, and her mom and dad, who were now well into their fifties, would have never opened their restaurant. And her sister, Mila, wouldn't have had the chance to go to the United States to study chemical engineering.

My sister. The engineer.

Thalia was so, so proud of her sister. The first in her family to go to college. That was an accomplishment on its own. And her par-ents—they looked so happy, so very proud of their restaurant. And they were grateful too. For years now they had begged Thalia to return home.

"Thanks to you, our beautiful and brave daughter, we have money now. We're not rich, not by any means, but we don't have to fight just to survive. We can live, Thalia. Really live," her father had said.

Her mom had chimed in too. "Come back home. Come work at the restaurant. I promise you'll like it. People are leaving reviews on the internet, Thalia. On the internet! For our restaurant!"

But Thalia kept on refusing, explaining that she was happy with her life in Macau. She was living the dream.

What her parents didn't know couldn't hurt them, right?

The reality was that the first thing that bastard Peiwu had done to her when she'd arrived in Macau was to take her passport away from her—for safekeeping, he'd told her. And from there, it had only gotten worse. Within the first month, Peiwu had raped her twice and had almost beaten her to death. But she hadn't complained. She had toughed it out. What other choice did she have? The police? Geng Peiwu was rich and influential. High-ranking police officers often had dinner at his residence. They would never believe her. She couldn't leave, either; Peiwu had her passport, and she had no money.

She was trapped.

Then a miracle happened. Mrs. Peiwu became pregnant, and nine months later, Jing, a beautiful baby girl, was born. From that moment on, there were no more rapes, no more beatings. Thalia would never truly understand why, but she remembered something her dad had once told her.

"You've changed my life, Thalia. The day you were born is the day I started to truly care about others. I became a gentler, more compassionate man. A better human being. So, thank you for that gift."

Was it possible that having a daughter had transformed Peiwu the way it had her dad? For a few years, she had believed so. Peiwu had even returned her passport. A gesture of trust, he had said. By then, Thalia had developed a deep, powerful bond with Jing. Thalia loved the young girl very much and had become her de facto nanny.

One night, while Mr. and Mrs. Peiwu were out, and after she had wished Jing good night, Thalia was tidying up Peiwu's office when she had spotted the picture of a young woman on the floor, halfway out from under a bookshelf. Picking up the picture, she had recognized Benifel, one of her cousins from the Philippines.

Thalia sighed as she remembered how excited she had been at the prospect of seeing her favorite cousin again. Was Peiwu really planning on hiring Benifel? Of course he was. Why else would he have her picture? Unable to control herself, she had tried to call Benifel's parents with her phone, but the call hadn't gone through since it was long distance. The phone Mrs. Peiwu had gotten for her had allowed only local calls.

Surely Mr. Peiwu wouldn't mind if she used his office phone to make a quick call? This time the call had gone through, and Thalia had learned from Benifel's parents that their precious daughter had disappeared one month ago. Apparently, the police had mistaken Benifel for a prostitute and had arrested her while she was walking home after her night shift at the grocery store. The police claimed they had released Benifel within the hour. They had the papers to prove it. They couldn't say why Benifel hadn't returned home afterward. And no, there was simply not enough information for them to open an investigation. Thalia had hung up, confused and angry.

Then, looking more closely at the photo, she'd found a phone number written on the back with a ten-digit alphanumeric code. In tears, she had dialed the number, hoping it would somehow connect her to her cousin.

An automated voice had answered and prompted Thalia to enter the ten-digit code associated with the item she was interested in. Thalia, her hands shaking, had punched in the code. The same cold, emotionless voice had begun to describe her cousin Benifel in detail. Age: Twenty. Sex: Female. Height: One hundred and fifty centimeters. Weight: Forty-five kilos. Eye color: Brown. Hair color: Brown. Virginity status: Virgin. Dental hygiene: Poor. The voice had gone on to inform Thalia that the bid placed for this item that had originated from that phone number hadn't been successful. The winning bid was US$23,000 and had been placed from Russia.

At that moment Thalia understood that her initial opinion of Peiwu had been the right one. He was an animal. He was a predator. He was a rapist who hurt and exploited women like Thalia and her cousin Benifel.

Thalia's father had shown her how to skin a chicken when she was eight years old. By the time she had left for Macau, she'd skinned more than one hundred of them. She was going to use the same skills on Peiwu. She just had to bide her time.

Her time came five nights later during a dinner party. Peiwu had invited six of his associates to celebrate the successful launch of a new business endeavor. From the kitchen, Thalia had studied the six men while sharpening a ten-inch chef's knife. With one exception—a tall American with an angular face and good-humored eyes who seemed to smile a lot—Peiwu's associates acted exactly like him. She listened to their sexist jokes and denigrating comments about women. The American was laughing, too, but it didn't seem sincere. At some point, their eyes connected, and he smiled at her. A genuine smile. A father-to-daughter kind of smile.

Then, when she thought all Peiwu's friends were gone, she had pretended to wash the dishes. When Peiwu finally walked by, cigarette in hand, she grabbed the chef's knife and exited the kitchen, fully intending to slash the man's throat. She had been only a few steps away from doing just that when someone emerged from Peiwu's office and grabbed her wrist, stopping the knife motion. She tried to scream, but a hand clamped her mouth. It was the American. One of Peiwu's associates, but unlike the rest of them, he wasn't drunk. Not one bit. He was strong and fast and managed to drag her back into the kitchen, where he quietly pinned her against the refrigerator.

"I'm not here to hurt you," the American said. "My name's Henry Newman, and I'm here to help."

She hadn't been ready to give up just yet, and she tried to knee Newman in the groin, but it was as if he'd known she'd do that and had bladed his body away from the blow.

"Listen to me," he said. "Even if, and it's a big if, you were able to kill that prick, what do you think would happen to your loved ones back home? You're from the Philippines, right? Do you really think his associates won't go after your family? In retribution for his death, they'll burn your family, your friends, and everybody else you care about. Do you understand?"

"I do. But I want him to die," she'd said.

Newman nodded. "I know. I understand. But what if I tell you there's another way to hurt him. Another way to make him suffer. Would you be interested in that?"

CHAPTER FORTY

Macau Special Administrative Region
China

Twelve years after her initial encounter with Henry Newman, Thalia was still convinced that if it hadn't been for his intervention on that fateful night, she'd be dead, and so would her parents and sister. Newman had saved her life. In exchange for her loyalty and for spying on Peiwu, twice a year Newman sent money to her family, but always anonymously, letting her parents and sister believe that it was her who was sending it to them. There was also money for her in an account in the Turks and Caicos, but she didn't care about it. Greed wasn't the reason she was spying on Peiwu and his Red Dragon Triad. She did it for Benifel and all the other women whose lives Peiwu had destroyed.

Thalia was just finishing up the dishes when Mrs. Peiwu stopped by the kitchen, her eyes unfocused and glassy but trained on her.

"I'm going . . . to bed, Tha-lia," the very drunk Mrs. Peiwu said. "Thank you . . . for every-thing. It was . . . deli-cious."

"Good night, Mrs. Peiwu. Sleep well. At what time would you like breakfast to be served tomorrow?"

Mrs. Peiwu placed a hand on the marble countertop to stabilize herself. "Tomorrow? You know what, Thalia? I . . . don't worry about the breakfast. I'll . . . I think I'll sleep in."

Thalia watched Mrs. Peiwu hesitantly make her way to her bedroom at the end of the long corridor, using the wall as her guide.

Thalia gave Mrs. Peiwu thirty minutes before she pressed her ear against the master bedroom's door. Mrs. Peiwu wasn't snoring, but Thalia heard the deep, heavy breathing of someone fast asleep.

Good.

Thalia wanted to take advantage of Peiwu's absence to search his office one last time. Although she was aware Peiwu was in Switzerland on a business trip, she didn't know when he was due to return home. Last night's search, which had lasted well over an hour, hadn't turned up anything of value. She had been looking for the black file she'd seen Peiwu carry with him when the Russian had come to visit him the week before. She didn't know if the file contained the information Newman was looking for, but when she had mentioned the visit to Newman, he said he'd be interested in anything she could find out about the Russian and the file she'd spotted in Peiwu's hands. Newman told her to be careful and attentive to her surroundings. Even more so than usual. She had asked him why.

"Because I think the bastard's working with the MSS," he'd told her.

It had scared her at first. She'd heard stories about the MSS and what they did to people who crossed them. Then she had remembered she'd been working with Newman for twelve years.

And Peiwu never caught me. The MSS won't either. I'm good at this.

Yesterday, she had carefully combed through everything on Peiwu's desk and his bookshelves. Tonight, she would open his filing cabinets and his desk drawers. She'd secured the keys earlier in the day while she pretended to refresh the master bathroom. She'd long ago found out the hiding place where Peiwu kept the keys to his filing cabinets and gun locker—a false bottom in the lowest drawer of his night table. Thalia's objective was to move quickly, but she had to balance that with caution. Peiwu was a methodical man, and if she wasn't vigilant, he would know she had gone through his files. It would be hard for Thalia to blame it on anyone else. Since she'd started working for Peiwu, she could count on two hands the number of times she'd witnessed Mrs. Peiwu enter her husband's office.

Thalia walked away from the master bedroom and down the hallway toward Peiwu's office. As she reached the living room, she stopped dead in her tracks. The door to the penthouse's private elevator opened, and Quon, Peiwu's main assistant—a former officer in a mountain infantry regiment of the PLA with whom Thalia once had a brief but somewhat passionate relationship—stepped out. Behind him, two men she'd never seen followed.

Her former lover's face was a mask of rage. Thalia did her best to force out the fear that had gripped her, but she was frozen in place, her breast heaving.

"What . . . what are you—"

"Be quiet!" Quon shouted, flecks of saliva from his words hitting her in the eyes. He slapped her hard across the face. The blow stunned her into silence, pain shooting through her upper jaw.

Apparently finding Quon hadn't used enough violence, a man who had come up the elevator with him shoved Quon aside. He jabbed Thalia in the abdomen with his right fist. As she doubled over, he buried his fingers in Thalia's hair. The man twisted and pulled, forcing Thalia to straighten again. She gasped in pain at the sudden burn across her scalp.

"Quon, get me Peiwu's wife," the man ordered.

Since he was the only one familiar with the layout of the penthouse, Quon obeyed.

Sensing an opportunity, Thalia kicked her captor on the shin. He yelled in pain and let go of her hair, but her freedom was short lived. The man's colleague, who'd been standing behind her, delivered a blow to her kidney. The blow paralyzed her, giving the man she had kicked the time he needed to strike back. His first punch came hard and swift and reached deep into her gut. She folded in two, her breath taken away. Then the man's knee crashed into her face, hitting her right below her nose and splitting her lips. But before she could fall, the man regained his grip on her hair and lifted her up. Thalia heard herself scream just before the man's knuckles slammed twice into her jaw. Blood gushed out of her mouth as two teeth became loose. Only then was she allowed to fall. A knee slammed into her upper back, and her arms were forced back.

You're getting arrested! Resist! Resist! her mind screamed at her. *Don't let them take you!*

The sound of a gunshot had the two men jerk their heads toward the hallway. The man who had pushed his knee into her back got up, and the pressure in her back lessened. She could breathe again. She turned her head and saw Mrs. Peiwu standing at the end of the hallway, a pistol in her hands. Thalia snatched the phone in her back pocket and started to dial a number Henry Newman had forced her to learn a long time ago but that she'd never felt the need to call until now.

"Who are you?" Thalia heard Mrs. Peiwu shout.

"Everything is fine, Mrs. Peiwu. We're with the Ministry of State Security. Where's Quon?"

"The idiot's dead," she said. "It's not a good idea to rush into a woman's bedroom unannounced. What do you want?"

"We want you to lower your weapon, Mrs. Peiwu, we're not here to hurt you."

"What is Thalia doing on the floor?" she asked, pointing her pistol at Thalia.

That's when the man Thalia had kicked in the shin made his move. He was fast, but not fast enough to not catch a bullet in his left arm before he could draw his pistol. His partner, benefiting from the extra second he had, drew his gun and fired twice. Mrs. Peiwu, hit in the neck and left shoulder, fell back against her pristine white wall, leaving a smudge of red as she slid down into a sitting position.

The injured man pressed a hand against the bullet wound on his opposite arm. He winced as he made eye contact with Thalia. Seeing the phone in her hand, he kicked it away, sending it flying across the room.

A knee was once again pressed into her back, and zip ties were used to secure her hands. They were so tight that Thalia felt their sharp plastic edges cut into her skin. Thalia was rolled to her side, and her captors searched her. Very thoroughly.

They found the keys to Peiwu's filing cabinets, but she was too dazed to comprehend the significance of that fact.

"By the time we're done with you, you'll wish you were never born," the injured man spat, the blood from his gunshot wound trickling onto the back of Thalia's neck as he spoke.

Then he kicked her in the head.

CHAPTER FORTY-ONE

Davos
Switzerland

Although most of Newman's entourage in Davos were high-ranking corporate officers of Newman Horizon Development mixed in with a few of Geng Peiwu's top lieutenants, there had been several people Newman hadn't recognized. But it didn't mean he didn't know which organization they represented. They might have looked like police officers. But they weren't.

They were with Chinese intelligence.

That meant that even though he was scheduled to be rewarded with the prestigious Golden Lotus Medal of Honor for his supposedly heroic action in Macau, Newman wasn't fully trusted by whoever controlled Peiwu. Newman suspected it was Ma Lin, the 4th Bureau director for the MSS, but he had no way to know with complete certainty who it was within the MSS.

The who didn't really matter. The most critical thing was to find what it was that Peiwu was involved in. The fact that the MSS was pulling the strings was of great concern for Newman. But, with a little luck, Newman would know a whole lot more by the time he got back to Macau.

He looked at his Rolex. Three minutes until his call with Veronica. *That's assuming she has received my note.*

He was aware she'd left him voice mails and text messages, but he didn't dare acknowledge receipt of her texts or return her calls. It was too dangerous. His phone was no doubt being monitored by the MSS. Newman wished she would leave him alone, but Veronica was tenacious, a character trait he usually admired very much, just not at this moment. Her unrelenting determination to reach him by any means was why he had stolen a phone. The woman from whom he'd taken it, the CEO of an alkaline spring water company from Canada, had sat next to him at a panel. The open purse she had set on the plush carpet next to her chair had been too good an opportunity to pass up. He had grabbed the phone, placed it between his legs, and switched it off.

The panel moderator, who had shared each panelist's phone number with the others when he had e-introduced everyone the week before, had been a blessing. Newman was sure the woman hadn't seen him snatch her phone, but by now she surely realized it had gone missing. As soon as Newman powered it up, she'd get a notification on her watch, tablet, or laptop. Because he didn't have the password to unlock the screen, there was no way to turn off the phone's location feature. Newman estimated he would have at best four to five minutes before the phone's owner came knocking at his door.

Newman took a long, deep breath to calm his nerves and told himself for the fifth time in as many minutes that it wasn't too late to change his mind. He could still decide not to take the call from Veronica and go back to Macau tomorrow.

That was probably the best thing to do. And the safest.

He ran a hand through his hair and rubbed his eyes. *Am I overthinking this?*

He had dealt with Veronica before, but it wasn't as if they were friends or business partners. He'd given her a substantial amount of money because he believed in what she was selling. Veronica Hammond was a force to be reckoned with, and not only because she had close to fifty million followers across all social media platforms and could sway public opinion with a single tweet but also because she was a gifted archaeologist and app designer who could potentially help to make the world a better place.

Something that, deep down, Newman really cared about. That's why he was doing what he did, right? Making the world a better place?

Well, if this is what I've been doing all these years, I took one hell of a detour, didn't I? No straight and narrow for me.

He was about to risk a lot on betting that Veronica had somehow learned about his phone call to Patrick O'Donnell minutes before the assault had started. But the odds were in his favor, weren't they? Why else would she keep calling? It was hard to imagine that the Secret Service and the FBI hadn't shared their findings with her or her fiancé, Clayton White, the man who had freaking killed a rogue Iranian spy by slashing his opponent's gut wide open.

On the official website of the White House, Clayton White was described as a special assistant to the president for the Office of Special Projects. Newman couldn't help but chuckle at the title. But, as funny as it was, it still meant that White yielded quite a bit of power, and, as a former Secret Service agent and combat veteran, the man had probably found a way to stay in the game.

Newman was aware how addictive it was.

If White or Veronica did know about the call, FBI special agents— Newman assumed it would be the elite fly team—were around and would try to either make an arrest or detain him for interrogation with the assistance of the Swiss authorities and Europol—the law enforcement agency of the European Union. He couldn't allow either to happen. He had to convince Veronica he was one of the good guys.

He looked at his watch one more time, then powered up the stolen phone.

It was showtime.

CHAPTER FORTY-TWO

Davos
Switzerland

Newman closed the bathroom door and turned on the faucet and the shower. He sat on the toilet and looked at the phone.

C'mon, Veronica.

The phone pulsed in his hand, and Newman almost dropped it. The caller ID didn't come up on the screen, but it had to be Veronica. His finger hovered above the green button for a moment; then he took the call.

"Yes?"

"Henry? This is—"

"Don't say your name. I know who you are," Newman said, just loud enough so that he could be heard. In case the MSS was listening, he needed to protect Veronica. She was his only chance to get the word out that there was an imminent threat. As he heard her voice, relief and fear ran through him simultaneously.

There's no going back now.

"I'm glad you called," Newman said. "First thing you need to know is that this is not my phone. I believe mine is being monitored by the Chinese MSS. The one you've just called belongs to someone else, a woman who has probably already received a notification that her phone is now back online. I have only a few minutes before someone comes knocking on my door. Can I assume you've listened to the very disturbing phone conversation I had with Patrick O'Donnell? If this is the case and that conversation is the basis for your call today, I'm ready to talk."

Newman held his breath, waiting for Veronica's reply. The seconds ticked by. Slowly. Newman supposed she wasn't alone and that she was getting advice from somebody by her side. Was it Clayton White? Someone from the Swiss police?

For God's sake, I hope it isn't the police.

"Yes. That is the reason for my call."

"Okay," Newman said, as he released his breath. "Clearly the recording hasn't been made public yet. If it had, the FBI, the Swiss police, or Europol would already have me in custody, and I'd be in a Swiss jail, waiting for my extradition."

"How do you know they're not on their way?" Veronica asked.

"I don't. Maybe they are. If that's the case, it's all over."

"What are you involved in, Henry? Help me understand."

Newman's heart rate increased. For over three decades, he had shared with only four people what he was about to divulge to Veronica. It was the beginning of the end for him. Newman Horizon Development had grown beyond anything his initial backers had thought possible. A combination of luck, talent, and hard work had made it happen.

But it had been a mirage. All of it.

It felt weird that he was about to reveal his secret to Veronica, a woman he barely knew, but Newman had always considered himself a good judge of character. The fact that he was still alive proved it. And Veronica was the daughter of the president of the United States, wasn't she? That wasn't lost on him either. If there was one person he could trust, it had to be her. Whatever it was that had Peiwu's Red Dragon Triad collaborating with the Chinese MSS was alarming. Everything was different since Russia had illegally invaded Ukraine. The world dynamics had changed. North Korea and China felt empowered. The hermit kingdom had increased the rate at which it was lobbing missiles over Japan, and the Chinese government was getting more aggressive by the day. The status quo was no longer. The players were making their moves.

The assassination of Patrick O'Donnell, combined with Peiwu's request to smuggle additional personnel to the United States, had startled Newman. The MSS wasn't messing around. They had gone on the offensive, and Newman needed to get the word out.

"Thirty years ago, at the direction of the CIA, I became involved with the Red Dragon Triad in Macau."

"The CIA? Henry, what are—"

"Let me finish, please," Newman said. "I don't have much time left. The initial objective was to understand what the dynamics between China and Macau would look like at a time when the Portuguese authorities were withdrawing from the region. The objective morphed into something else over the years. No one could have predicted that Newman Horizon Development would grow into such a huge corporation both in Macau and in the United States. A few weeks ago, Geng Peiwu, the Red Dragon Triad leader, someone I have been doing business with for years, ambushed me. I witnessed someone I suspect was an MSS agent kill a Macau commissioner. A crime I was supposed to be blamed for if I refused to collaborate with Peiwu and his masters at the MSS. Are you getting all that?"

"I'm still listening," Veronica said after what seemed to Newman like a long pause.

Glad Veronica hadn't hung up on him, he continued, "I'm not sure what's brewing, but I have a feeling it is something that could have a huge impact at home. You must understand that Chinese intelligence plays the long game. The MSS isn't to be underestimated. It's methodical, disciplined, and will wait for the right opportunity to strike. And now they've gone on the offensive."

"But you don't know what it is."

"I have an agent in Macau who's looking into it as we speak. There's a fair chance I'll know more by the time I get back to Macau tomorrow."

"Why are you telling me this, Henry?"

"Because I'm sure the MSS has taken control of all my communication devices. I'm being watched by them here and in Macau. I have no way of contacting Langley. I want you to do it, and I want you to tell them to take down the entire network. Now."

"The entire network? What are you talking about?"

A knock at the door made him jump. *Shit.* He looked at his watch. He'd been on the phone way too long.

"Someone's here. I need to go."

"Wait!"

"Just make sure I don't get arrested or detained by the FBI fly team I suspect is already here in Davos," Newman said rapidly, aware how stiff his own voice sounded.

There was another knock at the door, this time louder and more urgent.

"It's imperative that I get back to Macau. Contact Liz Maberry. She'll vouch for me."

Newman ended the call and was about to power down the phone when it emitted a loud ping, the chime cutting through the sound of the shower and faucet.

CHAPTER FORTY-THREE

Davos
Switzerland

The moment the call ended, White took charge.

"Special Agent Wong, where are your two agents?" he asked.

Wong spoke discreetly into the lapel of her jacket, asking her agents for a sitrep.

"One is seated by the elevators with an indirect look at Newman's suite, and the other is in the staircase. They know what to do. Don't worry. The question is, do you still want to proceed?"

White was worried, and it had nothing to do with the FBI. He was confident Wong's team could do what he had asked. Wong had asked the correct question. Was it still the correct strategy? If Newman had told them the truth and he was indeed with the CIA, was tagging him the right move? The tracking devices used by the fly team were state of the art, but they still emitted bursts of data every few minutes to ping their location. If the Chinese MSS happened to electronically sweep Newman for bugs while the tracking device wasn't dormant, Newman would be in trouble.

Then again, could they afford to let Newman go? White wasn't convinced of the man's honesty.

"Yes. Proceed as if we hadn't had that call with him," White said, having made his decision.

His next step was to ask Veronica to contact her father, but he saw that she was already on it. Veronica put the call on speaker. The president's assistant answered.

"I'm sorry, Miss Hammond, but the president isn't available at the moment. Would you—"

"Go get him, Madison," Veronica said. "It's urgent."

Ninety seconds later, Hammond joined the call. "I'm short on time, Vonnie," he growled. "What is it?"

"Dad, we have a problem."

CHAPTER FORTY-FOUR

Davos
Switzerland

"I'll be there in one minute!" Newman shouted.

Whoever was at the door had knocked for the third time.

Newman had managed to stop the chime within half a second, but had he been quick enough? He pulled a small pin from his pocket and used it to remove the SIM card from the stolen phone. He dropped the SIM card into the toilet but kept the phone. It was too big to be flushed down. He inserted the phone between two folded white towels, hurried out of the bathroom, and stood in the suite's entryway as he took a moment to compose himself. He yanked his shirt out of his pants, then looked through the peephole.

Peiwu was standing in the hallway, flanked by two men Newman had never seen before. He opened the door.

"Good afternoon, Henry," Peiwu said, a worried look on his face. "Is everything okay? You look distressed, my friend."

Newman shook his head and let out a light chuckle. "I was in the bathroom," he said, making a show of tucking his shirt back into his pants. "What can I do for you?"

"I was thinking we could go out for a late lunch," the triad leader said. "What do you say?"

Newman didn't have any excuses ready to go, but, even if he had, he would have accepted Peiwu's invitation. In his peripheral vision, he spotted the woman from whom he'd pinched the phone. She hadn't seen him yet; her eyes were fixed on her tablet. Newman had no wish to have an awkward conversation about a missing phone while Peiwu was there. Peiwu hadn't shown any indication that he had heard the chime through the two closed doors. Newman reached for the sport jacket that hung on a hook by the door and stepped into the hallway.

"Good idea. Why don't you lead the way?"

They walked together to the elevators, and Newman pushed a button.

"Mr. Newman? Excuse me, Mr. Newman?"

Newman turned toward the voice. A young and very pretty woman wearing a trim business suit, with a badge around her neck identifying her as an accredited journalist, was smiling at him. Peiwu's two goons had their eyes on her, but in a nonthreatening way.

"Yes?"

"I'm Simone Petry, *LA Times*," she said, showing him perfectly straight white teeth as she shook his hand. "I'd like to ask you a few questions, if that's okay?"

"Maybe later? We're on our way to lunch."

"Of course, I understand," she said. "Maybe I could go down with you?"

He nodded. "This is Geng Peiwu, Miss Petry. A very interesting man."

"An honor, Mr. Peiwu," Petry said. "My ex-husband and I once stayed at one of your marvelous hotels."

Peiwu flashed her a smile. "Really? Which one?"

"The Illusion," the journalist said. "Great view from the room, and the food was absolutely delish."

"I'm glad you enjoyed your time in Macau," Peiwu said.

The elevator arrived, and a horde of conference attendees rushed out as the doors opened. Once the elevator was clear of people, Newman signaled the journalist to go ahead, keeping a hand on the elevator door to ensure it wouldn't close before they all got in. As Simone Petry stepped inside, one of her heels got stuck in the crack between the elevator and the hotel floor, causing her to lose her shoe and her balance. She stumbled backward into Newman, who had to let go of the door to catch her.

"Are you all right, Miss Petry?" he said, helping her back to her feet.

"Oh my God, this is so embarrassing," she said, her cheeks turning red. "I'm so sorry."

Peiwu picked up her shoe, examined it, then brought it close to his face, as if he wanted to smell it, before handing it back to her.

"Thank you," she said, tossing back a length of hair.

"Who would have thought elevators could become such a dangerous place?" Peiwu asked.

The door closed, and they rode down in silence. Newman kept an eye on the woman, wondering if she was really with the *LA Times*.

On the ground floor, Petry thanked them again and said she would try to catch them later. Maybe at the bar?

"I thought she wanted to ask you some questions," Peiwu said.

"That was my impression. Maybe she's too embarrassed?" Newman said as they approached the revolving doors of the hotel. Peiwu's black Mercedes sedan was waiting for them at the front. Eu-Meh, Peiwu's niece, was outside by the front passenger door. She was wearing a tight-fitting long black leather jacket and a pair of high-heeled ankle boots. Her black hair was pulled back in a low bun, exposing her slender neck and graceful jawline. She was looking straight at Newman, her cold eyes boring deep into him. He met her gaze, and his chest tightened. It felt as if he was staring into an empty grave. Newman shivered, a deep chill in his bones settling in. He looked away and took in his surroundings.

A Mercedes SUV was parked in front of the sedan, its engine running. Newman had the feeling that getting something to eat wasn't in the cards any longer. A thin film of sweat made his shirt stick to his back despite the crisp Alpine air. In the distance, snow glistened on the faraway peaks, and Newman wished he had come to Switzerland more often to experience everything the country had to offer. Now he wondered if he would ever get the chance again.

"Why don't we walk?" Newman offered, doing his best to keep an upbeat tone. "There are plenty of great places within walking distance."

"The place I have in mind is too far. We'll take the car," Peiwu said. "I'm afraid I have to insist."

Eu-Meh, who Newman could tell was wearing the same perfume she had in Macau, opened the door, and he slipped into the rear seat of the Mercedes while Peiwu walked around the back. The driver didn't acknowledge Newman. Eu-Meh sat in the front passenger seat. Through the windshield Newman watched the two men who'd flanked Peiwu climb into the SUV. The door to his left opened, and Peiwu joined him inside the car. The two-car motorcade left the hotel and headed north on Route 28.

A thousand scenarios ran through Newman's mind. None of them were good. Glancing at Peiwu, Newman could tell he was nervous, which didn't bode well for him either.

"Where are we going, Geng?" Newman asked.

"You are being summoned," Peiwu said.

"Summoned? Are you kidding me? By whom?"

Peiwu didn't reply but took a bottle of water out of the seat pocket in front of him. He shook the bottle, then offered it to Newman.

"Drink."

"Are you out of your mind? Drink it yourself," Newman said, noting that Eu-Meh had unbuckled her seat belt.

"Take the bottle and drink, Henry. Or she'll shoot you in the knee."

Eu-Meh had a suppressed pistol pointed at Newman's left knee.

Newman let out a light chuckle. "I feel we've been here before," he said, removing the cap from the water bottle. "Can you at least tell me what's—"

Midsentence, Newman flung the bottle into Peiwu's face and rammed his left foot as hard as he could into the back of the seat in front of him. The impact was such that Eu-Meh was shoved backward, her head cracking against the windshield. Her gun fell from her hand. Knowing he had to get control of the weapon, Newman propelled himself forward, aiming for the space between the two front seats.

But he didn't make it.

Peiwu crashed into his left side. Newman landed on his back, wedged between the front seat and the rear seat, with Peiwu on top of him. Newman didn't have the necessary room to throw a punch or kick, but that was fine. He grabbed Peiwu by the collar of his shirt and yanked the triad leader toward him as he headbutted him, hitting Peiwu on the nose. Blood gushed out of the man's nostrils and into Newman's eyes and mouth. But he didn't care. He was in a fight for his life. He had to finish Peiwu now so that he could get to the gun. If he couldn't do that, he was dead. He wrapped his hands around Peiwu's neck and squeezed with all his strength, doing his best to crush the man's windpipe. Peiwu's eyes bulged, and air wheezed through his throat as Newman tightened his grip around his neck. Peiwu's eyes glazed over. Newman had him.

Just a few more seconds.

Then the car came to a screeching halt, and someone jerked the door open. Newman looked up just in time to see a high-heeled ankle boot crash into his face.

Once. Twice.

And then there was nothing.

CHAPTER FORTY-FIVE

The White House
Washington, DC

Hammond closed the file he'd been reading for the last twenty minutes and leaned back in his chair.

Wow.

He wasn't even mad that he hadn't been read in on this file. He had to give it to the CIA. This had been one hell of an operation. As the former JSOC commanding officer, Hammond knew how difficult it was to pull off such a complex operation.

Hammond was still absorbing all the details of the file when there was a knock at the door. He looked up and saw Mark Williams, the CIA director, and Liz Maberry, the deputy director of Operations, step into the Oval Office. Even from where he was sitting, Hammond could tell Williams was seething. Liz Maberry had had her ass chewed out on the ride to the White House. Hammond was sure of it.

Following his call with Veronica, he'd reached out to Williams to inquire about Henry Newman. The director had sworn to him that Newman wasn't an asset of the CIA and never had been. Hammond had asked Williams to confirm this with his DDO and to call him back. Five minutes later, Williams had called back with his tail between his legs to confess that Newman was indeed a CIA officer and had been for over thirty years. Hammond had ordered Williams and Maberry to the White House. While they were on their way, he'd read the simplified file Williams had forwarded him and called Veronica to tell her Newman was CIA. He'd promised his daughter that he'd let her know if he learned anything more from the meeting.

"Please have a seat," Hammond said, gesturing to the two leather armchairs in front of the Resolute desk.

"Thank you, Mr. President," Williams and Maberry said in unison.

"I've read the file, and I understand why the DDO, and the DDOs before her, haven't shared the information," Hammond said, his eyes on the CIA director.

"So, Maberry," Hammond continued, switching his attention to the DDO, "you're not gonna have your head chewed off twice today. At least not by me. Understood?"

Maberry nodded. "Thank you, Mr. President. And for the record, I understand why the director was pissed off. I would have felt the same way if I were in his shoes."

That seemed to calm Williams. A little.

At least his eyes aren't throwing daggers anymore, Hammond thought.

"What else can you tell me that isn't in the file?" he asked.

"I'll let my esteemed colleague explain the situation to you, sir," Williams said, nodding toward Maberry. "I'm not sure I understand all the details yet, but she did brief me while we were on our way here."

Hammond leaned forward on his desk and waited for Maberry to begin.

"Initially, and this is well before my time, most of the intel we got from Newman was political, which was exactly what we wanted since the need to have our finger on the pulse of the political situation in Macau was what had prompted the mission in the first place. Then, slowly but surely, and as the political environment in Macau stabilized, Newman's intel became focused on laundering operations in Macau. Although Newman's feed allowed us to keep track of the major Sinocentric players and we were able to run a few operations overseas to disrupt the money train when we thought it was headed to a terror training camp, it had no real strategic value. My hope, and I'm sure it was the same for my predecessors, was that Newman would one day give us something of strategic importance."

"Did that happen?" Hammond asked.

"Maybe. It's hard to say," Maberry admitted. "About a year ago, Newman began assisting members of the Red Dragon Triad to enter the United States legally."

"You let him do what?" Hammond asked, shaking his head. "These are the assholes responsible for the fentanyl epidemic we have on our hands, for Chrissake!"

If Maberry was shaken by the president's rebuke, she didn't show it. Instead, she took full responsibility. "That's true, sir, but the fentanyl would have found its way here one way or the other. If you want my resignation over this, I'll gladly hand it to you."

Williams's head snapped in his DDO's direction. Hammond, too, was taken aback.

She has guts.

She was direct, and direct was good. She wasn't afraid of him either. Maberry was in her forties, attractive, with dark green eyes and chin-length shiny brown hair. Hammond hadn't had the time to look at her file, but he would. Soon. He liked her. Maybe she could take Williams's seat when the man retired at the end of the year?

Hammond sighed. Clayton and his friend at the DEA had been right to be worried about the Red Dragon Triad.

"That won't be necessary, Liz," Hammond said. "Please continue."

"Thank you, sir. When Newman began to help these triad members gain lawful residence, we created a small task force within the agency whose sole purpose is to keep track of these triads."

"How small are we talking about?" Hammond asked, wondering how Maberry had been able to keep an actual task force secret from the director.

"Three full-time employees, sir."

"All right. So, we believe Geng Peiwu is the leader of the Red Dragon Triad, yes?"

"As his father was before him. Yes, sir. This is all based on Newman's intel, because without it, I'm not sure we would have known. Legally speaking, when it comes to Macau and China, Geng Peiwu is a well-respected businessman. At least that's what they say publicly. I have to say that Geng Peiwu does have a ton of legitimate businesses, many of them quite successful."

"Have you lost any of them? What I mean is, have you lost track of any of the triad members that came to the United States with your help?"

"So far, we haven't lost track of anyone. But I'll admit it's a possibility. We're not conducting active surveillance on any of them, but we have all the data. We know where they live, where they work, the kind of cars they drive, and the list goes on. Because we never directly interdicted any of their activities on US soil, these people truly believe they're here free and clear."

"If I was to ask the FBI to go and arrest them all, you'd be able to provide the necessary information for them to do so?"

"Yes, sir. Absolutely. But I don't think we should."

The CIA director almost jumped out of his seat. Clearly, he wasn't in agreement.

Hammond frowned. "Why not?"

"If I may, Mr. President," Williams said.

Hammond gestured for him to speak. "Of course, Mark. I'd like to hear your opinion on this too."

"I disagree wholeheartedly with Liz. We need to round those people up."

"Why?" Hammond asked.

"We believe that the people coming in through the breach that was created for this operation are no longer criminal elements. Liz's own task force's assessment is that at least twelve Chinese intelligence officers have recently used the channel."

Hammond looked at Liz, gauging her reaction. She didn't move, but her jaw was clenched tight. Hammond had had dealings with the MSS before. It was a cunning organization. The MSS didn't do things half-assed. But moving so many agents in such a short period of time was a bold move, even for them. Hammond was mindful of how easy it would be to destabilize his country right now. He had worked hard to bring the two political sides closer, but it was a work in progress. He had seen some positive developments since he took office, but the divide was gigantic, and it would take years to repair and heal properly. And Hammond had only three years to fix it all.

If I'm to keep my promise to Clayton.

In the meantime, radicals on both sides were looking for the match that could light the fire again. It wasn't far fetched to think that assets planted by the MSS could play that role.

"If we move in now, we might not learn their intentions, correct?" Hammond asked.

"Yes, sir. Your assessment is correct," Maberry said, not leaving Williams the time to reply. "And that's the risk with getting everyone rounded up. It's possible that the intelligence assets the MSS has recently deployed in the United States don't know why they're here. Strategically, it would make sense to keep the assets in the dark until someone high up in the food chain—it could even be the Chinese president himself—is ready to pull the trigger on whatever task it is that he wants them to perform. Furthermore, and I should have mentioned this earlier, Newman successfully recruited his own agent in Macau. I have no idea who that person is. Only Newman knows that. For us, the agent is a coded source."

"A coded source? That means you pay the source a salary or something like that?" Hammond asked.

"We do. It's based on the information the source provides. But it's not much, and I wouldn't be surprised to learn that Newman is contributing to his agent's financial stability. Before he left for Davos, Newman managed to send us a message indicating that his local agent might be able to find out why the MSS was sending officers to the United States."

"I get what you're saying, Liz. But there's also a chance the assets who are already in place know exactly why they're here," Hammond said, remembering the conversation between the now deceased FBI director and Newman.

What I'm asking here is to delay such an investigation into this specific triad for eight, maybe ten months at the maximum.

Hammond got up from his chair and walked to the bulletproof window behind his desk. The thickness of the window distorted his view of the Rose Garden. Behind him, someone's phone beeped.

"My apologies, sir. I need to look at this. It's the task force."

Hammond wasn't usually one to hesitate, but making the wrong call on this one could bring a whole lot of problems he didn't want. Maberry had a valid point, but Hammond agreed with Williams about how soon they should move on the MSS agents. Sometimes a leader needed to know when to take a win. There were a lot of reasons why the MSS agents could be here. Sabotage, psychological warfare, recruiting proxies to do their dirty work, and the list went on. Whatever it was they were planning, it wasn't supposed to last more than eight to ten months.

"Sir?" Maberry asked, bringing Hammond back to the here and now.

He turned to face her. Maberry's face looked much paler than it had only a few moments ago.

"I . . . I'm afraid I have bad news, Mr. President."

"All right. Lay it all out and don't hold back. I'm used to hearing bad news."

"I just received confirmation that Newman's agent in Macau, the coded source we were talking about, was arrested earlier today."

CHAPTER FORTY-SIX

Davos
Switzerland

White paced back and forth the length of the suite, his frustration growing with every step. The tracking device, which had been planted on Newman by one of the FBI fly team special agents posing as a journalist, had remained immobile for the last hour. The agent had said that Newman and Geng Peiwu were headed out for lunch.

Why drive an hour away from Davos when there were so many great eateries within a five-minute walk?

"Remind me. How precise is your tracking device?" White asked Special Agent Wong.

Wong, who was seated behind a desk, refreshed the image on her laptop's screen.

"It's very accurate, sir. The red dot you see is the device. Its actual position is give or take three feet from what you're seeing on the screen," she said, using her finger to draw a small circle around the red dot on the digital map. "As I said, very accurate."

Veronica stood behind Wong, looking over her shoulder at the computer screen.

"Is it possible that the device fell off his jacket?" Veronica asked. "Your agent told us she had only a brief moment to pin the tracker on Newman."

Wong scratched her head. "I suppose that's possible. Another possibility is that he left his jacket in the vehicle and went to meet someone."

"Or that he's been made and what we're seeing on your screen is the location of his body," White said.

Veronica shot him a look. "Don't say that, Clayton," she said. "We're not there yet."

White didn't agree with her but kept his mouth shut. He had watched with interest as the car Newman had climbed into with Peiwu had traveled north on Route 28 before suddenly stopping at the northern edge of Lake Davos for less than five minutes before continuing toward Chur, a lovely town on the right bank of the Rhine and the capital of the Swiss canton of the Grisons. An hour later, the vehicle had stopped in the narrow roadway at the eastern edge of Chur's city limits.

"Zoom in again on the tracking device's location," Veronica asked Wong, taking a seat next to the FBI agent and opening her own laptop computer. "Maybe we're missing something."

Veronica had identified three houses that used the roadway for parking, and Wong had run the addresses through the FBI databases. There hadn't been any hits on the three houses, but White hadn't expected her to get any. Their only chance to get additional intelligence on these addresses was to contact the Swiss police or Europol, something Wong had done five minutes ago through official channels. While Europol had no executive powers, and its officers couldn't make an arrest without the prior approval and support from competent local authorities, White had suggested that Wong contact them first. The Swiss police, who wouldn't be happy to learn about an undeclared FBI fly team operating in Davos, would need some convincing to help the American team, and Europol—whose mandate was to serve as a center for law enforcement cooperation—could play an important role in smoothing things out. However, as professional and competent as Europol was, White would be stunned if they were to hear back from them anytime soon. He had no doubt Europol could get moving if he was to light a fire under their collective asses, but there was no real reason to strike the match just yet.

There wasn't much else they could do at this point, and it irritated him. White wasn't the most patient man, and he hated waiting for anything. It made it hard to remain focused and alert. He was heading toward the kitchenette to pour himself his third cup of coffee of the day when his phone rang. He looked at the screen. The call was coming through a secure app the White House used to communicate with the senior members of the president's staff.

"Clayton White," he said.

"It's me," Hammond said. "There's been a development."

"Should I put you on speaker? I'm with Vonnie and Special Agent Wong from the FBI."

"That's fine. Do it."

White walked back to the suite's living room and pressed the speaker button. He placed the phone on the table.

"We're all here, Mr. President," White said, cringing at calling Hammond Mr. President, but since Wong was there, White wanted to maintain proper decorum.

"With me in the Oval Office are CIA director Mark Williams and DDO Liz Maberry," Hammond said. "I know you're presently tracking Newman, so I think it will be of interest to you to know that Newman has been running his own agent inside Macau for the last fifteen years. Unfortunately, Deputy Director Maberry just received confirmation that Newman's agent has been arrested earlier today."

"How was this confirmed, and by whom?" White asked.

"Mr. White, this is Liz Maberry, I'll answer that question for you. It's an old system we used for low-risk agents. The agent dials a specific phone number, one that can be called only once, and a distress signal is sent out. We got such a distress signal from this agent today."

White cursed out loud. "Damn it. That means Newman is compromised."

"No, what that means is that Newman *might* be compromised," the president said. "But it doesn't change the fact that we need to get Newman out of Switzerland."

"What about Newman's agent?" Veronica asked.

"We'll do what we can, Miss Hammond," DDO Maberry said. "But we don't have a lot of options when it comes to China or Macau."

"Where's Newman now?" asked the president.

"For the last hour, the tracking device hasn't changed location," White said with urgency. "Newman climbed aboard a vehicle with Geng Peiwu and drove to Chur, a town of approximately thirty-five thousand people an hour or so away from here. Right now, it shows the tracking device in a roadway."

"Mr. White, this is Director Williams speaking. Thank you very much for your assistance. We have a team in Munich that could potentially—"

"Are you serious?" White asked, cutting off the CIA director mid-sentence. "What's wrong with you? There's no time to wait for a team coming from Munich. Not after the intel you just shared with us. Get your head out of your ass, Mr. Director!"

"Wait a goddamn second—"

"No! You wait, dumbass. If Newman's local agent has indeed been captured, he'll give up Newman. It's only a question of time before that happens. And you want to send a team from Munich to get Newman when he could already be dead? Get lost."

There was a moment of silence at the other end of the line, but it was brief. When Hammond spoke, it was with authority.

"Okay, Clayton. Let's assume that Newman is still alive and I want him to be extracted. What would you need to make it happen?"

"What I would need isn't available on short notice," White said, his mind racing to find solutions. There was no point asking for a Tier One team to intervene. By the time they got to Switzerland, it would be too late. Then an idea came to him.

TIGRIS.

Task Force TIGRIS was a semicovert, specialized tactical police unit working under the auspices of the Swiss Federal Office of Police. Years ago, during a training exercise in Singapore with the Secret Service, White had met two members of TIGRIS, and he'd been impressed. Even to this day, many Swiss citizens weren't aware of the unit's existence. TIGRIS might not be a Tier One unit, and had a force of only fourteen operators, but they were trained in hostage rescue. Furthermore, White was convinced that for the duration of the World Economic Forum, the Swiss government had its elite unit staged not too far from Davos. If the Swiss would be willing to activate TIGRIS and White could get ISR in the area, there was a chance.

ISR, which stood for intelligence, surveillance, and reconnaissance, encompassed many platforms, including satellite imagery and drones. ISR oftentimes played a crucial role in operations.

"Maybe there's a solution," White said, once he had gathered his thoughts. "The first thing we need to do is to get eyes on the tracking device's location to know what's up. We need to get that done ASAP. If we could get some type of ISR set up, too, it would be great. It could even be a local plainclothes police unit drive-by if nothing else is available. At the same time, we would need to get Task Force TIGRIS activated. I'm sure the Swiss have the unit stashed away close by."

"If President Hammond agrees, I'll get to work on the ISR immediately and see what we can come up with on short notice," DDO Maberry said.

"Get on it," White heard Hammond say. "Can you take care of TIGRIS, Mark?"

"Well . . . I guess I could, Mr. President, but I've heard very little about TIGRIS myself," Director Williams said. "I'll contact my counterpart at the Federal Intelligence Service and inquire—"

"Screw that!" Hammond's voice boomed through the phone's speaker. "You'll do no such thing, Mark. In fact, I want you to stay on the sideline for this one. Liz will take the lead and link with Clayton directly. As for TIGRIS, I'll personally call the president of the Swiss Confederation and get the ball rolling. Stand by your phone, Clayton. You'll hear from me very soon."

CHAPTER FORTY-SEVEN

Chur
Switzerland

"Welcome back, Mr. Newman."

Henry recognized his interlocutor not by the sound of his voice but by his stale cigarette breath.

Geng Peiwu.

Newman opened his eyes but shut them right away, trying to block out the nausea and the splitting headache that assaulted him. At best he had a concussion, but Newman didn't rule out a much more serious brain bleed. He forced his eyes to open again, then blinked a few times, focusing on the silhouette in front of him.

It wasn't who he thought it was. It wasn't Geng Peiwu.

Though he'd never met the man in person before, he'd seen many pictures of him. The bland face and asymmetrical lips gave him away. The man staring at him with a sneer was MSS 4th Bureau director Ma Lin. He was dressed in a crisp gray suit and a red tie, holding a cigarette in his tobacco-stained fingers. There was a certain curiosity in his eyes, and he studied Newman as if he were a rare, exotic animal.

Newman was completely naked, tied to a cold, gray metal chair, his wrists and ankles secured with zip ties and many layers of duct tape. He wasn't going anywhere. He was in what appeared to be a damp, dark basement, and the only light was in the form of a single weak bulb attached to the ceiling. Newman's body was shivering non-stop, racked with feverish chills. His lips were swollen and cut, with crusted blood and vomit on his chin and chest. All his muscle groups hurt, but his already unbearable headache was getting worse. Newman had no idea where he was or for how long he'd been out.

As his vision continued to clear, Newman spotted two other people. One of them, a thin man dressed in a dark, ill-fitting business suit, was busy setting up a television on top of a workbench. The other was Eu-Meh. She had removed her long leather coat, revealing a blood-stained pink blouse with rolled-up sleeves. More worrisome were the heavy-duty black rubber gloves she was wearing and the bloodied butcher's saw she was holding in her hands.

Newman turned his head to his left, following Eu-Meh's gaze. That's when Newman found Peiwu. Just like Newman, Peiwu was fully naked and tied to a metal chair. But that's where the similarities ended. Unlike Newman, Peiwu wasn't breathing. His torso had a multitude of deep cuts and lacerations, and his face was still knotted with the agony of his final moments. His left hand was missing, cut off at the wrist. A similar thing had happened to his right foot.

Holy shit! Had Peiwu died at the hands of his niece? Why had she turned on him? Was she working with Ma Lin? It certainly looked like it. Then Newman remembered the words Peiwu had spoken in the Maserati:

Don't be duped by the look of innocence about her. She's a cold-blooded killer.

Peiwu hadn't lied. His torturer had been ruthless and pitiless.

The work of a true savage.

Newman wondered what had happened since he'd fought with the triad leader in the back of the Mercedes. Definitely something significant, but he didn't have the bandwidth to analyze the situation any further.

"You're wondering what happened, yes?" Ma Lin asked, taking a few steps toward Newman. "Do you know who I am?"

There was no point in lying. Everyone who lived in Macau knew Ma Lin.

"Yeah . . . Ma Lin. An . . . MSS shit," Newman said, his voice hoarse and strange.

Eu-Meh's eyes lit up, and she took two quick steps forward, raising the butcher's saw. She looked at Ma Lin, clearly hoping he would give her the authorization to start cutting Newman into pieces. But Ma Lin shook his head. Eu-Meh's face twitched with disappointment.

Though Newman had spoken only a few words, moving his jaw had done nothing for his headache. It was getting worse. He had to find a way to get under Ma Lin's skin. With some luck, Newman could inspire the Chinese spy to hit him a few more times in the head. Newman was confident he'd die from the blows, which was a better option than being tortured by that crazy bitch, like Peiwu had been.

Newman closed his eyes. The idea that he had only a concussion was now grotesque. The shivering, his incapacity to focus, and his limited ability to think all pointed to severe brain damage.

"I must be honest with you, Mr. Newman, you don't sound good at all," Ma Lin said.

Newman forced his eyes open.

"Well . . . I . . . I don't feel good . . . either," he said, the words like sandpaper against his throat.

Ma Lin took a long drag of his cigarette as he continued to study Newman.

"Here's the deal, Henry. I know for a fact that Peiwu wasn't in on it. Trust me, with what Eu-Meh did to him, he would have said so."

"In on . . . what?"

"Right. Let me explain the rules," Ma Lin said. "I ask the questions. You don't. I'm extremely low on time because you were out for much longer than I thought you would be. To be blunt, just before you came to, we were discussing if we wouldn't be better off just shooting you in the head. I honestly thought you'd become brain dead. My mistake. I'm glad you came back to us. I have a feeling our conversation will be . . . very productive. I wish I had more time to play with you, but I don't."

Ma Lin grabbed a remote control from the nearby workbench and switched on the television. After a few seconds, the image of Thalia Magallanes appeared on the screen, and Newman's heart sank. It was as if she was looking straight at him. Her face was a mask of pain, guilt, and despair.

Newman guessed she could see him, too, because the first thing out of her mouth was an apology.

"I'm sorry . . . I'm so—"

Her words morphed into a scream as something flashed four or five times across the screen. It happened too fast for Newman to understand what it was. Then, whoever was handling the camera angled it in a way that showed Thalia's hands. Two of her fingers had been ground to a bloody mess.

Newman felt like someone had punched him in the solar plexus, and for a long moment, he couldn't breathe. A cold, aching misery enveloped him. He wanted to scream. He would have given his entire fortune—his life, even—to get to whoever had done this to Thalia. He would smash her tormentor's body with a steel pipe until he broke every bone.

"Look at her, Henry. Look carefully at what you've done to this poor girl," Ma Lin said, lighting up another cigarette. "How much additional pain do you want to inflict on her?"

Newman was speechless. Ma Lin was right. He'd done that to her.

"You played a great game, Henry," Ma Lin continued. "Peiwu completely missed it and brought her into our midst. That's why he's dead. He was a loose end anyway. I have to say that it took us a while to find her. When we started doing our business with Peiwu, I ordered a thorough security check on everyone in his entourage. Thalia passed. There was nothing suspicious about her. I was about to drop all electronic surveillance on her when her parents called. It was interesting to listen to them talk about how well their restaurant was doing. Did you know they were begging Thalia to come back to the Philippines? But she didn't want to hear it. She said she was happy. Her parents ended the call by thanking her for the latest deposit."

Newman's stomach churned. He was the one who had set up the account.

"Upon hearing this, I decided to investigate them too. I knew there was no way that Peiwu was paying her enough for her to send money back home. Anyhow, from there it got easy. The account you set up for them wasn't as well protected as you thought. My men took advantage of Peiwu's presence in Davos to pay her an unexpected visit. We caught her at a good time. She had Peiwu's file cabinet keys in her pocket."

A new wave of dizziness washed over him. His stomach contracted, and Newman knew that if he'd had anything left to puke, it would have come out. The sharp stabbing pain in his head continued, and he squeezed his eyes shut. Even the faint light of the single bulb was too much.

"If it makes you feel any better, Henry, you weren't the first one she gave up. For almost thirty minutes, she held on strong, claiming that she had been romantically involved with our friend Peiwu for years and that he was the one who had opened an account for her parents. It's only when my associate started cutting off her toes that she gave you up. Brave girl. The problem is, she doesn't know more than that. It means you kept her in the dark too. She did talk about the number she dialed. She told us it was a number to call in case she needed help. I thought this was interesting. Who did she call, Henry? Who knows about her? And who do you work for?"

In Newman's mind, the whole thing was beginning to sink in. Renewed anger welled up inside him, filling him with a murderous rage, enough so that for an instant, he forgot about the agony he was in. Newman wanted to say something, anything, but he couldn't even talk. He didn't seem to remember how.

Ma Lin seemed genuinely disappointed. "Too bad." His statement was followed by an audible *tsk* and a nod.

A high-pitched scream came from the television speaker.

"E . . . e-nough," Newman heard himself plead. "E-nough."

"Enough? Then talk," Ma Lin warned him.

Newman knew he had lost. There was no point in resisting. He doubted Ma Lin and the rest of his sadists would stop hurting Thalia, but if there was even a chance they would, he'd tell them everything they wanted to know.

"C-I-A," he mumbled. "C-I-A."

CHAPTER FORTY-EIGHT

Chur
Switzerland

White heard the two light, multipurpose Eurocopter EC635s before he saw them. He and Special Agent Wong were waiting for them in a large field just south of Lake Davos. Twenty minutes after he had hung up with Hammond, Nicklaus Hauser, the commanding officer of TIGRIS, had reached out to him. White had expected some resistance from the Swiss officer, but it had been the total opposite. Hauser had been beyond thrilled to get called up. As he had explained to White on the phone—with a very strong Swiss German accent—Swiss politics made it difficult for his team to get deployed. By Swiss law, they were not allowed to be sent on a raid that could be performed by local Swiss canton authorities. For TIGRIS, that meant that real-life deployments were few and far between.

"Have you ever been in a helicopter before?" White asked Wong.

"Only once, when I was a kid. I did a fifteen-minute ride with my parents when we visited Las Vegas."

"I'm sure that was a ton of fun, but this will be much more noisy and probably not as comfy. Last chance to back out, Wong," White said, raising his voice over the approaching helicopters.

"No way in hell, sir!" Wong replied, a big smile on her face. "I'm exactly where I want to be."

White gave her a fist bump. He liked Wong.

The two choppers buzzed low over White's position once; then the pilots brought their birds around in a shallow circle before landing.

As soon as one of the birds was on the ground, a TIGRIS operator gestured for White and Wong to get in. They hurried toward the helicopters. White ducked his head to protect his eyes from the dust of the rotor wash. White and Wong climbed aboard the same helicopter. White strapped into one of the available seats while a TIGRIS operator helped Wong get set up. The man next to White handed him a headset.

The chopper's two Pratt & Whitney turboshaft engines roared, and the helicopter lifted off.

"I'm Nicklaus Hauser," the man said, speaking into the mic. He offered his gloved hand to White.

White shook the man's hand. "Clayton White. Thanks for being here."

"As I told you on the phone, this is the best thing that could have happened to us," Hauser said.

"Did you look at the ops plan I sent you?" White asked.

"I did," Hauser said as he pulled out a tablet from his combat pack and powered it on. Once it had started up, a three-dimensional map of the objective appeared. "But I made a few adjustments."

"Okay. Show me."

"The cantonal police in les Grisons are excellent, but they're not equipped for this type of ops," Hauser explained. "If possible, I'll try to keep the locals around the security perimeters. I've tasked one of my operators to coordinate with them."

"Good thinking. What about the changes you talked about?"

Hauser used his fingers to zoom in on the map. "The moment we got the green light for the operation, I sent four of my guys to Chur aboard a civilian helicopter. I have two guys conducting reconnaissance on foot in this area."

Hauser pointed to two blinking green dots.

"They've already taken numerous short videos and over fifty photos," Hauser explained. "I'll show you the footage in a minute, but they're sure that something is going on in this house."

Hauser pointed to one of the three houses Veronica had identified on Teuchelweg. He selected a photo and enlarged it. It was a picture of the house. The property, which was located near the end of a cul-de-sac, was quintessentially Swiss. It was built of stone, and its roof had dark wooden beams that contrasted with the white walls. The second floor had a large balcony that wrapped itself around the four corners of the building. Each of the many windows had wooden shutters. To the left of the house, a large shed had been converted into a double-wide carport.

"We don't have the schematics yet, but the cantonal police will send them our way within the next five minutes. They won't show any renovations the owners might have made in the last ten years, but it should give us a general idea of the interior layout."

"Why this specific house?"

"I don't know why they picked it." Hauser shrugged.

"No, that's not what I meant," White said. "What made your team so confident this was the right property?"

"Ha. Yes, I understand now. Because of these."

Hauser showed White a few more photos. Two of them were of the Mercedes sedan Newman had taken with Peiwu. The Mercedes was parked near the entrance of the house Hauser had shown him earlier. The other photos were of other cars parked close by.

"The license plates belong to a rental company near Zurich," Hauser said. "Very unusual to have that many rental cars at the same location. This is a private residence, not a hotel."

"Agreed," White said, truly impressed. For a team that hadn't seen much action since its creation, they sure knew how to conduct a good recce. But Hauser wasn't done; he had a few more surprises for him.

"I also deployed two snipers," the TIGRIS team leader said, once again selecting the three-dimensional map on his tablet. "One is already in position about one hundred and fifty meters away from the objective. He has good elevation and a clear view of the west side of the house. Unfortunately, the other sniper had to reposition due to poor visibility."

A note flashed at the top of the screen. Hauser clicked on it. It was a short video that had been captured by one of Hauser's recce operators. The clip lasted less than a minute, but it was enough for White to see two men jogging from the parked Mercedes to the house.

"You have ISR?" White asked, stunned at everything TIGRIS had been able to accomplish in such a short period of time.

"We do," Hauser said. "We might not have the real-life experience your Special Forces have in the US, but all of us have trained our entire life for a moment like this. We're ready, Mr. White."

White took a moment to look at the four other operators seated in the chopper. They were serious-looking dudes and extremely fit. They wore black uniforms with the word *POLIZEI* written on their shoulders and at the back and front of their plate carriers.

"Have you considered my request?" White asked.

Before ending their initial phone call, White, who wasn't the kind of man who would ever ask someone to do something he wouldn't do himself, had asked Hauser if he could join the team for the raid. Though White hadn't been able to see Hauser's reaction, he could feel his question had caught the Swiss by surprise.

"I'll consider it," Hauser had said without much enthusiasm.

White understood. TIGRIS and its operators were Hauser's responsibility. The last thing White wanted was to break the integrity of Hauser's team. The guys had trained together for years, and each man would know instinctively what the operator next to him would do and how he would react. White hadn't trained with them. If he had been in Hauser's shoes, he wouldn't have hesitated even one second. His answer would have been a categorical no. Still, just in case, White had changed into a pair of blue jeans, a dark-colored long-sleeved T-shirt, and a pair of black tactical boots. He'd also borrowed Albanese's black Secret Service wind jacket.

"Are you armed?" Hauser asked.

"Glock 19, with four spare magazines."

Hauser nodded. "I know what you used to do for a living," he said. "There's no doubt in my mind you're a capable operator and would be a great asset to us, but I can't let you join in on the raid. When we work, we speak German. For this reason alone, I'll ask you to sit this one out."

White wasn't happy, but he couldn't fault Hauser's decision. The language barrier was a good excuse and one that was hard to argue against.

But once again Hauser surprised him. "What I can do is to allow you off the chopper with us," he said. "As per the plan we hatched beforehand, me and the four other guys from Alpha team will land in the large clearing to the southwest of the property. The second team will be divided into two elements, the three operators of Bravo, and the two operators from Charlie. Bravo will rappel down into the driveway on the north side of the house, while Charlie will slide down onto the roof and access the property by the large skylight. I will lead the assault with Alpha, while my second-in-command will be with Bravo and will go through the secondary entrance. With my two snipers already deployed and two of my guys doing the recce, I'm short. So, if you and your friend from the FBI could watch the rear of the building, you'd do me a favor."

White looked at the tablet on Hauser's lap. The map showed that the back of the target house faced a large, densely wooded area. It would be easy for one of the bad guys to escape through a window and disappear into the mountains.

"You can count on us," White said.

Hauser grinned. "I know," he said, handing White a portable radio. "It's already set on the appropriate frequency. You won't understand what—"

"I speak German," Wong said in German, raising her hand. "I can translate if necessary."

Hauser gave her a thumbs-up. "Danke."

Turning to White, he said, "Now I'll get back to my team for a last-minute brief. I'll see you on the ground. But don't worry, my American friend. If Henry Newman is there, we'll get him back. And by the way, once me and my guys have cleared the chopper, look under the seats. We might have forgotten a couple of tactical vests and two SG 552s."

White clapped the Swiss on the shoulder. "Thank you, Nicklaus."

White was glad he wouldn't have to potentially get into another firefight armed only with a pistol. But as impressed as he was with Hauser and the rest of his TIGRIS operators, something was bothering him. It had started out as a nagging irritation in the back of his mind as soon as he had hung up with Hauser after their first phone call. But now that they were getting closer to the objective and the actual assault, he'd gotten more worried about it.

Being exceptional during training scenarios was a good thing, but running an actual rescue operation where real bullets whizzed by your face was a different ball game. Training and preparation were good, but nothing trumped real-life experience when it came to giving you the confidence to make real decisions under the stress of combat.

White had looked it up. In the few operations TIGRIS had been involved with, there had never been a single shot fired. If all hell was to break loose during the assault, White had no way to know how the TIGRIS operators were going to react since none of them had ever been fired upon.

White wondered if he had made the right call by asking TIGRIS for their help. He couldn't escape the feeling that he may have miscalculated.

CHAPTER FORTY-NINE

Samedan
Switzerland

Ulyana gasped as Babanin rolled off her, his breathing fast and her own heartbeat pulsing through her at a rapid pace. He pulled her into his chest and wrapped an arm around her, his hand resting on one of her breasts. He pressed his lips to her exposed neck and kissed her. Satiation enveloped her, and she wished they could stay in this hotel room for another week. The breathtaking views, the food, the fresh mountain air, and the sex—everything was perfection. Located at 2,456 meters above sea level between Samedan and Pontresina, Romantik Hotel Muottas Muragl was a true gem, and the last twenty-four hours she'd spent there with Sascha had been memorable.

Nature at its purest, she thought, the majestic landscape and incomparable views of the Bernina massif in her mind. She had needed the break. The forty-eight hours prior to their arrival at the hotel had been long and hard, and fatigue had started to set in. Fortunately, with the latest weather forecast calling for continuous blue skies for the next seventy-two hours, Yuri had made the call to send them to Samedan, which had been a major relief. That was the option she and Sascha had pushed for. It made sense since the plane of the American delegation was already at the Samedan Airport and would have repositioned to Zurich only if less than ideal weather conditions had been forecast. The honest truth was that she didn't think they would have had any success at shooting down the plane if Yuri had sent them to Zurich.

Sascha had agreed with her.

Both locations—Zurich and Samedan—had their pluses and minuses. Zurich's main advantage was how much easier it would be to disappear into the city after the attack. With an urban area of almost 1.5 million habitants, Zurich was Switzerland's largest city and a hub for roads, railways, and air traffic. After hiding for a few days, they could have taken either a train or a plane to reach another European country within the Schengen zone.

Ulyana, who had never traveled to Zurich before, had been caught completely off guard by the city's austere beauty and quaint cobblestone backstreets and the premedieval architecture of some of its buildings. The city, one of the most beautiful she'd ever seen, was set against a mural of snow-dusted mountaintops, green hills, and the iconic Lake of Zurich.

Though Ulyana and Sascha had been there to scout locations from which they could fire the surface-to-air missiles, Ulyana had allowed herself to forget who she was for a few hours. She enjoyed her time with Sascha. He was the perfect partner, a man she could see herself with years from now, which felt weird because it wasn't a feeling she'd had before. She was pretty sure he liked her too. She'd seen the heat in his eyes as they made love. He was falling for her.

Sascha had an easy laugh, and their long, idyllic walk down the serene Limmatquai—a street along the bank of the Limmat River—had been marvelous. She'd especially enjoyed their stop at an eighteenth-century restaurant where they had shared a large fondue on a sidewalk table overlooking the river. She'd even caught herself envying the couples holding hands or pushing strollers. She'd never longed for a family, but was it because she'd never found the right partner? Her and Sascha's line of work wasn't conducive to long-term relationships. She got that. She wasn't sure she was ready to quit either. She was having fun. Still, the pull she felt toward Sascha was hard to resist.

But as wonderful as Zurich was, it had proved to be a challenge finding two good spots from which they could fire their missile with a high probability for a kill. Moreover, the police presence in Zurich was problematic and the odds of being spotted by someone were much higher than at the Samedan Airport, a regional aerodrome in the Engadin valley eight kilometers from Saint Moritz.

Setting up for an operation at the Samedan Airport—which was also known as Engadin Airport—would be easier by a factor of ten. The major issue they would face in Samedan, a small village of less than three thousand people, would be during their exfil, right after they had fired their missiles. The location they had scouted to initiate the attack was east of the airport, about two-thirds of the way up Muottas Muragl, a summit with commanding views of the entire Engadin region, including its four lakes and the famous resort town of Saint Moritz, and, most importantly, a direct line of sight to the airport. But with no places to hide, they would need to use speed to create distance between themselves and their likely pursuers. To achieve that, they would count on Yuri's eight-man security force, who would run interference to cover her and Sascha's retreat to the Romantik Hotel. Once at the hotel, they would board the vintage 1907-built funicular with some other tourists and travel down to the parking lot, where a rental vehicle had been positioned. From there, they would take Route 29 south toward the Italian border.

A good, solid plan, she thought.

Tonight, under cover of darkness, Yuri's men would deploy the MANPADS to the prearranged locations. Then, tomorrow, it would be up to her and Sascha, posing as amateur hikers, to complete the mission.

She sighed, louder than she intended.

"What's up?" Sascha asked, squeezing her tighter.

"I love it here," she said. "I think it would be nice if we could come back one of these days."

Sascha didn't reply but began to trace circles across her upper back and neck and down her spine. She wondered if the *we* she had used had somehow scared him. She was testing the waters, trying to figure out if there was a chance they would continue to see each other after this assignment—if they were to survive, of course.

"I think it will be hard for us to come back," he said a moment later, "but I have other places in mind that are just as beautiful."

His choice of words soothed her qualms. She liked the way he had put emphasis on the word *us*.

"Oh yeah? Like where?"

"The Maldives are pretty nice," he said.

"I've heard that. But we shouldn't wait too long," she said. "Scientists say eighty percent of the islands of the Maldives will be uninhabitable by 2050."

"I don't think the rising sea levels is what will keep us from going," he said.

She felt a slight change in his tone.

"What do you mean?"

"This job, it takes a toll on you, you know?" he said. "The risks we take, the lies we tell, all of that will catch up to us eventually."

"O-kay. So, what are you saying?" she asked, part of her hoping he'd say that he'd like to disappear with her forever.

"I . . . I don't know."

She rolled over to face him, their noses almost touching. She felt the soft brush of his hands on her waist, and it electrified her.

"You can tell me, you know?"

Instead of answering, he kissed her. He slid his arms around her, rolled onto his back, and pulled her on top of him.

CHAPTER FIFTY

Chur
Switzerland

Ma Lin was taken aback. Newman had thrown him a curveball. It wasn't like Ma Lin to show much emotion, but he had felt a tightening along the right side of his jaw as Newman had shared with him who his employer truly was.

Or at least the one Newman claimed to be working for.

The CIA.

Could Newman be telling the truth? It seemed so improbable. The MSS was known for long, deep undercover missions, as were the Russians, but the Americans? Never. Not like this one. Three decades? How was that even possible?

It was too far-fetched to be taken at face value. Still, he couldn't take any chances. In the unlikely event Newman was telling the truth, that meant there was a distinct possibility the entire operation in the United States was at risk. Ma Lin had sent twelve of his best assets to the United States using Newman's network. All of them had reported arriving there without issue. None had been arrested, and not one of them had detected surveillance.

Ma Lin sighed, his annoyance with the Americans growing. He would have to validate everything by an enhanced interrogation, but he would have to be careful. Newman was weak, and dark blood had once again started to ooze out of his nose and left ear at an alarming rate.

But first, Ma Lin had to warn Yuri Makarov. With Peiwu dead, was there a way to call back the cargo ships or to at least ask them to change course? It would be madness to lose these surface-to-air missiles. Ma Lin reached into the breast pocket of his jacket and took out his phone. He dialed Yuri's number and waited for the Russian to pick up.

"Quick update," Ma Lin said. "I can't confirm any of what I'm about to share with you beyond any reasonable doubt just yet, but I wanted to let you know that there's a possibility that our entire operation is in danger of imploding."

"Your operation, Director. Not ours. My part in this was over the moment the cargo ships departed Macau," Yuri said. "I fulfilled all of my contractual obligations."

"Yes, of course," Ma Lin said, the Russian's arrogance irritating him. "But as we move forward to the reunification of my great nation, I'm sure you'd like to see FiveSeas high on the list of our trusted partners, am I right?"

"What is it that you want, Director?" Yuri asked a few seconds later.

"Is there a way for you to recall the cargo ships?"

"There might be. Why?"

"The Americans may have learned about the ships. It would be a shame to lose these missiles."

There was a long pause. "How did the Americans come to learn about this?"

"I'm dealing with—"

"How?" Yuri yelled.

Ma Lin wasn't accustomed to being screamed at. He was the one who did the shouting, not the other way around. But he needed the Russian's help, so he let it pass.

"Peiwu's longtime housekeeper was apparently working for Henry Newman, who just admitted he's American CIA."

"Henry Newman, an American agent? That's impossible. He's as corrupt as they come and has been in Macau for decades."

"One doesn't exclude the other. You can be a crook and work for an intelligence service, Yuri. You should know this better than anyone," Ma Lin said, unable to resist throwing a jab at the Russian. "Can you call back the cargo ships or not?"

"I will try," Yuri said. "But I can't guarantee the results. The crew is loyal to Peiwu, not to me."

"Understood. Do what you can," Ma Lin said, ending the call.

Ma Lin squatted next to Newman. The American had lost consciousness again.

"Wake him up," he said to Eu-Meh, who was still holding the bone saw.

Hurried footsteps coming down the staircase from the ground floor made Ma Lin look back. Two men, both dressed in dark jeans and black leather jackets, walked toward him.

"We found what we believe to be a tracking device, sir," the smallest of the two said.

"Didn't you search him?" Ma Lin barked.

"We did, well before we reached Chur. And we burned his clothes too."

"Then how did you miss this?"

"We hadn't physically searched the car until now. We did an electronic sweep, but the tracking device didn't register."

"Tell me, where was it exactly?"

"Wedged under the front passenger seat."

Ma Lin shook his head in disgust. Peiwu had told him about his fight with Newman. In his mind's eye, Ma Lin could see the two men struggling to get a punch in. In the scuffle, Newman had lost his tracking device. Someone had tagged Newman. Was it the Americans?

Ma Lin's mouth went dry, feeling as though his throat might close up, as he thought about the Americans. They could already be on their way to his location.

"Change of plans, and go tell the others," Ma Lin said to his people. "We're leaving in five minutes. Burn everything."

Ma Lin looked around the basement and saw what he was looking for behind the television. He walked to the work bench and grabbed the suppressed submachine gun—a QCW-05. He checked that the fifty-round magazine was inserted correctly and pulled the charging handle. He walked back to Henry Newman, whose eyes were still closed.

Ma Lin fired three times into Newman's heart.

And then he heard the helicopters.

CHAPTER FIFTY-ONE

Chur
Switzerland

White had been in some rough helicopter rides during his time as a combat rescue officer, but he didn't remember anything as bad as the last thirty minutes they'd just been through.

Or I'm getting old, he thought.

None of the TIGRIS operators had seemed to notice the major turbulence that had rocked the helicopter. Special Agent Wong hadn't stopped smiling the whole way, which could only mean she was a roller coaster fanatic. White was glad he hadn't eaten much because he would have left everything on the chopper's floor.

The operators of the second helicopter were already fast-roping down to the objective when White's chopper flared to make its landing. The moment it touched down, the five TIGRIS operators were on the move, advancing toward the house in a combat crouch with Nicklaus Hauser leading the way. By the time the rotor had stopped spinning, White had already geared up with his tactical vest and was putting extra magazines for the SG 552 Commandos into the pouches. Wong, who wasn't familiar with the SG 552, decided her Glock 19 was good enough. White disagreed, but he didn't have the time to argue or to show her the basics of the Swiss rifle. At least he got her to put on a tactical vest, which was way too big for her.

"Stay close to me and keep your eyes open," White said. "We're moving."

Having memorized the map Hauser had shown him, White was familiar with the area. The zone Hauser had asked him to keep an eye on was the dense woody area to the south of the objective, seventy-five meters away. White glanced to his left as he entered the wood, catching a glimpse of Hauser and his men as they got ready to breach the main door of the house by putting an explosive strip charge on it. White knew that the second-in-command was doing the same thing on the other side of the house. The team on the roof would wait for Hauser's signal to enter.

White took a knee and looked at Wong to make sure she was in position. She was, but her grin from earlier was gone, replaced by an icy look of determination.

And maybe a bit of apprehension, White thought.

From his position—fifteen meters from the house—White could see the four windows on the south side of the building and a set of french doors that led to a small deck. This was a new addition to the house. The french doors hadn't appeared on the three-dimensional picture Hauser had shown him. Looking left again, White wondered what was taking so much time. Hauser should have ordered Alpha, Bravo, and Charlie to breach thirty seconds ago. The explosives used to breach doors like these were designed to shock the people inside the property, but only if caught by surprise. It was taking so long for Hauser to give the order to move in that White feared the TIGRIS team had lost the element of surprise.

Damn it! What is he waiting for?

There was no way the bad guys inside the house hadn't heard the choppers coming. The Eurocopter EC635 was a great multipurpose helicopter, but it wasn't quiet by any stretch of the imagination. Hauser was wasting time. He had to move in before the defenders could dig in.

Ten seconds later, White, who was now royally pissed off, asked Wong for the portable radio. She was in the process of unclipping it from her belt when the front door was blown off its hinges.

Shiiit!

White turned his head toward the sound of the explosion. He watched as Hauser entered the house only to be shot in the chest as he reached the threshold. He fell backward into the next operator, who, instead of pushing forward, froze in place when he saw his team leader catch a round. Then his head snapped back, and he collapsed on top of Hauser.

Hauser's operation was falling apart.

———

Finally, a TIGRIS operator returned fire, allowing his two other teammates to drag Hauser and the other operator out of harm's way. Gunfire erupted from inside the house. It took everything White had not to run toward the main door and take charge. But the language barrier would only create more problems for the team. It was up to them to find a solution.

Wong's fierce determination had morphed into a controlled terror. White recognized the look. He'd seen it many times before. Combat—and this was combat—was scary. It didn't matter how well trained a person was; the first time that person realized that the shots being fired weren't blanks or that they were in the middle of a real-life gun battle instead of a training scenario—as realistic as those had become in recent years—that same look Wong had on her face came out. The key was to channel the terror into crisp action. But that took time. For now, White thought Wong was holding up pretty well. Her breathing had accelerated, but her eyes were still focused. She had moved behind a tree, which offered her partial cover.

Good. She's thinking on her feet.

White heard two more explosions that sounded like grenades, but he couldn't tell if they were flash-bangs or frags. Just then, four people rushed out through the french doors. The first two were holding assault rifles—that White identified as QCQ-05s—and were scanning in front of them, the muzzles of their rifles swinging left and right, covering their respective arcs of fire.

These two know what they're doing, White thought.

One man was wearing dark jeans and a black leather jacket, but the second, who was much thinner than the first, wore an ill-fitting business suit. Behind the pair, a medium-height woman, who seemed to be barefoot and whose pink blouse was smeared with blood, walked to the right of a man dressed in a gray business suit. Both were armed with rifles.

This was a lot of firepower, and at least three of four people White had spotted—Pink Blouse, Leather Jacket, and Tiny—weren't at their first rodeo.

They're all Asians, White noted. *Either MSS or Red Dragon Triad members.*

White looked in Wong's direction. The FBI agent nodded at him, letting him know she'd seen them too.

White wondered if one of the four knew Ian Miller. He still couldn't understand why Miller had turned. The former PJ had seemed to be living the life when he'd seen him in Saint John. Was it because of Daphne Cook? It had to be. The pictures Pierre Sarazin had sent didn't lie. White pushed all that out of his mind.

Focus.

White aimed the SG 552 at the lead man twenty-five meters away. He didn't have a shot yet. There were too many trees, and his four targets were moving too fast. In a few more seconds, they would have to cross an area not as dense, and White would take his shot, trying to get at least two. Knowing Wong had only her Glock and having no idea how she was going to react when the gun battle started, the last thing White wanted was to get into a four-rifle-against-one-rifle kind of fight. Patience and placement of shots were going to be the keys to this situation.

Then Wong fired, startling White.

What the hell?

If he didn't have a shot with his rifle, there was no way in hell Wong had one with her Glock. But that little fact didn't make her shy away from pulling the trigger of her pistol again and again. Pink Blouse, Tiny, and Leather Jacket had all disappeared behind a huge rock, and Gray Suit had taken cover behind a tree.

"Reloading!" Wong shouted.

White swore under his breath. If by some miracle the four tangos had missed her muzzle flashes, they'd sure as hell have heard her yell that she was out of bullets.

Shit! Wong was going to get them killed.

White aimed at the two locations where he'd seen his targets take cover and fired three to four rounds in each direction twice, hoping to keep their heads down for a few seconds. Then, he was on the move. He reached Wong in three long strides, and without slowing down, he grabbed her by the pull handle of her tactical vest before she could understand what was happening.

"Get up!" he barked at her, without realizing that her feet were barely touching the ground as it was. He managed six more strides before someone opened fire. Bullets battered the position where Wong had been just three seconds ago. White shoved Wong behind a large fallen trunk and jumped on top of her, protecting her with his body. It took half a second for White to understand that there were no rounds zapping above their heads or against the tree trunk. The shooters hadn't seen them move and were firing toward the location where they had spotted Wong's muzzle flash—or heard her.

"You've got to move, too, Wong," White whispered through gritted teeth. "You can't empty a full magazine and just stay stationary, for Chrissake!"

She nodded rapidly. "I almost got him!"

White ignored her. "Stay there."

He crawled the length of the fallen tree trunk, stopping every few feet to listen, but with the rounds he'd fired with the SG 552 plus the magazine Wong had gone through with her Glock, his ears were ringing. He buried his fingers below the trunk, where the soil was wet and muddy. He then applied the mud to camouflage his face, or at least break the lines. White could still hear the firefight raging inside the house. He chanced a peek, careful not to jerk his head up. He didn't move, and he let his eyes do the work. The air felt stiller, cooler than it had been when he had entered the forest. His clothes, fully wet, clung to his legs and arms. His fingers tingled from the cold and the adrenaline rush. The forest floor was spongy beneath his knees and elbows.

But somehow, it felt good.

His peripheral vision caught movement, but White didn't look right away. He lay still, letting his eyes do the hard work and praying Wong wasn't about to empty another magazine. White spotted Leather Jacket first. He was limping. Wong had hit the sonofabitch in the leg.

Leather Jacket's limp was getting worse with every step he took. He was moving from tree to tree, taking a short break before moving to the next. Where were the others? It took White another ten seconds to spot Tiny. He was ten meters behind his friend, taking cautious steps and sighting over his rifle. He wasn't looking exactly at White's emplacement, but he would very soon if White correctly read the manner with which the man was scanning. Slowly, White lowered his head and clutched his rifle against his chest, only now remembering he hadn't changed magazines. He had fired up to twenty-four rounds out of the thirty his magazine initially held.

For God's sake, Clay. Get your head in the game.

He was mindful that the QCQ-05s his adversaries were carrying held fifty-round magazines. There was no way he was going to engage the four of them with six rounds left in his. Doing his best to be as quiet as possible, White ejected the mostly spent magazine and inserted a fresh one. Satisfied he wouldn't run out of ammunition right away, White lifted his head. He had now lost sight of Leather Jacket, but he had reacquired Gray Suit. Tiny was a bit farther away than White had thought he would be. Pink Blouse, though, was nowhere to be seen.

White wondered if Wong had managed to hit her too.

Analyzing what he was seeing, White noticed that the tangos had picked up the pace.

They're eager to put as much distance as possible between them and the house, he thought.

With slow but unbroken movement, White settled into a good firing position. Although Gray Suit would be an easier shot, White was going to take Tiny first. White set the iron sights on the man's head and tracked him. Every two to three seconds, he had a shot. White couldn't afford to miss, because if he did, there would be four bandits converging on their position from different angles. White slowed his breathing and focused on his sight picture. His finger moved inside the trigger guard, and he began to apply pressure. White's SG 552 barked once, and Tiny collapsed, shot in the head, the bullet shattering his cheekbone before taking a downward trajectory and exiting through his neck. White transitioned to Gray Suit, but the man had already flattened out, surprising White with his speed. White squeezed the trigger five times, sending rounds in Gray Suit's immediate vicinity.

Short, controlled, and simultaneous bursts fired by Leather Jacket and Pink Blouse—who'd reappeared to the side of the same big rock she'd taken cover behind—hit the tree trunk, peppering White with wood splinters, one of them slicing his right cheek. White knew he had to move; Leather Jacket and Pink Blouse had zeroed in on him.

That was the moment Wong chose to go to work. If White had thought that Wong had emptied her first magazine rapidly the first time around, this time she was lightning fast, firing her fifteen rounds in less than four seconds. White rotated, keeping the tree trunk as cover, and looked in Wong's direction. She wasn't where he'd left her. Wong had taken it upon herself to shadow Leather Jacket on a parallel path, and when he'd turned to engage White, she had opened fire and hit him numerous times.

White chopped a hand in the directions where he'd last seen Gray Suit and Pink Blouse. Wong gave him a thumbs-up, and then she made a rookie mistake. Because the plate carrier was too big for her and went over her holster and spare magazine pouches, Wong found herself incapable of reaching her last spare magazine. Instead of staying low and using her hand to lift the side of the plate carrier, she got up.

And the moment she did, a multitude of shots rang out.

CHAPTER FIFTY-TWO

Chur
Switzerland

White watched in despair as at least two rounds hit Wong center mass. The FBI agent was shoved backward against a tree, her pistol flying out of her hand. White reacted instinctively and rolled three times to his right in an effort not to reappear at the same place he had the last time. Then he got to one knee and squeezed off two shots at Pink Blouse, one of his rounds ricocheting off her rifle before slicing through her left forearm. The woman yelled in pain and fell, holding her injured arm. Farther to his left, White caught a glimpse of Gray Suit as he dove behind a tree.

This time, though, White knew where he was. White took aim at the leg sticking out from the side of the tree Gray Suit was using as cover and fired once. Gray Suit's knee exploded, and the man fell to his side. White was making his way over to him when he spotted five TIGRIS operators heading toward Gray Suit while shouting "Polizei! Polizei!"

Gray Suit held his knee with one hand while raising the other above his head. He turned his head toward White and frowned when he saw him, as if he knew who White was.

White certainly recognized *him*. He'd seen plenty of pictures of Ma Lin, the director of the MSS 4th Bureau—a man for whom White had a ton of questions. But with TIGRIS converging on Ma Lin, it would have to wait.

White told the TIGRIS operators where the other tangos had fallen, letting them know one of them, a barefoot female wearing a bloodied pink blouse, might still be alive.

Satisfied TIGRIS had things under control, White rushed to Wong and dropped to his knees next to her. As a former combat rescue officer, White had patched up wounded servicemen for years and knew what he had to do. The way he'd seen Wong drop, he'd thought for sure she'd be dead, but the FBI agent was very much alive.

Thank God.

One of the rounds had sliced through the meat of her right arm while another had hit her in the chest. White took off the plate carrier that had saved her life. The ballistic plate had stopped the round from penetrating. White quickly assessed Wong's health and gently patted her down to see if he had missed another entry wound, but he hadn't. He examined the pectoral area where the bullet had hit. A significant, very dark red welt was already growing on her skin, but Wong was going to be fine.

"Sorry . . . sir, I—"

"You were great, Wong," White said, holding her hand. "You have nothing to be sorry for."

"It . . . fucking . . . hurts," she said, in between quick, shallow breaths.

"Yeah, getting shot will do that to you. You want to stay here and wait for the medics, or you want me to help you out?"

"Help me up," she said without hesitation.

White eased her into a sitting position.

Then Wong's eyes grew wide, and she shouted, "Behind you!"

———

White turned, just in time to see the muted sunlight flashing on the polished steel of the knife in Pink Blouse's hand. White moved to his right at the last second, and the tip of the knife sped an inch to the left of his neck. Pink Blouse had been aiming for the base of his neck, and without Wong's warning, he would have been dead.

White tried to seize the woman's wrist but missed, allowing her to slash the blade in a downward motion at his torso. He twisted his upper body out of the way and delivered a right hook to her left temple. His fist connected, but he had no leverage behind the punch, and the woman shook it off. With a cry of rage, and bleeding profusely from the large cut on her left forearm, the woman went on the offensive, knowing she couldn't allow White to create the distance he needed to draw his pistol or raise the rifle strapped across his chest. White, not willing to trade a punch for a stab, waited for the right opening. The woman feinted, then moved in for a thrust to White's throat. White deflected the strike and countered with a punch to the woman's ribs. Her knees buckled, and this time White didn't miss. He seized her wrist with his left hand and brought it down while propelling himself upward and ramming his right hand under her elbow once, twice, and then a third time with as much strength as he could muster. The arm already hyperextended to its maximum after the first blow, White's second strike snapped the ligaments. His third broke it. The knife fell from the woman's grasp, a raging growl escaping her lips. White swung a heavy fist that connected with her jaw. Knocked unconscious, the woman fell face first onto the soft, damp earth.

White secured the woman's hands with a pair of zip ties, then turned his attention back to Wong, who was in the process of picking up the pistol she had dropped.

"Let's get that arm of yours checked out."

He offered her his hand, and she took it. He pulled her up.

White observed the FBI agent as she fought against the pain and changed her spent magazine for a new one, not even a moan coming out of her mouth. This young woman had earned his respect. She had a bright career ahead of her, of that he had no doubts.

White reached into his jeans pocket and made a call. He had to let Veronica and Hammond know what had just happened in Chur.

CHAPTER FIFTY-THREE

Samedan
Switzerland

Sascha watched Ulyana as she walked naked toward the bathroom. She truly was a beautiful woman.

"You coming?" she asked, glancing back at him.

"As tempting as that sounds, I'll stay here to catch my breath."

"Your loss," she said, closing the bathroom door behind her.

He heard the toilet flush, and then the shower was turned on. He paid attention to the actual sounds coming from the bathroom, and once he was absolutely sure she was in the shower, he pushed back the cover and swung his feet out of the bed. He sat up at the edge of the mattress and listened some more, closing his eyes.

Was she actually singing in the shower?

She is. She's humming a lullaby.

Sascha shook his head. Ulyana was batshit crazy. How could she be so happy knowing she'd be murdering people the next day?

Unless she's playing you and knows who you are.

Sascha dismissed the idea. She was falling for him. She really was.

Ulyana's phone buzzed next to her pillow. Then his did too. It was a text message from Yuri.

Schedule Change. Schedule Change. Schedule Change.

American Delegation is shortening its stay in Davos. Plane will depart from Samedan Airport in two hours. Same tail number.

You are clear to proceed as per proposed operation plan. MANPADS will be in position in ninety minutes.

Acknowledge.

Sascha's body tensed, and his mind began working on a solution. First thing he had to do was to acknowledge receipt of the message with a specific code, which he did. Then, snatching Ulyana's phone, he typed the eight-digit code he'd seen her enter the night before while they were having dinner. With her phone unlocked, Sascha sent Yuri the same nondistress code he'd just sent from his own phone. Sascha deleted the message and left Ulyana's phone on the bed in the same position he had found it.

Getting out of bed, he realized the shower was no longer running.
Shit.

Sascha hesitated. It was now or never. If he didn't act now, there might not be another chance to stop this madness. He made his decision and rushed to his backpack. He unzipped it, pushed some items out of the way, and reached for a small hidden pocket in the lining of his bag. The pocket held a burner phone—a Samsung with a detachable battery—and a SIM card. He quickly hooked the battery to the phone and inserted the SIM card. He powered up the device and waited for it to pick up the signal.

C'mon, c'mon.

After what seemed like an eternity, the screen lit up. After a quick glance toward the bathroom door to confirm it was still closed, he began typing, wishing his fingers to move faster.

Time: TIMING CHANGE. Today Between 1800 and 2000 Local Time.

Target: Same as previous report.

Location: Same as previous report.

Weapon Location: Unknown at this time but will be on location approx. 90 mins after time stamp of this message.

Sascha pressed the send button; then the door of the bathroom opened.

"What are you doing?" Ulyana asked, sending his heart jumping into his throat.

With his back to her, he let the phone slip from his hand. It fell between a pair of socks and a T-shirt. He grabbed the T-shirt, rolled it around the phone, then turned to face Ulyana.

She was standing at the threshold between the room and the bathroom, dripping wet and fully naked. "I thought you'd have joined me," she said, pouting her lips.

"Honestly, I need to keep some powder dry for later. You're an animal," he said, showing her the navy blue T-shirt he'd pulled from the bag. "I was just looking for a clean tee."

She walked to him and gave him a long, passionate kiss. She looked down, then raised an eyebrow, clearly surprised her kiss didn't have the desired effect.

"So, it's true then. You really do need your rest, old man," she said.

"I'll take a quick shower. You want to grab dinner after?"

She grinned. "Sure. Whatever gives you back your strength."

As he walked past her, she slapped him on the butt cheek with enough strength for him to feel the burn. His arms involuntary jerked up, and the phone slid out from the T-shirt, landing on the carpeted floor behind him, its screen facing the ceiling and angled toward Ulyana.

He spun around, but it was too late. Ulyana had seen the phone and was just about to pick it up when it vibrated. Since the phone hadn't had the time to lock itself, the message was on full display across the screen.

Message received.

Will forward new intel.

You are clear to terminate.

Though he was looking at the screen upside down, Sascha had no problem reading the message. To her credit, Ulyana got the message's meaning instantly. Sascha kicked hard, aiming at Ulyana's head as if he were attempting a fifty-yard field goal.

Ulyana's arms shot forward, blocking his leg and avoiding much of the damage, but the strength of his kick shoved her backward, sending her rolling onto her back. She didn't fight it and let the momentum carry her back to her feet after she completed a full roll. They stared at each other for a moment. They were both naked and in fighting stances.

"Am I the one you were cleared to terminate?" Ulyana hissed.

Sascha wished there was something he could say to defuse the situation, but there wasn't.

"I guess the cat is out of the bag on—"

She attacked him like a demon, but with discipline. Ulyana threw punches and kicks that he parried or blocked until an elbow hit him on the chin, stunning him. Then there was a blur, and something hit him on the jaw with the force of a sledgehammer, sending him crashing against the wall.

Sascha found himself on all fours, wondering what had just happened. His head felt as if it had been split open by an axe. Before he could catch his breath, Ulyana kicked him in the ribs. Sascha grunted and held his side, pain radiating through his chest. The next kick was meant to land on his face, but he stopped it with a forearm and managed to grab the ankle of her other foot in a reverse grip. He pulled her toward him, and she lost her balance, falling on her back. He hurried to his feet, wincing in pain as he did so. If two of his ribs weren't broken, they were bruised, at the very least.

Pure hatred was oozing from her body.

"Who's that on the phone?" she asked.

He spat blood on the carpet. "Does it matter?"

He could see her eyes moving, looking for a weapon. Their pistols were in the room safe, but he kept a blade in his nightstand. And so did she. A knife fight was all about mobility, and with the searing pain in his ribs and the brain contusion he'd suffered with what he now realized was a powerful, well-timed roundhouse kick to his head, a knife fight was the last thing he wanted.

Knowing how Ulyana thought, Sascha presumed she had come to the same conclusion. She took a tentative step back, moving closer to her nightstand.

And that's exactly what he wanted her to do.

—

Ulyana had a hard time controlling her anger. Within the last two minutes, her entire universe had shifted on her. Who was Sascha—her Sascha—in communication with? Was it Yuri? Had her uncle turned on her? She tried to convince herself he wouldn't do that, but she knew it wasn't the truth. But why? Was it retribution for the death of the former US president? If so, why order Sascha to kill her in the middle of an operation? No. *That* he wouldn't do. Yuri might be heartless, but he was practical. Eliminating her made no strategic or tactical sense.

If it wasn't Yuri, then who?

She looked at Sascha. She had injured him, but he was still a threat. Wounded animals were often the most dangerous ones. It wasn't lost on her that they'd had sex no more than an hour ago. And now, they were still naked—at least that hadn't changed—but they wanted to kill each other.

Ulyana looked for something she could use as a weapon, but except for the corkscrew next to the minibar, the only other option was her knife since they'd both locked their guns in the room safe. If she could get her hands on her knife, she would cut him until he told her who had ordered him to kill her. Then she would go after that person. She had no other choice. She couldn't protect herself if she didn't know who wanted her dead. But she had to get to that knife first.

She took a step back, to see if Sascha would follow. He didn't. He still looked dazed from the perfect roundhouse kick she had delivered to his face. It would have knocked out most men, but here he was.

Still standing.

She visualized her next move. She was confident she could reach her nightstand in four strides. He would know what she was after, but with his reduced mobility, he'd understand he'd have no chance to intercept her before she reached the knife. He would also know he'd be no match against her without a knife of his own. Ulyana's mind calculated that there was a fifty-fifty chance she could grab her knife and stab Sascha before he reached his.

Good enough for me.

She pivoted on her right foot and dashed to her nightstand, reaching it in three strides instead of four. She opened the drawer with her left hand, gripped the handle of the fixed-blade Gerber knife, and slashed behind her as she turned, hoping to catch Sascha since she hadn't seen him race for his nightstand. The only thing she ripped was open air.

Her brain told her to run before she fully comprehended why Sascha wasn't there. As she sprinted around the corner and saw Sascha reaching into the closet, she understood. Conscious he stood no chance against her in his condition, Sascha had played her. He had never intended to go for his knife.

It's the gun he'd wanted all along.

She was only two meters away from him when he emerged from the closet, a pistol in his right hand. A moment later they collided, and she sensed her knife embedding itself deep into Sascha's flesh. Then there was a gunshot, and she fell forward. She landed on the floor, her brain already telling her she had to get control of the gun, or at least get her knife back.

But when she tried to get up, her body refused to obey. For the first time, she was conscious of a scalding burn in her gut. She looked down at her stomach and saw a neat hole an inch above her belly button, dark blood pouring out of it. The pain was sickening. It was like nothing she'd ever experienced before. She put a hand to her stomach to stop the flow of blood, but it was too painful. Sascha was seated only a few feet from her, on the other side of the corridor, his back resting against the powder blue wall. Her knife was embedded in his thigh, but he made no effort to remove it. His pistol was in his hand, but not pointed directly at her.

Ulyana moaned as she began to draw her knees toward her stomach to relieve the pain.

"Don't. You'll only make it worse," Sascha said.

He was right. It was worse. Her skin had become clammy, and her body had started trembling. She was going into shock.

Internal bleeding.

"I . . . I need help," she said, suddenly very afraid.

"Somebody heard the shot, I'm sure of it," Sascha told her. "But by the time anyone gets here, you'll be dead."

There was nothing malicious or mean in the way he'd said it. He was just stating a fact. Tears began to well up in her eyes. She didn't understand why.

"Who . . . with who were you—"

"My boss. At the DIA," Sascha said. "That's who I was messaging with."

She tried to make sense of what he'd just said. It wasn't easy. Not with the thick fog enveloping her brain. The DIA? As in the Defense Intelligence Agency?

"But . . . you . . . are . . . Russian," she said weakly, becoming light headed.

"No. My parents were. Like yours, I guess. But me? I'm an American. I approached the DIA when I was still in service and told them about my parents. They weren't arrested, so that I could keep my cover. There's absolutely nothing in Russia for me. It was never my home. I despise men like Yuri."

Ulyana tried to move, but her limbs became leaden. She was going to die naked on the carpet. This couldn't be. She deserved better, but she knew there was nothing she could do about it. She felt herself drifting off, grateful that the pain in her gut had subsided to a tolerable level. Maybe she was going to be all right after all.

Yes. I'll be fine. I just need to rest for a while.

And then everything seemed to ebb away as her heart beat for one last time.

CHAPTER FIFTY-FOUR

Chur
Switzerland

Following his call with Hammond and a short conversation with Veronica to reassure her he was fine, White had given his statement to a senior cantonal police officer, thankful he'd been allowed to make an oral statement instead of spending hours at the police station writing a detailed report of his actions.

White had also spoken to Nicklaus Hauser prior to him being airlifted—along with four of his TIGRIS operators—to a nearby hospital. Hauser was shaken, mentally and physically, but he'd live to fight another day. The same couldn't be said for one of his team members, the one who'd been shot in the face right after Hauser had caught a bullet center mass.

Though it would take months for the fourteen-man TIGRIS team to become operational again, and despite the initial hiccup on the breach, they had performed like the elite team they were. White hoped that the Swiss government would see that Task Force TIGRIS was worth investing in. Fourteen operators weren't enough, though. Today's raid should have called for an assault force twice as large and a support team of at least ten. Would the Swiss government realize that? That remained to be seen.

Following the arrest of Ma Lin and Pink Blouse—a female MSS agent named Eu-Meh—White had been allowed to enter the property. In the end, TIGRIS had faced eight heavily armed men. Two of the bad guys were dead, five more had been injured and were on their way to the hospital, and one had surrendered when he ran out of ammo. For White, the fact that TIGRIS hadn't shot the man revealed the high degree of professionalism with which the Swiss officers operated.

In the basement, he'd found Henry Newman. The CIA officer— and CEO of Newman Horizon Development—had died bound to a metal chair, shot three times in the heart. Next to him, Geng Peiwu, the Red Dragon Triad leader, had perished in what seemed to be a much more agonizing way. Deep cuts and lacerations were plentiful on his chest, and his left hand and right foot were missing.

For White, if this dipshit was the one responsible for the precursors for the candy-colored fentanyl pills that were produced in Mexico by the cartels and then distributed to kids in the United States, then he'd gotten what he deserved. White had looked for Ma Lin, hoping to get a few words with him before he disappeared in political and legal red tape, but no one seemed to know where he'd been taken.

All around the house, inside and outside, police officers—uniformed and plainclothes—were interviewing the TIGRIS operators still on scene while forensic techs were drawing up diagrams and taking pictures and measurements.

The sun was starting to set behind the mountains, and the temperature had dropped a few degrees since White had entered the house twenty minutes ago. Special Agent Wong, who was seated on the rear step of an ambulance, was talking with a paramedic, getting her arm bandaged and her lungs checked out. It was going to be dark soon, and White needed to find a ride back to Davos.

He'd called Veronica to give her a quick sitrep, and she'd informed him that due to what had happened in Chur, the American delegation was shortening its stay in Davos and was scheduled to leave sometime within the next two hours. A uniformed officer walked to White and asked him to hand him the rifle still slung across his chest, which White did.

"And your sidearm too," the officer said.

"No," White said and walked away.

"Sir! I must insist," the officer called from behind White, but White ignored him.

"It's okay, Officer," someone else said, his tone suggesting he was in charge. "I'll handle it."

White stopped and turned toward the voice. The man who'd spoken was tall, in his late fifties, and dressed in an expensive Italian-made business suit. He had a pleasant face and a smile on his lips, but his eyes were shrewd and serious.

"Mr. White, can we talk?"

"Sure."

"My name is Guy Delatte," the man said, offering his hand. "I'm the director of the Federal Intelligence Service."

"What can I do for you, Mr. Delatte?" White asked, shaking the man's hand.

"I'm not sure how familiar you are with Swiss politics, but although my predecessor was often seen as being cold to the idea of working with American intelligence agencies, I'm not. In fact, I just had a very fruitful conversation with Liz Maberry," Delatte said, pausing a beat to assess if White was aware of who she was.

White simply nodded.

"She asked me if it would be possible to allow you a few minutes with one of the suspects TIGRIS arrested during the raid," Delatte said. "Would that be something of interest to you?"

"You know where Ma Lin is?"

"I'm not sure who you're talking about," Delatte said.

White understood. Ma Lin, as a Chinese government official, enjoyed diplomatic immunity. But that privilege could be afforded only if the Swiss authorities were able to confirm Ma Lin's identity. The FIS director was telling White no such thing had been done yet.

"I'd love to talk with the suspect," White said.

"I thought you would. Please follow me."

Delatte led White toward a black Mercedes Sprinter van. Two serious-looking, heavily armed dudes were standing next to it. When they saw Delatte, they opened the rear doors. The van's interior space had been modified. Stainless steel shelves and cabinets lined both sides of the inside walls, and an ambulance-style stretcher occupied the center of the floor space.

Director Ma Lin, who had a piece of duct tape on his mouth, was strapped to the stretcher while two medical officers worked on his leg.

With a wave of his hand, Delatte ordered the two medics out of the van.

"Take all the time you need, Mr. White," Delatte said.

White climbed aboard and sat next to Ma Lin. Delatte gave him a nod and closed the van's doors.

"Hello, Director. I'm Clayton White."

CHAPTER FIFTY-FIVE

Chur
Switzerland

"You know who I am," White said, looking at Ma Lin's contorted face. "And you know who I represent."

The MSS director's eyes were fixed on the ceiling of the van, refusing to acknowledge White's presence. That was fine. He'd soon change his mind.

"I spent my entire military career as an air force combat rescue officer," White said, "so I know a thing or two about pain. I could give you a shot of morphine, but with the carnage I've seen in the basement, I don't think you deserve the relief it would give you. What do you think?"

Ma Lin tried to keep it in, but a moan escaped from deep down in his throat, his entire body heaving with pain.

"I don't do torture," White said. "I'm not the kind of guy who gets off by inflicting pain on others. But even if I was, what would be the point? You're in enough pain already."

White placed his hand against Ma Lin's forehead. It was cold and clammy. White examined the director's knee and shook his head.

"That's bad," he said. "I'm not a doctor, but I think your knee could be rebuilt, given it's done soon enough. If not, I'm afraid amputation is the only way."

That earned White a hateful look from Ma Lin, which White considered to be progress.

"The problem, and I'm sure you've already figured this out, is that this isn't a real EMS vehicle. My guess is that it belongs to the FIS. They're clearly in no rush to send you to a hospital, and they told me I can have as much time as I want with you. So here we are.

"You have two options moving forward. The first one is that you talk with me, answer my questions, and then I release you to the Swiss authorities, and they fix your knee. My government will ask for your extradition so that you can face trial in the United States for the murder of Henry Newman. That probably will never happen because you have diplomatic immunity. It might take a few months of back-and-forth between our two governments and the Swiss, but I think it's fair to say you'll be back in China in time for your summer vacation."

Ma Lin was breathing hard through his nose now, but White wasn't ready to take off the duct tape.

"The second option is the one where you refuse to provide truthful answers to my questions. In that case, you'll simply vanish from the face of the earth. You'll be in a CIA black site within the next twelve hours, a place where only very rudimentary medical services are available. Certainly not the ones you'd need to have your knee fixed. I know the Swiss would have no problem going out publicly to say you were never here."

White could tell that Ma Lin was considering his options, his mind working through the pain to find an exit solution. White counted to ten, then ripped the piece of duct tape from his mouth. It was time to find out if his pep talk had steered Ma Lin in the right direction.

White half expected Ma Lin to spit in his face, but he didn't. Instead, he fixed his eyes on White, sizing him up. Ma Lin's lips were quivering and his teeth chattering.

Ma Lin didn't speak right away. He was in a jam, and he knew it.

"Morphine," he said. "Please."

"I've already established I wasn't going to give you morphine," White said, refusing to be pushed around. "Talk first, then I might be willing to reconsider, but the clock's ticking for you."

"I'm already dead," Ma Lin said. "As far as the MSS is concerned, I failed. I have nothing to gain by talking with you."

White had hoped Ma Lin would say that, but it was Ma Lin who had to take the first step. Once the door was ajar, White could open it all the way.

"What if there was a third option?" White asked.

"You . . . make me disappear. But no black site?" Ma Lin asked.

White didn't reply. Ma Lin swallowed hard and drew a shaky breath. "You'd have to protect me," he said.

"We would."

"What . . . guarantees do I have you'll—"

"None," White said, cutting him off. "You'll just have to trust me, or we're back to the two options I presented you."

"What is it that you want to know?"

CHAPTER FIFTY-SIX

Nine Days Later
The Mediterranean Sea, North of Algeria

White looked through the open door of the Black Hawk helicopter as it flew over the Mediterranean Sea. Two hundred feet to their left, and traveling at the same speed, another chopper carrying a contingent of ten Navy SEALs was on its way to seize *Lancer*, Yuri Makarov's superyacht. White looked at his watch. In three minutes, they would fly over one of the two US Navy destroyers that was on its way to intercept the vessel.

One of the first things Ma Lin had given up was the name of the two cargo ships Geng Peiwu had used to transport the FIM-92 Stinger surface-to-air missiles. Navy SEAL teams had executed perfectly coordinated raids on the two cargo ships and had seized the missiles without firing a shot. Peiwu's men aboard the vessels, who had somehow learned about their leader's demise, had realized how futile it would be to resist and had simply surrendered. White prayed their luck would continue. With two destroyers, two choppers full of SEALs, and a possible F/A-18 flyby, White couldn't imagine Yuri ordering his force to engage them.

But Yuri was Russian, and Russians had a tendency to make bad decisions recently.

On a brighter note, the FBI, using the intelligence Henry Newman had provided, had arrested the twelve MSS agents Ma Lin had sent to the United States. Again, not a single shot had been fired.

Now, White and the Navy SEALs were on their way to pay a visit to Yuri Makarov. *Lancer* was presently fifty miles north of Algiers, Algeria, and sailing east toward Libya. Earlier that morning, it had picked up a shipment of heavy machine guns, and it was now on its way to make a delivery to a Libyan militia group. Thanks to Pierre Sarazin, who had come up with the blueprints of the yacht, the SEALs had been able to plan their assault meticulously. Any edge they could get, they would take.

So, it had been a long—but very rewarding—seven days since White had left Washington, DC, to oversee the two raids on the cargo ships carrying the MANPADS. After his talk with Ma Lin in Switzerland, White had flown back to Washington, DC, with Veronica to brief the president and DDO Liz Maberry. To his surprise, two people White hadn't expected to see had also been present in the Oval Office: Lieutenant General Kenneth Burgess, the director of the Defense Intelligence Agency, and Ian Miller, who turned out to be a senior agent with the Defense Clandestine Service of the DIA.

White had learned that Miller's parents, who were now deceased, had been deep-cover KGB agents. They had moved to the United States in the mid-1980s and begun their lives as sleeper agents. When Miller turned seventeen, his parents had shared with him their true identities but hadn't done so with much enthusiasm. Miller had been out of boot camp for less than a month when Yuri Makarov contacted him through his parents. The following week, Miller had reached out to the DIA. White still didn't know if Miller had been with the DIA when they'd worked together in the air force—Miller was sketchy about the details of his employment—but when Miller had left the military, the DIA had sent him to Saint John in the US Virgin Islands.

The objective had been to infiltrate criminal entities in the Caribbean to monitor and to hopefully stop the flow of military-grade weapons transiting through the area—oftentimes originating from Russia or China and ending in the hands of the drug cartels in Mexico. White was only half-surprised when he learned that it had been Miller's tip that had led to the operation in California where they had seized a record amount of fentanyl. White hadn't made a final decision yet, but he wondered if Miller would be willing to get a temporary assignment to the Office of Special Projects. White wouldn't mind working with him again.

"Five minutes. Five minutes," the SEAL team leader told his men, showing them five fingers.

White took a deep breath. Like he'd felt in the chopper en route to Chur, he wished he could have been part of the raiding force. But this time, he hadn't even considered asking the SEAL team leader.

No point in pissing the man off.

White was grateful to be allowed to tag along. He'd watch the raid from above.

CHAPTER FIFTY-SEVEN

Aboard S/Y Lancer
The Mediterranean Sea

Yuri Makarov stood on the upper deck of his yacht, wondering when his lunch would be ready. *Lancer* was making its way east across the Mediterranean after a successful weapons pickup in Tripoli. The wind was more intense than it had been earlier in the day, but the water was surprisingly smooth, allowing the bow to cut through the sea easily. Hungry, and upset at the time it was taking his chef to prepare his food, Yuri descended the stairs to the main deck.

At least the table was ready and the Grüner Veltliner he'd asked for had been chilled.

Yuri was barefoot, wearing only a pair of white shorts. The stress of the past few days was apparently showing on his face—or so that dumb bitch Irina had said. Yuri had thanked her for her insolence with a bear slap that had nearly knocked her out.

But maybe she'd had a point.

He was feeling tired. It had been a terrible few weeks. He'd lost eight good men to the Swiss authorities, and three of his deep-cover intelligence assets had been killed—including his dear Ulyana.

His failure in Switzerland hadn't done anything to improve the Russian president's already cranky mood. He had ordered Yuri back to Moscow—a directive Yuri wouldn't obey even if it meant FiveSeas wouldn't get any more contracts from the Russian government. Yuri wasn't worried. Given time, the president would eventually come back to him and realize Yuri was too valuable to make an enemy of. In the meantime, he was happy smuggling weapons in and out of Africa. It wasn't as lucrative, but how much money did a man really need?

Seeing his chef approaching, Yuri sat down at the table.

"About time," he spat.

Yuri grabbed an Alaskan king crab leg, cracked it, and removed the meat with a small shellfish fork.

The sonic boom of two American fighter jets caught Yuri completely by surprise. The commotion shook his yacht as if it was a rubber boat, and his expensive bottle of Austrian white rolled off the table and shattered on the deck.

What the hell?

He got up and walked to the gunwale, trying to catch a glimpse of the fast-moving jets. He stepped on a shard of glass and cut his foot. He swore out loud and bent over to remove the piece of glass that had embedded itself in his flesh. As he straightened back up, he spotted what looked like a warship. It was still far away, but there was no mistaking it for a cruise ship. Its bow was pointing right at *Lancer*. As he searched for the two fighter jets, Yuri sighted another warship coming from a different direction.

A bad feeling began to build in the pit of Yuri's stomach. The Americans were coming for him. Yuri's mind switched to overdrive, and he began to think about his options. There weren't that many. Even with the weaponry he'd picked up in Tripoli, there was no way he could hold off what were probably two US Navy destroyers and a pair of fighter jets.

And there's probably fast boats or choppers with boarding teams already on their way, he thought.

Within minutes his yacht would be seized. Why hadn't his captain warned him? Surely, he must have seen the destroyers on the ship's radar a while ago, hadn't he? If he'd been warned in time, Yuri could have asked the captain to race back into Algeria's territorial waters. The Americans wouldn't have dared follow him there.

There were only two options left, and both ended with him losing his yacht. He could surrender and negotiate with the Americans, or he could take his helicopter and head toward Algerian airspace, taking the risk that the American fighters would shoot him down.

Would they dare do that? It wasn't a bet he was ready to make.

And it was too late anyway. The first Black Hawk was less than two miles away.

Yuri smiled. There was a way out of this. The Americans weren't stupid. They wouldn't kill him. With everything he knew about the Russian state and its president, he would have the upper hand. He'd give them the intel bit by bit in exchange for his safety and a nice, fat American life.

Lancer's captain had finally cut the engines. Yuri stayed immobile, making sure nothing he did could be interpreted as a threat by the boarding party. The first Black Hawk was hovering over the bow, with Navy SEALs rappelling down. The second Black Hawk was hanging in the air about fifty feet above the stern of his yacht, men in tactical gear sliding down nylon ropes.

One man didn't come out, though. But he was looking at Yuri, a huge grin on his face. The man waved. Yuri gave him the finger. Then the man's smile disappeared, and Yuri felt a presence behind him. He turned around.

Irina.

The first thing he noticed was the big purple bruise she had on her face where his hand had connected with her flesh. Only then did he see the gun.

Irina smiled. "The president sends his regards."

Yuri didn't hear the gun go off, but he did see the muzzle flash a millisecond before the bullet tore through his brain.

EPILOGUE

Five Months Later
The White House, Executive Residence of the President of the United States
Washington, DC

Although it was four o'clock in the morning, White couldn't remember the last time he'd felt so positive about life. He'd never been the grumpy type, but it seemed that life had gotten even better since their little Charlotte was born. He felt like his heart had been tinged by something magical. He quietly left the bedroom and closed the door behind him. The nursery Veronica had set up on the third floor of the Executive Residence was only a couple of steps away from their bedroom. At first, White had wanted Charlotte to sleep in their room with them. He had even set up the crib he had built for her at the foot of their bed.

Veronica had vetoed it, citing no less than three books that had been written by pseudoexperts about the importance of having a separate room for the baby. He had decided wisely not to push the argument and had moved the crib to the nursery. White looked at his daughter fussing in her crib. She'd eaten thirty minutes ago, and Veronica had just fallen back asleep. Even though White knew he shouldn't—Vonnie had given him a million reasons why this was a bad idea—he leaned over the rail of the crib and picked up his baby girl. He snuggled her to his chest. Charlotte grabbed his thumb and squeezed, letting out a loud, cute squeal. White kissed his daughter on the forehead and sat on the rocking chair, feeling blessed.

———

Veronica woke with a start and sat straight up in bed. One-month-old Charlotte wasn't in the habit of sleeping past six. She looked at the alarm clock.

It's seven thirty!

Still heavy eyed, she swung her feet off the bed but thought about glancing over to Clayton's side before allowing herself to panic. Clay was gone.

He's with her.

She sighed in relief.

She had no idea she would become such a worrier. It seemed that worrying was the only thing she did nowadays. That and breastfeeding.

She got out of bed and stretched for five minutes. She went to the bathroom to brush her teeth and tiptoed her way to the nursery. The door was ajar, and she peeked inside but didn't enter.

Veronica smiled and observed the scene from the hallway.

Clay was in the rocking chair, slowly rolling back and forth, holding Charlotte tight against his chest while talking to her. Had he memorized one of the storybooks? She tried to identify the words he was saying to match them to one of the dozens of stories Clay liked to read to Charlotte but couldn't.

Closing her eyes, Veronica focused on Clay's voice.

". . . and I promise you, baby girl, I'm not gonna let any of those cute teenage boys around you until you're at least twenty-one. And I'm gonna kick anyone's ass who tries to hurt you. And . . ."

Veronica chose that moment to enter the room. Clay looked at her.

"Good morning, beautiful woman," he said, beaming. "Did you sleep well?"

"I did," she said, stretching her arms over her head. "Thank you for letting me sleep in, babe. I needed it."

"You know, Vonnie, most people wouldn't call seven thirty sleeping in."

A smile played on her lips.

"Yeah, I know," she replied as she walked past two large stacks of unopened toys. "But we do, don't we?"

She examined all the new gifts that had come in the last forty-eight hours. She would open them today, but they kept coming faster than she and Clay could unwrap them. After the riot act she'd read them last night during their most recent video call, Veronica hoped Auntie Emily and Uncle Pierre would stop sending toys and clothes to the White House.

She chuckled. *Fat chance of that happening,* she thought.

Veronica kissed her husband. "You spoil her too much, hon."

Clay grinned. "Well, that makes two of us, doesn't it?"

ABOUT THE AUTHOR

Photo © 2013 Esther Campeau

Simon Gervais was born in Montréal, Québec. He joined the Canadian military as an infantry officer, and in 2001, he was recruited by the Royal Canadian Mounted Police, where he first worked as a drug investigator. Later he was assigned to antiterrorism, which took him to several European countries and the Middle East. In 2009, he became a close-protection specialist tasked with guarding foreign heads of state visiting Canada. He served on the protection details of Queen Elizabeth II, US president Barack Obama, and Chinese president Hu Jintao, among others. Gervais lives in Ottawa with his wife and two children.